DEATH AT THE BAR

They'd barely slurped the snow-white foam off their first beers at the bar when a voice cut through the saloon chatter and the drunken laughter.

"Weeel Leweees!"

Will turned slowly, stepping away from the bar. There were two men facing him from about eight feet away. The speaker was Mexican, with long, greasy hair and a drooping mustache that hung two inches below his jaw. His holster, tied low on his thigh, held a Colt .45. "You have someteeng my fren' Meester VanGelder wants."

The second man was white, short, and scruffy, looking like a cowhand at the end of a drive, except for his tied-down holster.

"Your friend VanGelder is a fat, cowardly pig, an' you two sows look like you came from the same litter," Will said in almost a conversational tone. "You got something to take care of with me, let's get to it."

The Mexican's eyes were coal black and glistened like those of a snake. "You make beeg talk," he snarled, "but now you die. No?" His hand swept to the grips of his pistol . . .

Paul Bagdon

BAD
MEDICINE

Dorchester
Publishing

DORCHESTER PUBLISHING

September 2011

Published by

Dorchester Publishing Co., Inc.
200 Madison Avenue
New York, NY 10016

ISBN 13: 978-1-4285-1166-8
E-ISBN: 978-1-4285-0959-7

The "DP" logo is the property of Dorchester Publishing Co., Inc.

Printed in the United States of America.

Visit us online at www.dorchesterpub.com.

ACKNOWLEDGMENTS

This one is for Don D'Auria, the absolute best editor a writer could possibly have, as well as for the cover art folks, the promotion people, the proofers, and the contract people at Dorchester/Leisure.

As my protagonist would say, "Damn! They don't come no better'n that."

—PB

BAD
MEDICINE

Chapter One

The sun hung over Will Lewis and his Appaloosa stud, Slick, like a gigantic, flaming brass disk, sucking all moisture from the earth, the desiccated prairie grass, and the man and his horse. An endless sweep—a swell—of merciless heat had begun shortly after first light and had escalated almost exponentially since then.

Slick was dragging his toes and weaving slightly, even at his plow-horse walk. His head hung low, muzzle barely a foot from the ground.

Will reached forward and took a pinch of hide from Slick's neck, stretched it up an inch or so, and released it. The flesh moved back into place slowly, lethargically—Slick was baking in his own hide and not far from going down. Lewis knew that it was a sure bet that if Slick did go down, he'd never get up again.

Will hefted his canteen: it was maybe a quarter full. His throat was a sandpit, his lips cracked and weeping blood, his entire being screaming for water. He reined in, slouched down from his saddle, dumped the canteen into his Stetson, and held the hat to Slick's muzzle. The horse sucked once, emptying the hat, and eyed Will, demanding more, begging for more.

Lewis stepped back onto his saddle, red and black spots floating in his vision. He pulled in a long, deep breath. The spots didn't disappear but they diminished in size and number.

His words weren't anywhere near perfectly formed, and he could barely hear himself speak. "We shoulda hit th' town if Hiram's directions was right. Hiram—he's a idjit. He jus' mighta up an' killed me an' a good horse."

Slick was weaving more noticeably.

"Sonofabitch," Will mumbled, and heeled Slick to keep him moving.

At first Will thought it was just another oddly shaped cholla. As he drew closer he saw it was a sign. Like all the signs of jerkwater West Texas towns, it was a slab of barn wood with hand-painted text. It was pocked with bullet holes and speckled with shotgun pellets. The sign read DRY CREEK.

Slick's head shot up as if he were suddenly checking the sky, his nostrils flared, his breath huffing through them. He smelled either humans or water—it made no difference to him. Either one promised the end of his thirst. He picked up his pace without urging from Will.

Another couple hundred yards later the tinkling notes of a honky-tonk piano reached Will. A vision of a schooner of beer the size of a hog's head popped into his mind and refused to leave it. His throat moved up and down in a swallowing motion without his volition.

They came down a grade and Dry Creek spread before them, such as it was. There were the usual false-fronted structures on either side of a pitted and rutted street that put a tail of dirt and grit in the air behind each horse and wagon. The town offered a mercantile, a shoe and boot, an undertaker and furniture maker, three saloons, and a sheriff's office. At the end of the street was a small church, and beyond that, a livery and blacksmith operation. The reason the town existed—a railroad depot with stock fences—rested at the far end of the street, beyond the church and stable.

Each gin mill had a watering trough in front of it, partially under the hitching post. The scent of water goaded Slick into an awkward, shambling lope and Will gave him all the rein he wanted. The horse slid to a stop at the first trough and buried his muzzle in the water, sucking like berserk bellows. Will climbed down and fell to his knees next to Slick. He pushed some of the horse spittle and green scum to the side and planted his face in the water.

The water was piss warm, metallic tasting, with a good growth of stringy, weedlike scum at the bottom—and it was the finest thing Will Lewis had ever tasted in his life. He drank until he puked, stood, dragged Slick's head out of the trough, and stepped into a stirrup. Slick fought him, rearing and snorting, but Will wheeled him around and jabbed his heels into his sides, pointing him toward the blacksmith shop. Too much water at one time to a dehydrated horse could cause founder or twisted gut. If Will's old man had taught him anything, it was this: "Ya take care of yer horse 'fore ya look after yerself."

The smith was a barrel of a man with forearms like hams, a full beard, and the chest of a bull buffalo. His hair, twisted and greasy, hung well below his shoulders. He came out to meet Will as he dismounted.

"Nice animal," he commented in a deep, hoarse voice, " 'cept the poor fella's dryer'n a dust storm in hell. You oughta know better'n to—"

"That horse an' me just crossed that goddamn desert out there," Will snarled. "I gave him the last of my canteen an' both of us come close to croakin'. You got a problem with me, do somethin' about it. If not, shut your yap an' listen. You water this boy every twenty minutes, maybe a quarter bucket. I want shoes all around—not keg shoes, neither. I want you to turn them outta good bar stock and bang in an extra nail at each toe. Give him small rations of molasses an' oats, maybe some corn, a few times a day, an' all the good hay he wants—not this burned-out shit you got stacked up here, the trefoil an' clover I see there in the back. Got it?"

The smith grinned. His teeth were an almost startling white. "Feisty, ain't you? Now look—all that's gonna cost you some money," he said.

Will flipped a double eagle to the big man. "You need more, let me know."

The blacksmith raised the coin to his mouth and bit down on it—hard. Will saw the muscles at the man's jaw flex and harden.

The smith wiped the coin on his muleskin apron and dropped it into the pocket of his denim pants. "Look here," he said, "we got off to a bad start. I had no way of knowin' you crossed the sand. I figgered you was another twenty-five-a-month-an'-chow cow-puncher who'd run a good horse to death. I was wrong." He extended his right hand. "Lucas Toole," he said.

Will took the hand. It was like grasping a brick that had grown fingers. "Lewis," he said, "Will Lewis."

Lucas grinned again. "I got me a bottle out back—real whiskey, not 'shine. I was wonderin' maybe you'd like a little taste after drinkin' some of that good water outta the barrel there with the scoop hangin' on it. Pure deep well water it is, cold 'nuff to crack yer teeth."

"No more'n I want to wake up tomorrow morning." Will grinned, heading to the barrel. "But maybe first, my horse . . ."

"I was hopin' you'd say that," Lucas said, stepping ahead of Will with a bucket, filling it a quarter full, and holding it to Slick's muzzle.

It was good whiskey, just as Lucas said: the label was real, not a sloppy counterfeit, and the booze tasted of woodsmoke and fresh prairie grass. Will took three long sucks. "Damn," he said almost reverently, handing the bottle back.

Lucas lowered the level of the bottle a good two inches and wiped his mouth with his arm. "Done some time, Will?" he asked.

Will's eyes showed nothing. "Time? What makes you think that?"

"Well, hell," Lucas said, "there's jus' somethin' about a man who been inside for a good bit—his eyes ain't never still, and he don't seem to ever relax. He's always tight, like he's waitin' for a punch he knows is comin' but he don't know exactly when."

After a long moment, Will said, "I done four. I was movin' some beef that maybe had the wrong brand on 'em. An' I lost the bill of sale, too. Musta flew right outta my pocket with the wind. The fact I was movin' 'em at night toward Mexico didn't impress the law positive."

"That'll happen to a man," Lucas said. "Where they lock you up?"

"Folsom."

"Damn. Hard time."

"Yeah."

"My younger brother done three in Folsom," Lucas said. "That's how I knew about how a fella looks when he first comes out."

There was a long and somewhat uncomfortable silence. Lucas broke it by asking, "So—what're you gonna do now?"

"My brother, Hiram, has a cattle spread not far from here. I've got some money I hid out before I went to prison. Me an' Hiram are gonna expand his place a lot—more land an' more beef. Hiram, he's a hell of a hand with . . ."

Lucas's grin dropped as suddenly as it would have if someone had sucker punched him. "Hiram Lewis, that'd be?"

"Well, yeah. But what . . . what . . . ?"

"Take this," Lucas said, handing back the bottle. "Have a good belt an' then sit you down on a bale of hay."

"Why? What's . . . ?"

"Jus' do it, OK?"

Will, confused, did it, eyes locked with those of the smith.

"Ain't no good way to say this," Lucas said. "I knew Hiram real good—done business with him, drank with him, played cards, broke bread with him an' his family. Good man. Sarah, his wife, was sweet as August honey, and their two daughters—why, you couldn't find better kids. Twins, they was, musta been born 'bout the time you went inside."

Will didn't realize it, but he was holding his breath.

"Was renegade Injuns and crazies from the war," Lucas said, each word straining his voice. "Killed 'em all, burned the house an' barn, made off with the cattle. I went out an' put them in the ground nice an' proper, Will."

"What about the law? The sherrif?"

"A Mex gunfighter killed him about three, four months ago. Nobody wants the job."

"The place—was it bad?" Will asked in a monotone.

"You don't want to know, Will."

"Tell me," Will said in the same flat, emotionless tone.

Lucas took the bottle back and sucked a deep swallow. "I . . . I guess you got a right to know," he said. He paused for a moment, avoiding Will's eyes. "You know how them renegade Apaches treat women, right? An' this One Dog, the leader, is worse 'n most."

"The twins, too?"

Lucas nodded. "Killed 'em, Will. Bullets, not arrows. Leastwise, it was fast."

"How'd they do Hiram in?"

"Nailed him to a fence post, scalped him, shot him fulla arrows, an' burned him."

Neither man said anything for what seemed like a long time. Finally, Will rose from the hay bale and walked out of the barn. It was twenty minutes before he walked back in, and his eyes were red rimmed and his nose running. "How many head was Hiram running?" he asked, his voice on the cusp of cracking.

"Maybe a hunnerd or so branded, an' maybe twenny youngsters, more or less. Couple of good horses. Sarah, she had some goats, a slew of chickens. There was three dogs. They was fine cattle dogs—friendly cusses, too. They . . . well . . . gutted the poor critters. I put them in the ground, too, off ta Hiram's side. Like I said, they was right good dogs."

Will was silent for a moment.

"I'm purely awful sorry I was the one to tell you, Will."

"Don't matter none who tells it—the facts don't change," Will said.

"No—I don't guess they do."

"How many renegades?" Will asked.

"Maybe twenty-five or thirty all tol', from the tracks. Only eight or ten horses was shod. See, Hiram an' Sarah had 'vited me out for dinner. That's how I found what happened."

Will remained as still as a statue, staring out of the barn into the sunbaked street, seeing nothing.

"What're you gonna do, Will? I s'pose you own the land now. It's all registered with the property office, an' you bein' blood kin an' all—"

"What I'm gonna do," Will interrupted, "is take a few days to get Slick back in trim, then go out to the ranch."

"An' then what?"

"Stock up, buy a good rifle, track this One Dog down, an' kill him an' each of his followers."

Lucas shook his head. "Big order," he said.

"Me an' Hiram always got along good," Will said. "He even come all the way out to Folsom to see me. That's when we decided to partner up on his operation. I had money to buy more stock, fatten 'em up, and drive 'em into Dry Creek to the train, an' be a real, legal cattleman. We figured to build up his house some, too. I sent Hiram to one of my stashes to get money to get some good fencing up, buy me a solid horse, an' get him an' Sarah whatever they needed. Sarah, she played the piano. Hiram said he was gonna order one from Susan Robucks for her . . ." His voice trailed off to silence.

"That all sounds real nice, Will. Woulda been, too, an' that's for—"

"So," Will interrupted, "I don't have a choice. I gotta go after them, take them down. You can see that, can't you, Lucas?"

There was another stretch of quiet broken only by the creaking and complaining of the barn beams and a Morgan mare in a stall crunching corn.

Lucas spat off to the side. "Seems to me the boy you rode in on is all the horse you need," he said. "Hell, I got nothin' even close to him in my string."

"You're right. Thing is, he's stole. I picked him up the day I got out. He was the warden's horse. He had spur gouges on his flanks, and ol' Slick, he was wild as a hawk. I seen he was top stock, an' he's proved me right. Any other horse'd be out in the sand feedin' vultures right now."

"He's branded, though," Lucas said.

"Yeah. I was kinda wonderin', maybe you might have a runnin' iron around here somewhere, an' could be, a good bill of sale, too. I'll pay good."

"Hell," Lucas said, "there ain't a brand I can't change and make look real legal, and I got more bills of sales than I need. I guess the warden, he figured them bars was right cute—like the bars of a cell. I can make them into a *HW* if that suits you—ya know, Hiram an' Will."

"Sounds real good, Lucas. Thanks. Even as kids

me an' Hiram planned on the H an' W brand. I guess maybe it was an omen or something—but a piss-poor omen."

"Only thing is, I can't do no brandin' 'less you run over to the saloon an' fetch us a bucket of cold beer. Fair deal?"

Will didn't waste a minute getting through the batwings. The bartender was a black man, huge, sweaty, and alone in the joint except for a few cow-hands slugging down shots of whiskey.

"Lord, Lord," he said, chuckling. "Ain't you the fella tried suckin' my trough dry not long ago?"

"That was me," Will said. "Me an' my horse, we always been partial to trough water—'specially when it's nice an' warm with lots of horse slobber in it."

The 'tender laughed, the sound deep and rich. "You want somethin' from here or you gonna go back out to the trough?"

"I need me a big bucket of the coldest beer you got for me an' Lucas, the smith. And maybe I'll try a taste of decent whiskey while I'm here."

"I can do that," the black man said. He put a gener-ous double shot glass in front of Will, topped it from a bottle he took from under the bar, and turned away to draw the beer. The booze went down like liquid fire, but it felt good to Will, pushing what Lucas told him back a tiny bit in his mind. Will put a five-dollar piece on the bar as the 'tender set down the beer bucket.

"Lemme fetch your change," he said.

"Ain't no change comin'," Will said. " 'Cept maybe another taste of that whiskey." The coin disappeared into the bartender's left hand as he filled Will's shot glass with his right.

Will trudged back to the livery, walking carefully, sloshing not a single cold, precious drop from the bucket.

Slick was in crossties, with his right front leg jacked up and lashed in a V position by a long, thick leather strap that immobilized him. The acrid stink of burned hair and flesh was heavy in the air. Slick's ears were laid back tight to his head, and his eyes were mere slits, behind which a feral fury seethed. His muzzle was drawn back over his teeth, which clattered like castanets.

"He'd sure love to take a bite outta your ass, Lucas," Will said.

"Madder'n a pissed-on hornet," Lucas said. He smiled. "Gimme that bucket."

Will noticed an inch gash over Lucas's left eye. The cut was held closed tight with a glob of hoof dressing. The dried blood was pretty much the same color as his beard.

"Little tussle?" Will asked.

"Sumbitch caught me soon's as I put the iron to him. That's why I got him rigged like that." Lucas grabbed the beer bucket with a hand on either side and drank it dry in four long, gargantuan glugs.

Will moved to his horse's flank. The new brand was covered with udder balm, but the livid pink-red flesh showed through. It was a fine piece of work: the *IIII* had been transformed into a neat *HW*.

"You done real good, Lucas. I'd be mighty proud to buy us beefsteaks an' maybe another beer or two."

"Lemme put your horse in a stall an' dump some laudanum in his yap 'fore he busts up all his teeth."

Will watched as the smith put his shoulder against Slick's right shoulder and took a good grab on the horse's pastern. Will shook his head in awe. Lucas was damned near carrying a twelve-hundred-pound horse into a stall.

The tincture of laudanum was in a brown glass bottle with a capacity of a pint or so. Lucas took a hard twist on Slick's nose. The teeth chattering stopped. The smith poured half the bottle and maybe a bit more into Slick's gullet. Three minutes later Lucas unfastened the rig. Slick stood on all fours for a bit of time and then nuzzled Lucas like a foal begging for a piece of apple.

The few folks at the rickety tables in the hotel dining room barely looked at Lucas and Will as they walked in and sat at a table. Lucas took over the ordering when the waitress—a hefty lass with a sweet smile that'd make Satan head for the nearest church to repent—walked up.

"What we need is this, Millie: two of the biggest beefsteaks ya got, barely cooked, a heap of mashed taters, maybe some of the carrots you do up with butter on 'em, an' six schooners of cold beer."

Millie brought the tray of beer first. The men lit into it.

Lucas set an empty schooner down and caught Will's eyes, holding them.

"Somethin's been itchin' me, Will, an' I'm tryin' to figger her out. Not much more'n a hour ago I tol' you your bro an' his family was killed an' his place burned to the ground. You took you a little walk and then come back an' that was it. See? Now here we are gnawing beef an' suckin' beer, like nothin' bad never happened. Why's that, Will?"

Will Lewis held the blacksmith's eyes.

"I don't know that it's your business, Lucas, but you been real good to me—busted a couple of heavy laws with your runnin' iron an' your papers—an' you deserve a answer."

Will hesitated for a time. "I took a floggin' in Folsom—thirty strokes—for killin' another con in a fight. I'd seen other men under the lash screaming an' cryin' and beggin', an' it made me sick. When it was my turn I made me a promise: there wasn't nothin' I couldn't take—but what I could do was find a way to make things even."

Will took the last beer from the tray and drank half of it. "After I stole the warden's horse, I went to the cabin of the man who laid the whip to me an' hung the sumbitch from a tree by his wrists an' put an even thirty on him. See, Lucas, what I done was mark that bill as paid. That's what I'm gonna do with this One Dog an' his crew—mark their bills paid in full."

"We need more beer," Lucas said. "You want some red-eye, too?"

"Beer's fine. I already got me half a stumbler on."

"Ya know, tryin' to do what you plan is pure crazy. Some more men . . ."

"I'm more'n likely gonna get killed doin' this, right? That's OK. But if I brought friends in, the whole mess wouldn't be all right. 'Cause those boys'd be killed, too. I'll hire me some guns when an' if I think I need 'em. Nobody cares if those types get killed, not even their own selves."

The steaks came—an honest two inches thick and dropping off all the way around the big dinner platters. They were singed outside but bleeding inside—cooked perfect. The mashed potatoes were as white as a new snowfall, and the serving spoon stood up like a soldier at attention in the middle of the bowl. The carrots were soaked with melted butter with a touch of garlic, an' they tasted just fine.

Lucas wiped his mouth with his sleeve and chuckled.

"What?"

"Ain't real hard seein' you et in stir."

Will was confused for a moment and then looked down at the table and at his right hand. His left arm was wrapped protectively around his plate, his hand in a tight fist. When he used the knife to cut his steak, Lucas saw that the handle was tucked into Will's palm and that the blade was between his thumb and forefinger, ready to attack in any position.

Will chuckled softly. "Ol' habits die hard. In Folsom, a man who doesn't guard his plate is gonna go hungry."

"You have much trouble inside—'sides killin' that fella?" Lucas asked.

"Everybody has trouble in a prison like Folsom," Will said. "Some real bad boys in there. Show some weakness an' you'll end up bent over a barrel with your drawers down."

"What about the guards?"

"The screws? They'd be first in line at the barrel."

Lucas began to speak but stopped. The two men finished their meals and called to Millie for another tray of beer.

"You got somewhere to stay while you're in Dry Creek?" Lucas asked. "Thing is, I got a decent li'l room up in my hayloft I usta live in 'fore I was married. It's got a real bed. It's a tad warm durin' the day, but cools down good at night."

"I'll take it an' pay up when I leave. Thanks."

Lucas wiped foam from his mouth with his sleeve and looked down at the table, avoiding Will's eyes. "About Hiram's farm . . . ," he began.

"What about it?"

"Ain't no reason to go out there, Will. None 'tall."

"I gotta pick up a trail somewhere."

"Nothin' to pick up," Lucas said. "We had rain since, and some hard wind. Anyways, the sonsabitches headed for Mexico with the beef, jus' like they always do."

"OK."

"You're goin' anyhow, right?"

"Yeah—if you'll rent me a horse. Slick's gonna be on vacation for a bit."

"I don't have nothin' with the class of your Appy, but I got a couple head of good horses got some manners an' will take you where you want to go."

"Sounds good. Say—ain't it about time to have us some more beers?"

"*Some* more, my ass." Lucas grinned. "I'm wantin' a *lot* more."

The ringing and clanging of Lucas's work the next morning as he shaped a piece of stock felt and sounded like he was using Will's head for his anvil. "Damn," he grunted, sitting up very slowly. He noticed he was wearing only his left boot. The right one rested next to the bed. As he leaned forward to tug the boot on, a spinning dizziness captured him. He lowered his head between his knees and sucked in deep drafts of air. Quite slowly the earth ceased spinning. He sat up again, found his hat next to where the boot had been, and put it on. He had no recollection of what had happened after the steak dinner and the ocean of beer he had poured down.

"You didn't quite make it." Lucas grinned as Will stepped slowly down the ladder. "There's prolly some beer left in town, an' last night you swore you was gonna drink all there was."

Will stumbled to the water barrel, doused his face and head, drank deeply, and then vomited the water next to the barrel. "Damn," he grumbled, "you musta had as much beer as I did last night, an' here you are workin' away, makin' more goddamn noise than a locomotive hittin' a brick wall."

"I'm used to it," Lucas said. "Hell, you jus' was sprung from four years in hell. You gotta build up what they call 'tolerance.'"

Will rolled a smoke with slightly trembling fingers, lit it with a wooden lucifer he snapped to a flame with his thumbnail, and inhaled deeply. "Damn," he said.

"You're lookin' a mite shaky," Lucas said. "Have you a belt from my bottle an' you'll be fine—hair o' the dog." Lucas tossed the half-empty quart to Will. Will grimaced but was able to choke down a good slug—and keep it down. The results were almost instantaneous.

"Hard to git it down, but it sure does the job," Will said. He held his hand in front of him: it was rock steady.

"What're you gonna do today?" Lucas asked after helping himself to a suck at the bottle.

"Well," Will said, "I'm gonna buy me a Winchester Model 1873—the .32-caliber, lever-action model— an' a whole lot of ammunition, an' then sight her in. I'll pick up a couple hundred rounds of .45s—

Remington, not that army crap. I gotta see can I still draw an' shoot. It's been a long goddamn time."

"That 1873's a fine rifle," Lucas said. "They come kinda dear, though."

"Well, it'll be the second one I've owned. The first one took a round in the lever mechanism that warped it all up the time the law got me. You're right, though—the '73's a hell of a weapon. That first one of mine never jammed or screwed up the six years I carried it. Oh—I need to rent a horse, too."

"*Rent*, my ass, Will. You paid for all the beer an' grub last night. That buckskin down at the end stall is a honest horse—he'll do for you. Toss your rig on him. Take a set of hobbles along—I don't know how he'll act when the shootin' starts."

Will fetched the buckskin from his stall and put him in crossties. He worked the horse over with a currycomb and brush, checked all four hooves. The gelding was put together nicely: broad chest, slanting pasterns, good-sized rump, and prominent withers. Slick's saddle fit the buckskin well. Will noticed that the horse didn't suck air to bloat up a bit when Will pulled the cinches—always the sign of a willing cayuse. Will led him out of the barn, climbed into the saddle, and headed for the mercantile.

The store smelled good, just as most mercantiles did. The scents of leather, gun oil, the tang of the bundles of new shovels, picks, and axes, tobacco, new denim, and the barrels of apples and buffalo jerky combined, merged, into a partnership of promises of new goods that'd get the job done—whatever the job was.

Will knew he was wasting his breath, but he asked the clerk anyway, "I don't suppose you got a Sharps?"

"Wish I did, but I ain't," the shopkeeper said. "What the armies—both sides, mind you—didn't snap up, the wooly hunters bought."

"Yeah, I figured," Will said, and walked over to a long rack of rifles, his boots loud on the polished wood floor. He pulled out a Winchester '73, held it to his shoulder, worked the lever, and dry-fired it. He put it back and tried another and then another. He settled on the fourth one.

"Somethin' wrong with them first three you tried?" the clerk asked, curious.

"Not a thing. But this one here feels like it was made for me. That's somethin' a man knows when he's choosin' a rifle or a pistol. Know what I mean?"

"No," the clerk admitted, grinning, "but I'll take your word for it."

Will bought a couple hundred rounds of .32-caliber cartridges and a hundred .45s for his Colt. He'd been lucky to get his pistol back when he was released from Folsom. Ordinarily, its bone grips and filed-down front sight would have caught a guard's eye, and the pistol and gun belt would have gone home with him. Will's weapon was buried in a pile of beat-up rifles and shotguns and, beyond being dusty, was in fine shape. He set the rifle on the counter and began to walk the aisles of the mercantile, picking up a good bedroll, a poncho, a nine-inch knife in a sheath to carry in his boot, a little derringer .25 for his vest pocket, four canteens, a handful of stogies, and a few packs of Bull Durham. Finally, he bought a pair of denim pants, a set of long johns, and a good work shirt. The clerk let him change in the back of the store. Will tossed his old clothing into a trash barrel. The pants felt like slabs of wood against his legs, but he knew they'd break in soon enough.

The clerk, grateful for the big sale so early in the day, tossed in a rifle-cleaning kit and a can of gun oil for free. Will paid up and hauled his purchases out to the hitching rail. He tied the bedroll snugly behind the cantle of the buckskin's saddle, distributed the ammunition into the right and left saddlebags, and slid the rifle into the sheath in front of his right stirrup, where a cowhand would carry his throwing rope. Will had no use for a rope. He led the horse across the street and tied him at the saloon hitching rail.

He had a single belt of whiskey and a mug of beer and bought a sack of empty whiskey bottles from the bartender.

It was a nice enough day for a ride, and the buckskin had a sweet rocking-chair lope that was a pleasure to sit to. Will put maybe six or eight miles between him and Dry Creek and reined in at an outcropping of rocks. He slid the hobbles on the buckskin's pasterns and, as an extra precaution, tied the reins securely at the base of a stout rock.

The sun was flexing its muscles as Will walked out into the arid land, dropping a bottle here, standing a line of three there, throwing a couple out as far as his arm could hurl them, and dropping others randomly until the sack was empty.

Will already knew that the action of his new Winchester was as smooth as the workings of the best regulator clock and that the *snick* as he worked the lever indicated perfect lubrication. Nevertheless, he levered and dry-fired a few times for the simple joy of using a well-made tool. He loaded the rifle.

Will eased himself down onto the sand in the sit/ fire position and fit the butt to his shoulder. The first round he fired spurted grit into the air a couple inches to the left of his intended bottle. The buckskin snapped his head toward Will, eyes wide, but settled down quickly. He'd heard gunfire before. Will used the tip of his sheath knife to adjust the tiny setscrew and fired again. The bottle exploded, spewing bits and shards of glass, glinting like diamonds high into the sky. He blew two bottles apart without removing the butt from his shoulder: the action of flicking the lever was smooth and sure, and his index finger barely moved from the trigger.

He needed the remaining bottles for practice with his Colt. He took some long shots with the rifle, spurt- ing chunks of pulp out of a cholla about seventy-five yards away. With his last two rounds he reached out farther—at least a hundred and twenty-five yards—to a rock he could barely see and punched it twice, the slugs ricocheting into the vastness with a sharp whine. Will held the barrel of the rifle against his cheek: it was warm but far from hot. "Hell of a weapon," he said aloud, smiling. "I can trim the hair off a flea's nuts at half a mile with this baby."

Will stood and meandered off from his sit/fire site, very conscious of the stiffness of his new drawers against his legs. The leather of his holster was warm and slightly oily feeling from the neat's-foot oil he'd rubbed into it, his gun belt, and the piece of latigo he'd used to tie the holster to his thigh. The oiliness would dissipate quickly, leaving the leather smooth and supple.

The bone grips of his Colt .45 fit his hand as easily and naturally as the hands of two lovers as they meet. He crouched slightly and drew a dozen or more times, until the process began to feel as effortless as it needed to. He knew he'd lost a little speed, and that a speck of time could kill him. He wiped sweat from his forehead with his sleeve, walked over to the buckskin, drank a couple sips from his canteen, and poured the rest into his Stetson for the horse.

He worked on his draw an hour without firing a shot, breaking only to build and smoke a cigarette. When a good bit of his confidence had returned he slid a half dozen rounds into the pistol's cylinder. His first draw and fire brought a curse from him: he'd missed the bottle by four inches. He dropped the pistol back into his holster, let it settle itself, and tried again. He missed by three inches.

"Shit," he said disgustedly, "I can creep up on it a inch at a time, but there ain't a lot of gunmen who'll give me the time."

Will put perhaps twenty rounds through his Colt before he made a good, solid hit. Grinning, he took out two more bottles, reloaded, and blasted his final targets into smithereens. He fired until all he could hear was a buzzing in his ears and his right hand was scored and scraped by blowback. An unlucky rattler chose the wrong time to slide out from a small group of rocks. Will decapitated the snake with a single shot. He stood, pistol hanging at his side, sweat stinging his eyes, and watched as the snake's mouth on the raggedly severed head opened and snapped shut several times, as if it were attacking an enemy. Amber-colored venom dripped from the sizable fangs.

Time had passed unnoticed. Will was surprised to

see the sun beginning to touch the horizon to the west. He loaded and holstered his Colt, slid his rifle into its sheath, removed the hobbles from the buckskin, and rode back to Dry Creek, the image of a cold beer floating in his mind. The horse, too, was anxious to get back to the stable where water, hay, and grain awaited him. Will had to rein him in several times—it was still too damned hot to run a horse unless it was absolutely necessary. He held his mount to a walk the last half mile into town.

Lucas, finished with his day's work when Will rode in, was sitting on a hay bale with an empty beer bucket next to him. "Damn, boy," he called out, "I'm hungry 'nuff to eat my saddle an' thirsty 'nuff to drink the damn Pecos dry!"

"Well, I'll tell you what," Will said with a grin. "Lemme brush out this good horse an' look to his feed an' I'll show you how to eat a steak and drink some beer."

"I put fresh water, grain, an' a flake of hay in his stall, Will. All you gotta do is run a brush over him an' we're on our way."

Twenty minutes later the two men were seated at a rickety table on equally rickety chairs in the saloon, each with a schooner in hand and another full one waiting to be imbibed.

"So—how'd the shootin' go, Will?"

"Piss-poor at first, but then it all started comin' back to me. Some more practice will help."

Lucas finished off his first beer and picked up his second. "Was you . . . I dunno . . . like a hired gun, 'long with rustlin'?"

Will laughed. "Hell, no. I ain't a gunfighter, Lucas. I robbed me a couple banks an' two, three stage coaches, but I give all that up to move cattle. Only thing I was ever caught for was them cattle—that's why I only drew four years in Folsom."

"They didn't tack nothin' on for killin' that con?"

"Jus' the floggin'. The man was bad news—waitin' to be strung up for rape an' murder. I saved the prison some money, I guess."

"You shoulda got a medal 'stead of a beatin', then."

"That's how I see it," Will laughed. He finished his second beer. "Seems to me it's your turn to git your ass over to the bar. I'm damn near dyin' of thirst here."

Lucas began to stand and then sat back down, his eyes focused over Will's shoulder. Will turned in his chair. A fat man in a dude suit with a watch and chain and polished boots stood a few feet back from Will. His face, as round as a muskmelon, was red, and his bulbous nose had the wandering veins of a heavy boozer. He wore a bowler hat that would have been as handy as teats on a shovel in the sun.

"Mr. William Lewis?" he asked, ignoring Lucas.

Will nodded without speaking.

"I'm Cyrus VanGelder," the fat man said in a voice that was almost feminine. "I deal in land."

"Good for you," Will said. "But I don't like bein' disturbed when I'm talkin' with a friend, and I got no land, anyhow."

"Ahh, but you have," VanGelder said. "All the land and property of the late Hiram Lewis, recently deceased, now belongs to you, my friend. I'm prepared to make a very generous off—"

Will moved a bit more in his chair, now facing VanGelder. His fist went out like a piston, burying itself in eight inches of flab at the land speculator's waist. The fat man landed on his back on the floor and immediately curled into a flaccid ball, clutching his gut, gasping, his face now a pale white.

"You come near me again an' I'll show you what a real punch feels like, you fat vulture. That jus' now wasn't nothin' but a little shove." Will turned his chair back to the table, speaking over Lucas's laughter. "Now 'bout that trip to the bar—unless you're scared this lard bucket here'll take after you, maybe boot you 'round a bit."

"I'll chance it," Lucas said, "but I'm purely scared, Will." He shoved his chair out and strolled to the bar. VanGelder managed to get himself up from the floor, still hunched over. "I won't forget this," he said, stepping clumsily toward the batwings.

When Lucas returned to the table with a tray of six beers he had a frown on his face.

"You're lookin' worried," Will said.

"Well, maybe I am a tad. See, the thing is Van-Gelder has a pair of gunhands workin' for him an' they're both bad news—a Mex an' a Anglo. Both killers. The Mex is the one who gunned the sheriff a while back." He paused for a moment. "You'd best watch yourself, Will."

"I always do." Will grinned. "C'mon—let's have at those brews."

Slick was gaining weight and strength daily. Out in the pasture now, he'd established himself as the top gun, and the other horses kept their distance from him, moving away from the water as he approached the trough and grazing with a good bit of ground between themselves and the Appaloosa.

One morning, as Will and Lucas leaned on the pasture fence, Lucas said, "I guess I might owe you a stud fee."

"How's that?"

"Yesterday, when you was out shootin', my bay mare come into strong heat, struttin' 'round with her tail up, drippin' like a leaky roof durin' a rainstorm. Slick, he figured he'd calm her down some—humped three times that I saw an' probably a couple more times I didn't see."

Will laughed. "Slick likes the ladies OK," he said. "That mare is a real good looker, built nice, handy an' quick on her feet. If she took, you'll end up with a hell of a foal."

"That's how I see it." Lucas smiled. "An' I got no doubt she took, after all the times Slick climbed on her."

Will rolled a smoke, eyes still on his horse. "I'm gonna bring Slick in today, look him over. If he's back in shape I'll ride him out to Hiram's place."

Lucas nodded. "I figured that was comin'," he said. "I guess I can't talk you outta it."

"Nope."

"Gettin' a li'l weary of pumpin' lead at rocks an' suckin' beer like you done the last week or so?"

Slick, standing in the crossties in the barn, was rock hard and twice as feisty, stomping his hooves, snorting, ready to feel Will's rig on his back. The new brand was crusted over nicely with no moisture weeping from it. Will filled two of his new canteens and secured them with latigo strings around his horn and saddled the Appaloosa up, slipped the low port bit in his mouth, and led the horse out of the barn. Lucas stood by the pasture fence, chewing on a blade of grass, waiting for the show he was pretty sure would come.

Will stepped into a stirrup, swung aboard—and Slick sunfished, all four hooves off the ground, all his pent-up energy released. He went up again like an unbroken bronc and Lucas yelled out, "WHOOOO—EEEE! Ride 'em, Will!"

Will waved his hat, face showing his joy. "Mr. Blacksmith," he yelled, "you tol' me this horse was broke when I bought him off ya!"

"Well," Lucas called, laughing, "kinda *green* broke. Give him eight, ten years an' he'll calm right down."

Will allowed Slick to play for a few more moments and then reined him in. He waved to Lucas and set out at a quick jog toward what had been his brother's home—and that of his brother's wife and twin daughters.

Slick shook his head, trying to get under the bit. Tired of wrestling with him, Will gave him all the rein he wanted. The Appaloosa surged ahead as if he'd been fired from a cannon and was in a full gallop within a bit of a second. Chunks of dirt and grass leaped into the air from under all four hooves as Slick stretched out and poured on all the power and speed he had. As it always did, the rush of pure strength and willingness of the animal at speed cleared Will's mind of everything but the hot wind whipping his face, the smooth pumping of Slick's shoulders, and the sensation of flying rather than riding.

Will checked the horse after most of a mile, tapping lightly at his mouth with the bit to slow him from the headlong gallop. Slick, initial burst expended, slowed to an easy lope, his chest and flanks breaking sweat.

The West Texas sun beat down on man and horse as if it had a personal vendetta against them. Will shared his first canteen with his horse and rode on.

The first indication Will had that he'd come upon his brother's ranch was a tall pile of rough-cut fence posts and two coils of barbed wire. One of the top posts had an arrow sticking in it, surrounded by a dinner-plate-sized scorch mark. Maybe because the posts were too green, the intended fire never got started. In the distance Will saw a stone fireplace and chimney standing guard over the rubble around it.

The house hadn't been large—probably two bedrooms and a loft above. There'd been a porch around the front, and part of an overturned rocker lay on the burned surface. Pieces of glass sparkled in what would have been the inside of the house, no doubt from Sarah's canned fruits and vegetables exploding in the conflagration. There was no discernable furniture: all the wood and fabric must have been consumed by the fire. A singed arm and hairless head of a rag doll protruded from under a collapsed, burned-through loft beam. A cluster of wires and burned wood confused Will at first. Then he saw the few piano keys that had partially survived. A lump rose in his throat, making breathing difficult. He wiped his face on a sleeve and swung Slick to the barn, a couple hundred feet from where the house had stood. There was next to nothing left of it. Will figured Hiram must have had his first cutting of hay in for the summer—and hay burns as readily as gunpowder.

Grass was already growing well on the six mounds off to the side of the wreckage of the barn—four large mounds and two small ones. Will sat and stared at the overgrown little hills until Slick began to dance nervously, not understanding the strange, choking sounds coming from his owner.

Will swung his horse away from the barn and house and rode toward Dry Creek.

Lucas was whacking away at a horseshoe on his anvil. When he was satisfied with the shape he looked up at Will.

"I'll be headin' out in the morning," Will said. "I figure to buy you one of them steak dinners an' all the beer you can drink as a send-off tonight." He held out five gold eagles to the blacksmith. "This oughta take care of your work on Slick an' his feed an' the rent on the room."

"Bullshit," Lucas said. "I don't take money from friends—an' that's what you are, Will. A friend. Plus, looks like I got a prime foal outta the deal if my mare took good, an' I think she did. So put your money away."

Will had anticipated just such a reaction. Five gold eagles rested on the table next to the bed in the hayloft, along with a note that read, "Thanks, Lucas. See you soon, my friend. Will Lewis (of the H&W Cattle Ranch)."

The steaks that evening were prime—thick, juicy, and perfectly cooked. The beer was bitter cold and tasted sharply of hops—the kind of beer a man could drink all night and thoroughly enjoy each and every glug. When they'd finished their meal, Lucas handed over a bill of sale with a crude map drawn on the blank side, showing a few towns and the spot he figured One Dog would swing across the river and into Mexico. Will studied it carefully. "What're these round things?" he asked.

"Water. Ain't much of it out there. Far as I know, these here got at least a trickle year-round."

"Good. Thanks." He folded the map carefully and put it in his shirt pocket. "What say we belly up to the bar? This brew is tastin' awful good."

They'd barely slurped the snow-white foam off their first beers at the bar when a voice cut through the saloon chatter and the drunken laughter.

"Weeel Leweees!"

Will turned slowly, stepping away from the bar. There were two men facing him from about eight feet away. The speaker was Mexican, with long, greasy hair and a drooping mustache that hung two inches below his jaw. He was tall for a Mex—maybe five feet ten—and his holster, tied low on his thigh, held a Colt .45. "You have someteeng my fren' Meester VanGelder wants. Meester VanGelder, he always gets what he wants."

The second man was white, short, and scruffy, looking like a cowhand at the end of a drive, except for his tied-down holster. He took a couple steps to the side of his partner.

"Back away, Lucas," Will said quietly. "You ain't armed, an' this is my fight."

"But—"

"Do it!"

Lucas reluctantly stepped toward the end of the bar.

"Your friend VanGelder is a fat, cowardly pig, an' you two sows look like you came from the same litter," Will said in almost a conversational tone of voice. "You got something to take care of with me, let's get to it. If not, get out an' don't bother me."

The Mexican's eyes were coal black and glistened

like those of a snake. "You make beeg talk," he snarled, "but now you die. No?" His hand swept to the grips of his pistol.

Will drew and fired twice before the Mexican cleared leather. Both rounds took the man midchest, hurling him back onto a table, which collapsed under his weight. The other was leveling his pistol at Will when Will's third round plowed a hole in his throat. Blood spurted a foot from his neck and his gun dropped to the floor. He collapsed slowly, clenching his neck, making a liquid, gurgling sound. He was dead before he hit the floor.

There was utter and complete silence in the saloon for a long moment. Then, one of the men who'd scurried away from the bar whispered, "Holy shit."

Will nodded to the bartender. "Draw us a couple of buckets of beer an' we'll drink by ourselves, somewheres else. Tell you the truth, some of your customers kinda piss me off."

Chapter Two

One Dog would have been a strikingly handsome man—except for his eyes, which were narrow, reptilian, constantly in motion. His features were finely chiseled and his skin the hue of aged brass. His muscles weren't prominent, but the flesh of his arms, body, and legs was tight—taut, actually—and he moved with the economical stealth and agility of a mountain cat. He wore a Confederate shirt with the sleeves torn off and Union Army pants. A pair of ammunition bandoliers crossed his chest and a rifle on a sling rested across his back.

One Dog rode a tall pinto bareback. There was no bit in the animal's mouth; instead he was controlled by heel and leg commands and a strand of tanned and supple deer hide loosely wrapped around the animal's muzzle, leading back to reins.

None of One Dog's men had ever seen him smile, much less laugh. They'd all seen him kill numerous times. He rode ahead and to the side of the herd of thirst-crazed cattle as his men prodded them into a gait far too fast for the stultifying heat. Many of the animal's tongues protruded limply from their mouths, coated with dirt and dust.

In the distance One Dog saw the pale smoke rising

from the pit of stones being prepared for his sweat lodge. He rode in that direction. The four men he'd sent to prepare the lodge had done a good job. The sapling frame shaped a dome about ten feet in diameter, and buffalo hides covered the frame, making it all but airtight when the entrance/exit flap was closed. Inside, centered in the lodge, was a pit a couple of feet in diameter and a foot deep. One Dog swung down from his mount and inspected the pit where the stones were being heated. Several already were brilliant orange red. He nodded to his men; they'd done good work.

One Dog hadn't partaken of a sweat lodge in well over a year. Within the last week or so, however, he'd felt a cloud of death—his death—winding its way around him, invading his sleep, confusing his thoughts. He could not allow this to happen. He could not fear death nor anything else if he was to keep his magic, his medicine. The sweat lodge, he knew, would cleanse him of the dreams and the sense of foreboding that haunted him and would surely replenish the power of his medicine. He'd taken neither food nor water for the last two full days, and earlier that morning had forced himself to vomit what little was in his stomach. Now he walked a couple hundred yards from the lodge, sat in the sun, closed his eyes, and reached inside himself in meditation.

The black cloud remained around and over him, even through his long meditation. Darkness had fallen. One Dog walked to the glow of the stone pit. All the rocks were red now. They were ready. He ordered his men to fill the central pit of the lodge with the superheated stones. The men prodded individual stones into the small hole using long shafts to do so. Nevertheless, each of them broke a heavy sweat although several feet from the stones.

One Dog entered the lodge and pegged the entrance flap to the ground. Then he sat cross-legged, facing east. The intensity of the heat made him dizzy, and breathing was difficult. He fumbled at the small deerskin sack in the pocket of his shirt and leaned forward to pour the contents into the center of the searing-hot pit. The mushroom buds immediately burst into flame and just as quickly became thick, acrid-smelling smoke that brought spasms of racking coughing that shook One Dog's entire body. He forced the coughing to stop by holding his breath and then began to sip the smoke as one would sip a small bit of water. The holy magic of the mushroom buds touched him and he breathed more easily, without coughing, drawing in the sacred smoke, feeling his spirit loosen to accept whatever truth lay ahead of him.

One Dog drifted from the sweat lodge to the place of his birth. Although he'd left his mother's womb only an hour ago, the vision of his naming came to him: his mother stood holding him at the front of the tepee. His father, massive, strong, stood in front of her. A group of wild dogs approached, bodies low to the ground, teeth bared, their growling like mounting thunder. His father nocked an arrow and pulled it to the full bend of his bow—and then released the arrow. The shaft flew faster than an eye could follow, and its flint head sank four inches into the space in front of the dog's right foreleg, piercing his heart, killing him instantly. The other dogs scattered.

"My son's name will be One Dog," his father declared. "One day he will kill as easily as I killed this dog. He will be a great warrior."

One Dog floated—drifted—to his first kill. He was but twelve years old but handled a bow like a man and was feared by the other boys his age. The victim was a miner leading a loaded-down donkey. The miner was a big man, broad shouldered, with a beard that reached his belt, and bare arms with bulging muscles that stressed his skin. He carried a pistol in a holster and a rifle in his right hand. It was a rocky, hilly area: it would have been easy to take the white man from cover. One Dog spat on the ground and made his way past the man and the donkey, keeping outcroppings and hills between them. When he stepped out from behind a tepee-sized rock, his bow was pulled and ready. "White snake!" he called.

The miner began to raise his rifle when the arrow struck his throat. One Dog took the man's hair and slit the donkey's throat. "I am a warrior!" he shouted, listening to his voice echo, as pleased and proud as he'd ever been in his life. It was there, he believed, that his magic was born—the medicine that had protected him all these years, through all the battles, all the killings, all the tortures and burnings. He heard his twelve-year-old voice cry out again, "I am a warrior!" and it was true and it was good.

Long Nose bragged about the speed of his paint horse. One Dog believed his bay was faster. The bet was horse against horse: the winner took the loser's animal—and the pride of its rider. It was a long and very close race. Long Nose won, and his victory was seen by the tribe. One Dog slid down from his heaving, sweat-dripping horse, pulled his knife from its sheath, and plunged it to the hilt into his bay's eye. "Here's your horse," he said to Long Nose as the bay crumpled to the ground.

Long Nose held One Dog's eyes for a long time before he swung his horse away and rode off. So strong was One Dog's medicine that Long Nose never returned to the tribe.

The first farm attack sprang into the air in front of One Dog, without the cloudlike drifting that had carried the other visions. It hadn't been at all difficult to assemble a group of crazies: deserters from both sides, drunks, gunfighters, drifters, murderers running from the law. One Dog killed a couple of them in front of the others to establish his superiority. He expected no loyalty from his gang, but he demanded their fear of him, and got it. The crew was without prejudice, as was One Dog. They hated everyone—whatever the race, creed, color, or tribe—equally.

What bonded them together was their bloodthirstiness—killing for the sake of killing.

The farm was a small cattle operation: a hundred acres or so, perhaps two hundred head of beef, the owner, his wife, and two hired hands. One Dog hit both the house and the bunkhouse fast and hard. His fire arrows and those of the other Indians sent the occupants scurrying out, to be mowed down by gunfire. The three men were killed first. It took the wife a much longer time before death released her. The crew carried off nothing and didn't bother to collect the cattle. They watched the house and barn burn to cinders, passing bottles of rotgut tequila among them, laughing, recalling the woman's screams.

The smoke from the peyote mushrooms became dense again, darker, more pungent, burning One Dog's nose and throat as he inhaled.

The vision, at first, was of an Appaloosa horse, riderless, breathing fire, hooves striking blue sparks from the ground as the massive animal galloped toward him, teeth bared, keening a quavering death canticle. The horse burst into flames and was gone. A man far larger than life, faceless, appeared. He held a long-bladed, bloodied knife in one hand and a pistol in the other.

Behind the giant came a man, a woman, two children,

and two dogs. They were of normal size. Each person had the fangs of a viper at the corners of his or her mouth. One Dog felt a terror, a cold, lashing wind, such as he'd never experienced before.

One Dog, whimpering, lumbered to his feet and drew his knife. He slashed the buffalo hide of the sweat lodge and fought his way through the supporting saplings, tumbling out of the smoke and the intense heat onto the ground.

Will Lewis drank coffee with Lucas in the predawn before he set out to find One Dog. Slick was packed, saddlebags bulging. Will had cleaned and lubricated both his rifle and his pistol the night before, although neither had needed any attention.

"Got the map I made?" Lucas asked.

Will patted his chest pocket. "Yep."

"Grazing is going to be piss-poor—everything's burned out this time o' the year—but I showed some places where ol' Slick can get some grass in his belly."

"I noticed," Will said. "And it's mostly near water. That'll make things easier."

"That's how I figured it."

The silence between the two men stretched into a state of discomfort. Both were aware of the burgeoning friendship that had grown between them—and both knew it was quite possible that they'd never see one another again.

"Well, hell," Will said, finishing his coffee and setting the mug aside. "I might just as well pull out, Lucas—use all the daylight I can."

"I guess. One thing, Will: there ain't no shame nor dishonor in picking One Dog offa his horse with your rifle at a hundred yards or so. Then you can take his men down as you see fit. One Dog is purely evil—you'd be doin' the world a favor."

"That ain't my way, Lucas."

Lucas sighed. "I figured you'd say that." The men extended their hands and shook, peering into one another's eyes, seeing the friendship there.

"Watch your back, pard," Lucas said. He turned away and began shoveling pea coal into his forge.

"I'll do that," Will said. He mounted and clucked to Slick.

He could have cut off a few miles by not riding out to the ranch, but for some reason it was important to him that his journey start there. He didn't dismount at the mounds; in fact he spent only a few moments gazing at them. The image, he knew, he'd carry forever, and it would push him on when he was too weary to take another step.

Will didn't mind traveling alone. In fact, he preferred it. He'd deserted the Confederate Army after the Third Battle of Petersburg, where Grant overwhelmed Lee and the rebels in sixty-five. Since then he'd drifted alone, putting together a few men when he needed them, and leaving them as soon as the job was done.

The sun, Will realized, was his most powerful enemy. Early on he'd loped Slick a bit, but as the heat became more debilitating, he held the horse to a rapid walk, broken every few miles for more miles of a slow walk. Both man and horse were dripping sweat by midday.

At dusk they struck a tiny oasis with a few scraggly, desiccated desert pines around the puddle of sulfur-smelling water, right where Lucas had placed it on the map. Both Will and Slick drank: Will figured that using as little canteen water as possible made good sense.

Will hobbled Slick and let him graze on what little grass there was and walked out on the prairie. He didn't have to go far before he spooked a fat jack-rabbit out of some scrub and took it down with a single round from his Colt. He skinned and gutted it, built a small fire from sticks and broken branches, skewered the carcass, and sat back as the meat sizzled over the flames.

He used canteen water to brew coffee in an empty sliced-peaches can that had been with him since he left Folsom. Coffee was not only a necessity, but was precious, and brewed from sulfur water, it would have tasted like runoff from a hog pen, but it was coffee, and that's what counted.

The days passed, one a precise mirror of the one before and the one to follow, except that Will knew each mile brought him closer to One Dog and his band. He lived on jerky, rabbit, prairie dog, and a couple of times skinned-out rattlesnakes. Slick maintained his strength on the sparse grazing, but he was losing a bit of weight.

The town of Lord's Rest had seemed impossibly far off when he left Dry Creek, but now he was a few miles from it and his mouth was watering as he imagined a good meal, a few beers, and maybe a shave. A bath would have been a foolish luxury: he'd be soaked in sweat as soon as he was back on the trail.

Slick, he knew, could use a day or so off, some good feed, lots of clean water, and some rest, and it was possible Will could pick up some information in the town.

*   *   *

The coach stop had two saloons, a mercantile, and a livery. There were other single-story buildings but they were boarded up. One of the saloons had a hand-painted sign over its batwings saying EAT DRINK—BEER—WISKEY—NO CREDIT TO NOBODY. There were a couple of cow ponies tied to the rail in front of the place. The gin mill across the street either had walk-in drinkers or none at all—there were no horses at the rail.

He left Slick to the care of the blacksmith at the livery after looking over the other horses in stalls and out in a corral. They all looked good—brushed, shod, and well fed. He knew his horse would get good care—and his overtipping of the smith wouldn't hurt, either.

Will walked down to the "Eat Drink" joint and pushed through the batwings, the hinges of which were in dire need of grease or oil. He stood just inside for several moments, letting his eyes adjust to the murky light. There was a pair of men slouched at the far end of the bar. All but one of the few tables were empty. The one closest to the back wall looked as if someone had thrown a pile of rags on it, along with an empty whiskey bottle. Will looked closer. The pile of rags was a man, obviously passed out.

The bartender was squinting at the print of a dime novel, his lips moving as he read. He put his book down and faced Will.

"What'll it be?"

"A couple of cold beers and a shot of redeye," Will said. "And give the boys down at the end the same."

"I can't serve ya nothin' 'til I see your money," the bartender said. "Too many goddamn freeloaders drift through here."

"Sure," Will said, and dropped a pair of gold eagles on the scarred and sticky bar. "That do it?"

"Hell, you can buy the dump for that." The barkeep grinned. "I ain't seen nothin' but nickels and pennies for better'n a year now." He pulled a pair of schooners of beer and set them in front of Will.

"No business?" Will asked.

"No people. A buncha religious nuts decided to build a town here an' got a pretty good start. Even the L an' J Coach Line set a stop here. Thing is, there wasn't no law. The church the loons was buildin' got burned down, an' the bidnesses all went to hell, an' the God folks started pullin' out when they found they couldn't grow nothing but scrub an' rocks, even with the Lord helpin' 'em." He drew beers for the fellows down the bar and then came back to Will to fill a double shot glass from an unlabeled bottle. "They was strange folks but harmless 'nuff. They done that speakin'-in-tongues stuff an' we could hear howlin' and yellin' comin' from their gatherings. Some say they handled snakes, but I never seen that myself, so I dunno."

"What about the gent at the table? He need a drink?"

"Hell, no. What he needs is a new mind an' to be run through a sheep dip to kill his stink. I dunno where his money comes from but he buys a bottle every mornin', goes over there, sets down, an' commences to drink it. Then he passes out an' sleeps for the rest of the day. I don't even know his name, or if he's got one."

Will drained the shot glass and coughed as the sensation of a yard of barbed wire being stuffed into his mouth, down his throat, and into his gut struck him. "Damn," he gasped.

"You git used to it," the 'tender said.

"I s'pose I could get used to a kick in the eggs," Will gasped, "but that don't mean I'd like to try it more'n once."

The bartender nodded toward the end of the bar. "Them boys has grown right fond of it."

Will watched as the two downed the whiskey as if it were milk and lit into their beers.

"What brings you to Lord's Rest?" the bartender asked. "If you're runnin' from the law it don't make no nevermind to me."

"Hey, fellas," Will called to the other drinkers, "come on up here so we can talk a bit. Drinks're on me." He answered the bartender's question. "I'm lookin' for some men—a bunch ridin' together," he said.

The pair of boozers moved amazingly fast down the bar to stand next to Will, empty schooners and shot glasses in their hands. Will pointed to the glasses and the bartender complied.

"You?" he asked.

"Beer. No more of that panther piss you call whiskey."

" 'Bout these men you're lookin' for—you wantin' to hire them on for a drive or somethin'?" the fellow closest to Will asked.

"No—just lookin' for 'em, is all." He sipped his beer. "You boys ever hear of One Dog?"

The bartender's well-tanned face went ghostly pale. The silence in the saloon was like that of a crypt at midnight. The pair of boozers started toward the batwings, leaving their drinks on the bar.

"Git back here, you two," Will growled. "I bought drinks an' I'll keep on buyin'. All I want is some information."

"One Dog is somethin' we don't talk about," the 'tender said. "We want to keep our hair."

The boozers nodded, standing at the bar, not touching their abandoned drinks.

"Here's the thing," Will said. "You either talk to me or you don't. You talk, that's the end of it. I never saw or heard of you boys or this crummy li'l town. You don't talk an' when I find One Dog I let him an' his gang know I got info from you 'bout where he was."

The boozers looked at one another for a long moment. Finally, one spoke. "Couple weeks ago One Dog an' his riders come upon a saddle bum 'bout three, four miles outta town. A kid out rabbit huntin' found the drifter's head stuck on a tall shaft pushed into the ground. Other parts of his body was around, too. Poor fella's nuts was jammed in his mouth." He downed the whiskey and motioned for another.

"You sure it was One Dog?" Will asked.

"Oh, yeah," the bartender said. " 'Cause a couple days later a sodbuster was burned out an' him an' his family killed. There ain't 'nuff rogue Injuns 'round these parts to take down a wooly, much less pull shit like that. The sodbuster, he come in here every so often. Had him a wife an' seven kids."

"One Dog was headin' toward the Rio Grande?"

"I s'pose so."

"Nobody track them? No posse or nothin'?"

"We got no law here an' the army don't bother with us," the bartender said. "An' you can bet any bunch trackin' One Dog is ridin' into a ambush—an' after a lot of pain, is gonna be real dead. No two ways about it."

"Maybe," Will said. "Buy these boys drinks until one of them eagles is worn out. You keep the other one." He turned from the bar and then turned back. "Say—anywhere in town a man can get a shave?"

"Jus' down the street—big buildin', used to be a cathouse. It's boarded up, but the door opens. Fella there is a doc—kinda—an' a barber."

"Likes his ganja, the doc does. But it's early 'nuff—he should be OK," one of the drunks said.

Will walked down to the old cathouse and pushed the door open. A barber's chair sat in the middle of a small room. The room itself was filled with grayish smoke that smelled a bit like cedar. "Shit," Will grumbled, and began to go out the door.

"Now hold on there," a raspy voice called from an adjoining room. "I heard you mumble a profanity when you saw my barber chair—which is manufactured by the finest firm in Chicago, Illinois, and cost a pretty penny—and I think I deserve an explanation." The speaker stepped into the room with the barber chair. He was of medium height, grossly fat, and quite neatly dressed. He held a meerschaum pipe in his left hand.

"It ain't your chair I object to," Will said. "It's the weed you're burnin'. Hell, I'm lookin' for a shave an' you're liable to cut my throat."

"I resent that," the fat man said. "It's true that on occasion I may take a few puffs of a plant the good Lord put on earth for my use and the use of those fine and noble people, the Mexicans. But my skills are in no way impaired. Perhaps later in the day wouldn't be the best time for a shave, but, sir, I've barely left my bed."

"Yeah. Well, I don't—"

"And, since you're a new customer to my emporium, I'll add a hot bath at no price, and provide you with a fine Cuban cigar and a taste of brandy while you wash and soak." He paused and then added, "If I may say so, sir, you're looking a mite soiled."

Will's beard was driving him nuts with its itching, and the bath sounded awfully good. The cigar and brandy sweetened the offer. "OK," he said, "you got a deal. But you cut me an' I'll shoot you full of holes. Fair 'nuff?"

"Indeed. Take a seat in the chair an' I'll get the water boiling. Perhaps a brandy now while you wait?"

Will nodded. "Sure. It can't be no worse than the swill I downed at the saloon."

The barber waddled into the other room and returned in a few moments with a tumbler of amber liquid. He handed the glass to Will and said, "Now I'll see to heating the water."

Will sniffed at the glass. It had the scent of fresh-cut hickory wood and brown sugar. He took a cautious sip. It was the best booze he'd ever tasted. While the big man wrestled wood into his stove and placed buckets of water on the cooking surface, Will settled back in the chair, sipping and putting together what he'd learned at the saloon. It wasn't long until he heard water churning and boiling. The barber returned with a white sheet—and another tumbler of brandy, which Will accepted without argument. "I'll shave you first, and then you can luxuriate in your bath in the next room." He spread the sheet over Will's lap and around his neck, and stirred a mug of soap into a creamy, clean-smelling froth, which he spread with a hog's-hair brush over Will's neck and face. His straight razor moved easily, slowly, not tugging at whiskers. In a matter of a few minutes, Will's face was as pink and smooth as a young virgin's ass.

"Bath's ready," the barber said, handing Will the promised cigar, already lit and burning evenly and aromatically, and his glass of brandy. Will stood next to the tub, stripped, and sank his body into the still-steaming water. The barber handed him a long-handled scrub brush and a chunk of lye soap and then stepped out to the other room. Will soaked, drank brandy, smoked his cigar, and watched the water he was in change color from a sparkling clear to a brownish hue as sweat and dirt lifted away from his body.

The cathouse was totally silent, as was the town of Lord's Rest. Will's mind drifted like the smoke from the cigar clenched lightly between his teeth. *Coulda been different—a lot different,* he thought. *Maybe me an' Hiram would be cattle barons, or could be I'd have a wife an' a passel of kids an' so much prime land somewhere it'd take a good man on a strong horse a week to ride around it. I'd set on the front porch at dusk with a glass of bourbon an' watch my horses out on pasture an' listen to my kids rippin' 'round after each other. I'd have a little gut from eatin' so good an' so often, an' my neighbors would wave— Ahhh, bullshit.*

That wasn't me. The first Colt .45 I bought—with its taped-up grips an' rusted finish an' a trigger that had to be yanked rather than eased—changed my whole life. That gun gave me the power I needed to do anything I wanted, get anything I wanted. Hell, the first mercantile I robbed, I wasn't but thirteen years old an' nervous as a whore in church, an' my voice squeaked when I demanded the money. He chuckled out loud. *Made off with four dollars an' fifteen cents, but it was a start, an' it felt better than anything had ever felt before.*

First man I drew against was a drunken cowpuncher who'd been slappin' me 'round in a gin mill for no reason. I took it for a bit an' then faced him. I had two rounds in his chest 'fore he was able to fumble his pistol outta his holster.

I never cared for killin', but I've done 'nuff of it. Thing is, I never killed a man who didn't need killin'. Now, this One Dog . . .

That thought raised him from his languor. He put the brush and soap to good use and then stepped out of the foul water and dried off with a rough towel. He dressed quickly, tugged his boots on, and went out front. The barber was sucking at his pipe, smiling. "What do I owe you?" Will asked.

"A dollar'll do her."

Will gave him two. "Anyplace in town I can get a room for a couple nights an' a decent meal?"

"Hell, boy," the barber grinned, "this place was a cathouse. I got more damn rooms'n a ol' whore has crabs. Cost you a dollar a night. Only real grub in town is the saloon on the other side of the street, but it isn't a half-bad feed. That 'Eat Drink' sign on the other gin mill don't mean a thing 'cept the sign was there when the owner bought the joint."

Will handed over another pair of dollars. "I'll be back later," he said.

The meal at the saloon wasn't half bad: the steak was large and thick and cooked so that thin blood ran from its middle. Will sat at his table, drank a pot of coffee, and then started on beer. It was good beer—not cold, but not warm, either. He rolled smokes until his fingers no longer obeyed and he scattered perfectly good Bull Durham all over his table, put a bunch of money next to his empty plate, and weaved back to the cathouse. He slept the rest of the day away as well as the full night.

In the morning he ate a half dozen fried eggs and most of a pound of bacon, along with a helping of thin-cut fried potatoes and several cups of coffee. He walked down the street and checked on Slick, who snorted at him and then dropped his muzzle back into a nice serving of crimped oats and molasses.

Will spent the rest of the day sitting in the shade of the saloon's overhang, went inside at late dusk, drank too much, and crossed the street to his room. He flopped onto the bed fully dressed except for his hat, which he tossed toward the door, and slept deeply and dreamlessly for the night.

The screams he heard at first light tried to work themselves into a dream, but failed. Will sat up as the howls of pain from the street brought him to full wakefulness. The window of his room no doubt hadn't been cleaned for years, but it was possible to see through parts of it.

There were two men on horseback—Indians, obviously—and a white man with a rifle.

The two drunks from the day before were yelling with pain, screaming for help. The Indians fired arrows at the drunks, starting low—just above their heels, and then moving upward. The Indians were good: their shafts went where they wanted them to. Their speed and skill with their weapons was nothing short of amazing. A man barely had time to scream before the next arrow was unerringly on its way.

Some grunted words were exchanged between the two Indians. They laughed and nodded to one another. The next two arrows severed the spines of the two harmless drunks at about midback. They fell clumsily, with no control of their limbs, like a child's rag doll hurled against a wall.

Will scrambled from his room and down the stairs, his right hand checking the position of his Colt. He burst out of the cathouse a few seconds too late. The two men were facedown in the dirt of the street with arrows buried several inches into the backs of their heads—the final punishment for speaking of One Dog.

An arrow slashed a shallow furrow across Will's cheek and blood cascaded down the side of his face. He was on the ground, rolling in the dirt, before the next arrow from the second Indian missed his face by a couple of inches. It was hard to keep moving and fire accurately at the Indians, and even if he dropped them, there was the white man with the rifle.

Will fired twice at the Indian who'd cut his face and he got lucky: a slug tore through the archer's shoulder and the second entered his right eye socket. The second Indian was drawing his bow as Will got his balance on the ground. He put two bullets in the man's chest.

The rifleman was the problem now and Will rolled again, just as a gritty volcano of dirt spurted an inch from his face. He blinked away the grit, and as the rifleman worked the lever of his weapon, Will blew the top of the man's head off, blood, bone, and brain tissue scattering in a pinkish red mist.

The rifleman collapsed from his horse. Will recognized him—the rag-dressed boozer in the saloon who was slumped over the table with the empty bottle in front of him.

Will walked to the pair of dead Indians. Both wore war paint on their faces, but their clothing was strange—one wore a rebel outfit with bullet holes in the shirt that were there long before he met Will Lewis; the other, butternut drawers and a Union shirt. The rifleman looked like a down-on-his-luck cowhand who hadn't seen a new shirt or pair of drawers for a good long time. The serape he wore was too large for his body and there were bullet rents through it—mainly in the back.

Will slid the cylinder of his pistol to the side, let the empties drop to the ground, and replaced them with fresh cartridges. He holstered the Colt and raised the fingers of his right hand to his cheek. Blood was gushing, cascading, onto his neck and shirt.

A quick flash of a thought flicked into his mind and he forgot his wound and his flowing blood. He set out at a clumsy run to the saloon where he'd asked questions about One Dog. He pushed through the batwings and breathed a sigh of relief. The 'tender was peeking over the bar, unmoving.

"I'm glad you're OK," Will began as his vision cleared in the dreary light. "Those two boys . . ."

He looked more closely. The bartender's head was planted on the handle he used to draw beer from a barrel. Will looked closer, wiping blood from his face. A long tube of bloody, glistening intestine snaked out of a lengthy gash in the man's stomach. His pants were at his knees; his groin was a bloody, sexless mess.

Will turned away, gagging, choking, bile burning in his throat, dizzy from what he'd just seen and from his loss of blood.

He stumbled out of the saloon and down the street

to the barber's place. The usual thick scent of ganja filled the room. The barber was in his corner chair, almost invisible behind a shroud of smoke.

"How screwed up are you?" Will asked. "I need some stitches bad."

The barber smiled. "I'm jus' havin' my mornin' smoke, is all. I can sew you up right fine." He laughed then, totally inappropriately. "I seen what happened. Them Injuns was for sure handy with the arrows. An' you—"

Will stepped closer and backhanded the barber—hard. "You drink a pot of coffee an' then git to work on my face 'fore I bleed to death. Hear? You don't, I'll gun you as dead as them bodies out in the street."

"I don't need coffee. I can stitch you up just fine. Thing is, it'll hurt like a bitch. How about you take a few sucks on my pipe—relax a bit, kill the pain?"

"No. Jus' do your sewin'."

"Maybe some booze? Like I said, this is gonna hurt bad."

"Goddammit . . ."

"OK, OK—no need to get feisty an' outta sorts." He fetched a leather kit box such as surgeons used during the War of Northern Aggression and selected a hooked needle and a long length of suture material. "Too bad I don't have some chloroform, but I don't. See, chloroform will put a man to sleep an' he'll—"

"Do your work an' shut the hell up," Will interrupted.

"Yessir."

The suturing was an ordeal that had Will digging his fingernails into his palms until they bled. After an eternity the barber placed the last of thirty-seven stitches and tied off his handiwork. "Gonna leave a scar, but what the hell," he commented. "You wasn't all that pretty to begin with. Now—here's what you gotta do. Go over to the mercantile an' pick up a quart of redeye an' a clean bandanna. Every mornin' you soak the bandanna in booze and wash down the wound.

"Take a nip if you want—the cleanin' is gonna sting some. After maybe twelve, fourteen days, cut the first suture an' pull the whole length out. Don't yank—kinda use steady pressure an' she should come right on out, slick as can be."

Will stood up from the chair woozily, but quickly regained his balance. The side of his face felt like a mule had kicked him. He handed the barber a gold eagle. "Thanks. You quit burnin' that weed an' you might could make a good sawbones."

The barber pocketed the coin and mumbled something that ended with "... an' the horse you rode in on."

Will strolled on over to the mercantile, weaving slightly but walking fairly well. It was the messiest, most poorly kept store he'd ever been in. The storekeeper was a large—very large—woman who quickly brought the image of a Brahma bull to Will's mind. He wandered the aisles until he came to an uneven pile of bandannas and pulled one out from the bottom of the pile. He went to the counter. "I need a quart of decent whiskey," he said, "an' this bandanna."

"What happened to your puss?" the woman asked. There was no sympathy in her whiskey-and-gravel voice, only mild curiosity.

"I bit myself," Will said. "How much for the booze an' the bandanna?"

"Say—ain't you the gunman who put an' end to them three this morning?"

"No."

"Yes ya are—I seen it from my window right here. Ornery sumbitch, ain't you?" She turned and plucked a bottle from under the counter. "This here's a good sippin' bourbon," she said. "Aged."

Will looked over the bottle. The label was slightly crooked, and the print on it was fuzzy and next to impossible to read. "Old . . . old what?" he asked. "I can't read this."

"Says Ol' Kaintuck Home—brung here all the way from Kaintucky."

"Brung all the way from the barrel of this crap you got in the cellar—right? Aged maybe part of a day?"

"Buy it or don't buy it—makes no nevermind to me. You ain't gonna git a chance to drink it 'fore One Dog rips yer guts out, anyways."

"You pretty sure of that?"

"Damn right. You pissant gunsels don't scare Dog none."

Will dropped some coins on the counter. "You talk to One Dog, do you? Tell him he doesn't have long to live."

The woman laughed, and it was a cruel laugh—like one would give to a fool. "You ever had yer nuts ripped off when you was alive? You ever git to see how long your guts is? You ever had yer head boiled while you was tied upside down over a fire?" She laughed again, that same witchlike laugh. "Yer a fool—an' right soon yer gonna be a dead fool."

Will smiled. "Jus' tell him, OK?" He tipped his hat. "Been real nice doin' business with you an' chattin' with you, too." He took his bottle and his bandanna and left the mercantile. The air outside smelled very good after being in the store.

Slick was out in the small pasture the stablekeeper maintained for his own stock and for the horses he boarded who'd kick hell out of his stalls out of boredom. That, or cribbing—chewing on the crosspieces of their stalls. The swallowed chunks of wood could kill a horse, and it made his stalls look terrible.

As usual, Slick was a good bit away from the other animals. He'd either mounted them or fought them, and they wanted no part of him.

Will leaned against the fence, his face throbbing as if he'd taken a punch every few seconds. He soaked his bandanna with whiskey and gently rubbed it along the line of stitches. It felt as if he'd lit the wound on fire.

"Dammit," he said, tossed the bandanna to the side, and took a long suck from the bottle. It wasn't as bad as the saloon booze, and even if it were, it cut the pain. Will took another suck and put the cork into the bottle. That's when the arrow buried its head in the board he'd been leaning against. He dropped to the ground, Colt already in his hand, and saw an Indian riding toward him, a fresh arrow already nocked. Will's finger was on the trigger and the muzzle of his pistol was chest high to the galloping attacker.

He lowered his weapon and put a slug into the Indian's knee. The bow and arrow dropped into the dirt of the street; the man screeched and grabbed at his leg with both hands and tumbled from his war pony.

Will walked to the Indian, his Colt steady in his hand, muzzle centered on the Indian's head.

"Bad shot," Will said. "Now I can send you away, no? To the place where all your relatives will shun you, laugh at you, and you'll be alone, eating snake and prairie dog, no woman, no horse—no pride. Why? 'Cause you're a coward who was scared off by a white eyes you didn't even know."

"I piss on your mother," the Indian snarled. "I know you." He grasped his knee with both hands. His face was contorted with the pain.

"You know me? Damn, coward, I never seen you before."

"One Dog, he had a vision. He will himself kill you."

"I'll do this: You can crawl to your pony an' some-how git on him. Then you ride back to One Dog an' tell him Will Lewis is gonna kill him—an' all you're getting is some time, 'cause I'm gonna kill all of you who ride with One Dog."

"A corpse—you're a . . ."

Will nudged the Indian's knee with the toe of his boot. "You remember the name I gave you?"

"You said, Lewis—Will Lewis."

"Very good. An' you'll tell One Dog this: He's a cowardly chunk of yellow dog shit—a killer of chil-dren an' of women. Tell him he'll suffer before I kill him."

The Indian spat again. "One Dog cannot be killed. He has medicine—bad medicine—that protects him from white men. You will—"

"This is gettin' tiresome. You gonna do what I said?"

"One Dog will carry your hair on his belt and your head will—"

"Like I said, this is gettin' tedious."

Will fired, the slug giving the Indian a third eye.

"Dumb sumbitch. All you hadda do was make it to your pony, an' ride off. Now, you ain't ridin' nowhere—'cept maybe to hell."

Chapter Three

The saloon on the other side of the street was doing business, as usual. Will saw that the bodies were still in the street, although there was a difference: the Indian's bows, quivers, arrows, and moccasins were gone. The two drunks were drawing hordes more flies than the Indians, probably because of the manner in which the Indians had slaughtered them. The white man with the rifle lost his boots, horse, weapon, gun belt, and hat—and anything he had in his pockets.

"One hell of a sweetheart town," Will said aloud, disgustedly. "Even in Dodge the furniture maker hauled the dead gunsels outta the street. 'Course he got money for boxin' 'em up an' plantin' 'em."

An old gaffer with a patch over one eye sat on a bench in front of the mercantile—all mercantiles had to have benches—whittling aimlessly, not forming anything from the rough block of wood he held, merely cutting thin and narrow strips from it.

"Kids got the bows an' the arrows an' such," the old fellow said. "Ain't nobody in this here town got the balls of a turnip to touch One Dog's men." He thought for a moment.

Will stepped toward the batwings.

"'Course One Dog would up an' gut them kids same way he would a full-growed man. Don't matter none to him.

"You're prolly wonderin' why I got this patch over my eye. Thing is, there ain't nuthin' but a hole there. I lost the eye at Antioch to them sonsabitch bluebellies an' their grapeshot." He paused again. "I s'pose you wanna hear the story."

"No—not at all," Will said, pushing his way into the saloon.

Will stood at the bar and swilled beer and the occasional shot of redeye. He hadn't gone after One Dog immediately, suspecting that the posted guards would be the heaviest after the shootings in Lord's Rest. His face throbbed with his pulse and his head felt as if someone had split it with a dull ax.

The bartender fetched another schooner for Will and asked, "Want me to run a tab for ya for a couple days? Be easier than you haulin' coins outta your drawers."

"No. I'll be ridin' out early tomorrow. I'll pay my way tonight."

"I don't think you'll be ridin' out. We got a nor'easter comin' on like a damn locomotive. Ain't gonna be nobody ridin' nowhere. You don't believe me, you go on out an' take a gander at the sky."

"I've rode in rain an' wind before," Will said. "I guess I can do it again."

"Nossir. I don't think so. Even the goddamn wooly hunters hunker down under cover when something like this comes on."

Will walked to the batwings and out onto the street, beer in hand. The sky in all directions was a roiled, dirty gray, like soiled, fresh-sheared wool, and the temperature had dropped like a rock down a well. Chain lightning flickered and flashed as if spearing the clouds, and thunder grumbled, although the sound was muffled, muted, like the sounds of a far-off cannonade.

A few fat, stinging drops of rain struck Will's face as he stood looking at the sky. The choice was an easy one: go back to his room at the cathouse or into the gin mill. He chose the saloon.

"See wad I mean?" the 'tender said. "An' damn, I was supposed to git some bidness late tonight or tomorra—a bunch of fellas ridin' through. Shit. They ain't gonna be thirsty if they ride in this sumbitch storm, an' that's for sure." He considered for a moment as if working a puzzle in his mind. " 'Course they might like a taste of whiskey."

Will's head was still throbbing. The stitches seemed to be holding well, weeping only minute bits of blood. He ordered a bucket of beer and walked over to a table with his bucket and an almost empty schooner, and rolled himself a smoke.

There were eight, maybe ten, men in the saloon—no women. A couple were playing checkers at a table. The balance were standing at the bar in various states of intoxication, from the gent stretched out on the floor to those who stood straight to those who looked like they'd join their colleague on the floor before long.

The storm was like a living thing, with its massive paws around the saloon. The entire building shook when blasts of wind struck it, beams groaned, and the sounds of shingles ripping from the roof sounded like heavy cartridges striking. The rain—now sheets rather than drops—was lashed almost parallel with the ground by the snarling, howling wind.

Will was building another cigarette when the batwings slammed open, one ripped from its hinges, and three horsemen, as wet and dripping as they'd be had they been dragged across a wide river, swung down from their saddles and hauled off their ponchos. "Whiskey—lots of it," one rider said, using his hand, curved as a scoop, to sluice water off his horse.

"You can't bring them horses . . ." the bartender called. "I ain't gonna clean my floor in the . . ."

The rider who'd dismounted first drew his .45 and put a slug into each of the prominent, almost crab-apple-sized nipples on the nude poster over the bar. The 'tender went back to pouring liquor.

Will stood—somewhat shakily—and faced the horseman. "You never did have no manners," he said. "Ridin' yer damned horse into a fine place like this an' then shooting at the only tits we got to look at. Why hell, I oughta kick yer ass back out into the rain."

The gunman swung toward Will, crouching a bit, planting his boots one a foot ahead of the other, his Colt already in his hand—and then his hard, bearded face broke into a broad smile and he ran to Will. The two men embraced, cursing one another, pounding each other's backs, laughing.

"Yer jus' as ugly as you ever was," the gunman shouted. "You still chasin' them sheep when you get lonely?"

"Seems to me you put the wood to the fattest, ugliest, smelliest whore in Fort Worth an' then never paid the poor heifer. Ain't that right, Austin?"

"Paid her? Why hell, I give her the biggest thrill in her life!"

The other men were shedding their ponchos and dragging the saddles from their horses. They were young, perhaps eighteen or twenty, but it was obvious to Will that these boys were gunfighters—or at least, young fellas who knew about killing.

Will nodded in their direction. "Who's the crew?"

"They ain't mine. We done a little bank together and that's the end of it. We split equal four ways an' then we'll ride off in four different ways."

"How about you pull the saddle offa your horse an' we'll set at a table an' drink some beer an' talk things over?" Will said.

"You betcha," Austin answered. "Hell, I ain't seen you in . . . what, six, seven years? Not since you—"

"Closer to eight," Will interrupted, moving to a table. He watched as his friend pulled cinches.

There'd been four of us figurin' to take the Wells Fargo stage. Rumor had it the coach was carrying pay for silver miners—American bills, not army script. The trail at one point was a long, sweeping curve around a marsh and there were trees on both sides. We heard the rumble and rattle of the coach long before it came into sight. Each of us outlaws pulled his bandanna up over his nose, covering most of his face.

"Don't feel right," I said quietly, our horses standing together.

"Why? It ain't the shotgunner's nor the driver's money. They ain't gonna die for it."

"I dunno. Seems like we been tappin' coaches a little too hard around here, Austin. This one's it for me—I'm takin' my split an' haulin' ass."

Austin thought that over as the sounds of the stage

grew louder. "Might could be you got a good idea there, Will."

We had planned the heist out pretty thoroughly. Austin and me would come out from the trees in front of the coach and hold our guns on the shotgunner and the driver. The other two men would drag out any passengers and get the cash box secured under the front-facing seat. We'd collect the guns any passenger might be carrying—and those of the shotgunner and the driver—and ride off, rich, happy, without having spilled a drop of blood.

That's when the plan went straight to hell.

The fellow riding shotgun raised his weapon toward me and I shot him in the chest. The driver reached for a holstered Colt and Austin put a slug into his shoulder, slamming him off the seat and onto the ground.

There was a barrage of pistol shots and the percussive boom of a shotgun at the passenger door, and both of our partners went down. Three Pinkertons shoved their way out of the coach and opened fire on Austin and me. Austin's horse—a strong, fast bay—caught a bullet that tore off one ear and a good piece of his head, and he went down, hard. Austin did his best to push off, but his horse came down on his lower left leg and boot, pinning him. He fired at a Pinkerton as he struggled to get free, but missed. His second round took the man in the stomach. He screamed and went down. The Pinkerton with the shotgun was looking for me, butt of the weapon to his shoulder, but the coach horses were between us. The battle was over. We were outgunned, and Austin, although he was able to free himself, was a target for a pair of angry, bloodthirsty hired guns who'd just seen their partner gutshot.

I spun my horse away from the carnage and slammed my heels into him. Then, after a couple of long strides, I *hauled back on the reins, rolled the horse back over his haunches, and pounded back to the stagecoach, thinking what a damned fool I was. I wrapped the reins loosely around my saddlehorn, pulled my hide-out derringer, drew my rifle from its scabbard at my right knee, and rode in firing and shouting like a goddamn madman.*

The Pinkertons hustled to the rear of the coach. Austin, face as pale as that of an alabaster doll, leaned against the open stagecoach door, his left foot held off the ground. I galloped directly at him, my good horse picking up speed, coming at Austin like a runaway train. Austin latched onto my horn with both hands and swung on my horse behind me. A cluster of pellets from the shotgun snarled by us like a swarm of angry hornets, and a couple of pistol rounds weren't too far off—but we made it.

"My foot's busted," Austin yelled into my ear, "but I can ride OK."

"Ya damned idjit," I called over my shoulder. "You let that pissant Pinkerton kill your horse . . ."

"I figured I'd git us a bottle of rotgut, too." Austin grinned as he set a tray of beer and the bottle of whiskey on the table.

"I shoulda warned you," Will said. "The whiskey here tastes like it run straight outta Satan's boot."

"Don't make no matter. Booze is booze, no?"

"Not this dragon piss."

Austin drank off a half schooner of beer and poured from the whiskey bottle until the mug was full. He tasted it and smiled. "Ain't bad this way," he said.

"Well."

The silence between the two men settled in very quickly and very uncomfortably.

"Look," Austin said, "I never seen you since you

dumped me off onto that sorrel stud. He was a good horse."

"Yeah. He was. Best in our crew—'cept mine. His owner didn't have no use for him, not with all that Pinkerton lead in him."

"Mmmm. What was that feller's name—you recall?"

"No."

"Me neither. Decent fella, though."

Will took a sack of Bull Durham from his vest pocket, offered it to Austin, who refused, and rolled himself a smoke.

"Ya know, I never knew why you come back when the Pinkertons was gonna shoot my ass off," Austin said. "Thing is, Will, I never got to tell you thanks or nothin'."

"No need," Will said. "I guess I woulda done it for any outlaw."

"Well, here's the thing: I owe you, Will, an' I wanna pay you off."

"I got all the money I need, Austin. There's—"

"That ain't what I'm talkin' 'bout," Austin said. "I . . . uhhh . . ."

"What?"

"I worked for Hiram for a bunch of months when the law was hot after me while you was in Folsom, Will. He was a good man. Me an' him, we usta throw horsehoes an' so forth. He was my boss, but he was my friend.

"An' when his ol' . . . when Sarah wasn't about, I used to ride the girls on my horse—at a gallop, Will. They loved it. They'd laugh an' so forth an' have one he . . . heck of a good time."

Will nodded and began to roll another cigarette.

"I wonder, can we talk about somethin' else—?" Will began.

"No. No, goddammit, Will Lewis. That devil One Dog killed folks I . . . I loved. I'm goin' to put a lot of lead into them sonsabitches—but One Dog, he's all yours, Will. That's the way it's supposed to be. That's the way it will be."

Will sucked down a beer, thinking. "You ride with me, you'll more'n likely die," he said, "an' probably die hard."

Austin grinned. "So will a pile of them murderin' scum."

Will considered for a long moment. "This ain't a pleaure ride, Austin—no robbin', no stealin', no whorin'. It'll be hard ridin' an' lots of blood."

For the first time in the saloon, the grin disappeared from Austin's face. His eyes caught and held Will's. "Understood," he said. Then, he repeated, "Understood."

Will shook his head. "Dammit, Austin, you don't know what you're gettin' into here. One Dog an' his crew are—"

The grin came back to Austin's face as he interrupted Will. "What those loons are is not as tough as we are. Right? All we gotta do is kill the whole goddamn bunch an' then we'll be all set. Right?"

Will shook his head again. "Damn," he said.

"Looky here, Will," Austin said. "You ever seen a man as good with a gun as me?"

"Yeah. Me. An' I seen this gunnie standin' on one leg waitin' to see how many holes the Pinkertons could put into him."

"Well, hell. They up an' shot my horse an' he fell on me. Other'n that, I was good."

"Good with a busted-up foot an' no ammo an' standin' there like a cigar-store Injun."

Austin's grin disappeared again. He leaned across the table until his face was but a few inches from Will's. "I'll say this: I'm ridin' with you no matter how you flap your mouth. See, all you do is think on your own self. Hiram, he was my friend. I rode his girls around, an' I paid a whole ton of respect to Sarah. I whacked fence poles for Hiram, an' I hefted bales. Like I said before, he was my friend. An' Sarah an' the girls . . ."

"You got supplies?" Will asked quietly.

"I will have, come tomorrow morning," Austin said. "A goddamn prairie dog could bust in that mercantile there an' clean 'em out."

"OK. Grab me a bunch of Bull Durham—the sacks with the papers. We'll ride at first light."

Austin held out his hand across the table. Will took it and they shook.

"You still handy with that Colt?" Will asked. "I mean when you ain't clumsy enough to let a horse fall on you an' you got no ammo?"

Austin drained the schooner he'd been holding and picked a new, full one from the tray.

"Name a target, Will." Austin began to stand.

"Stay sittin' right where you are." Austin sat back down. "See them shot glasses on the shelf under the lady whose tits you shot off?"

"Sure."

"When I say shoot, you pick off every other one from right where you are."

"They're kinda tight together, Will."

"Yeah. They are. So will One Dog's men be if we get to them at the right time."

"Hell, man—this ain't no contest." Austin grinned. "I could do this here in my sleep. But look—s'pose you pick off the ones I leave? I don' wanna ride with no ol' fart who can't handle iron. You got some years on you, Will—an' you was locked in Folsom for—"

"Shoot," Will said.

Austin had pushed his chair back, balancing it on its hind legs. His pistol was in his hand with speed that brought a smile to Will's face. The six shots were thunderous in the saloon, but still not as loud as the storm outside.

"You nicked the fourth one."

"Yer ass, Will Lewis—the sumbitch already had a notch in it. Now, 'cordin' to what we agreed, you was—"

The shot glasses Austin left seemed to disintegrate at the same time. Will holstered his Colt. "OK?" he said.

Austin reached across the table once again. Once again the men shook hands.

The men Austin rode in with were having a fine old time, shooting holes in the walls, blowing bottles to smithereens, drinking with both hands and paying with neither.

"Your boys are tearin' hell outta this place an' they're not payin' a dime," Will said. "I was wonderin', could you get the whole goddamn bunch outta here?"

"I'll make sure they pay up, Will."

"Ain't the point. That ol' fella don't need this horsehit. He ain't a bad ol' guy and I come to like him while I been here. I can see cowhands at the end of a drive with some money in their pockets raisin' some hell, but these clowns of yours, they piss me off. If you don't shag 'em out, I will, Austin—and then the damn fools'll be carried out boots first."

Austin drew his .45, tipped out his cylinder, and filled the empty spaces with fresh cartridges. He pushed his chair back and stood, right hand all but touching the grips of his weapon.

"Hey," he hollered. "Hey. You boys put your rigs on your horses an' git out. We was together for one thing—that bank—and we done it good. Now, git."

"Austin," one of them said, "the storm an' all . . . We ain't goin' nowhere. Not nowhere. We're real happy right here."

"Well," Austin said, "let's talk about this, OK?"

"Ain't nothin' to talk about. We—"

Austin drew and fired his Colt twice. Both slugs found a home in the outlaw's gut.

"What you boys gotta do is split his take, an' like I said, git outta here, storm or no goddamn storm. Ever'body understand? Oh—an' take that mouthy sumbitch's body out an' toss it in the street."

No one answered, but the two outlaws began slapping wet blankets on the backs of their mounts.

"An' lemme say this: I never seen nor heard of none of you. We never rode together. Any one of you who says different faces me—an' if you back-shoot me, my pardner here will do what needs to be done." Austin picked up a schooner and drained half of it. "You boys worked out OK. We all got money an' that's all we was after. But don't cross my path . . ."

The men began to saddle up. Austin stood by the table, his Colt comfortably fitting his hand. When they'd all ridden out of the saloon, hats pulled down, slicker collars wrapped around their necks, Austin pulled a sheaf of bills from his pocket and strode to the bar.

"This oughta do it," he said to the bartender, dropping the money. "If it don't, there's more where that come from."

"That'll do her fine," the 'tender said. "I'll thank you, sir."

"Ain't no 'sir' involved. I'm a common thief jus' like the boys I chased outta here." He grinned. " 'Cept I'm a bit faster an' a whole lot smarter."

Will shook his head slowly from side to side. "Jesus," he said. "He ain't changed a bit."

Will and Austin drank their fill, wrapped themselves in their ponchos against the storm, and fought the wind to the cathouse. The barber was passed out on the floor by his table and the *hempa* smoke was as strong as a skunk trapped in a closet.

"Damn," Austin said, "if that don't smell good, I dunno what does. I ain't had me a decent smoke since me an'—"

"There'll be no smoke and damned little booze, Austin. I remember you after suckin' that weed, an' you was as crazy as a shit-house rat. I'll plug you myself, you start that craziness."

"Feisty as ever," Austin grumbled, following Will up the stairs.

"Take any room you want," Will said. "They're all empty."

Austin tried the doorknob of the room next to Will's. "Sumbitch's locked," he said, and kicked it hard. The door was stout; it stayed closed.

"Take another one," Will said. "They're all the—"

Austin drew and emptied his Colt into and around the doorknob. He pushed the door lightly with his boot, and it swung open with only a tad of metal-to-metal squealing. He grinned at Will, said, " 'Night," and pulled the battered door closed.

The storm and the rain hung around like stink on a manure pile through the night and into the day. Will and Austin stood glumly at the cathouse door.

"Well hell, we might jus' as well get some grub, Will," Ausin said. "Don't make no sense to ride in this shit—an' any tracks there was is long gone."

"Yeah. Rain's fallin' on One Dog, too, though, an' I doubt he's stupid 'nuff to try to move cattle an' horses in this storm. I figure he's holed up somewhere. We'll catch up soon's we can ride. This mud is like greased ice; we'd be sure to bust up our horses, slippin' an' slidin' an' goin' down." He watched the windswept rain for a minute. "Food across the street ain't too bad. Don't matter if it was, howsoever—it's the only choice we got."

Will had always been amazed at Austin's ability to consume food. A Mexican gunslinger in their gang years ago had referred to Austin as *el gordo*—the fat one. The gunsel had told Austin the Spanish term meant "the fast gun," which had pleased Austin immensely.

Will ordered a couple eggs and some bacon and coffee. Austin ordered a dozen eggs, fried; the biggest steak the joint had, cooked bloody rare; a pair of helpings of hashbrown potatoes; a soup bowl of grits and hot sauce; a pot of coffee; and a quart of liquor. "We ain't goin' nowhere today," Austin said defensively about the booze. "A li'l taste won't make no difference." He poured a pair of inches into Will's coffee cup. Will didn't refuse it.

Austin ate like one of those newfangled threshing machines chopped wheat: there was a constant input of food into his mouth until his plate was as empty and barren as a harvested field. He sat back, belched loud enough to scare a good dog that had been sleeping near the door, and filled his coffee cup with booze. "I once heard," he said, "breakfast is a important meal. That's why a ramrod will always make sure his men are fed good of a morning on a drive."

"I never been on a drive where the grub—any meal—was decent," Will commented. "Beans an' salt pork three meals a day ain't what you'd call fine eatin'. What me an' the other hands would do was to put a bullet into a beef every so often, bust one of its legs, an' tell the trail boss the poor critter stuck a hoof in a prairie-dog hole. 'Course there was no reason to waste that meat, so the cook'd grill up a slew of steaks an' chops an' so forth."

Austin nodded, smiling. "Them trail bosses was awful careful about their herds, but a accident sure can happen. A cow is 'bout as bright as a wore-out boot. A drive is jus' bound to lose a few."

The wind and rain stopped sometime during the night, and the following sunrise showed a clear sky and promised a return to the scalding heat that is a West Texas summer. Will and Austin were saddling up when they still needed a lantern to cut the dark in the barn. Will overpaid the stableman for the care of both horses and tossed a five-dollar bill to the boy who cleaned stalls and ran errands.

"You must have a ton of money, Will," Austin said as they rode out of the end of Lord's Rest.

"I got money. What I don't have is a brother or his wife an' children."

"Yeah. That's why we're here, no?"

"Yeah. That's why we're here."

They stopped about midday when the heat was making both the men and the horses drip sweat. Austin sighted in the rifle he'd taken from the mercantile and found it to be a fine weapon.

"We should come to some water 'fore too long, if this map is right," Will said. "We'd best have a sip an' give what we have to our horses."

"Yeah—they're both sweatin' buckets an' the fastest we gone is a slow lope. That kinda worries me, Will. One Dog an' his men will run their horses 'til they drop. We could be losin' ground."

"Maybe so. But even if them killers are good enough to ride the unbroken horses they stole, they'll ride them to death, too. An' I figure most of them deserters never rode nothin' but a plow horse 'fore the war. They don't know how to treat a animal, an' the Indians don't care. We're doin' the right thing, Austin. We'll catch them."

Austin took a quick sip from one of his canteens and poured the rest into his hat for his horse. Will did the same. When the animals sucked the hats dry, both men emptied their second canteens into their hats, and again the horses sucked them dry in moments. Austin put his hat on and walked to his saddlebag. He removed a quart of whiskey, yanked the cork with his teeth, and poured a good three inches into his gullet. "Damn," he said. "Don't taste real good, but least it's wet."

He handed the bottle to Will. Will looked at it longer than Austin thought he would and then tipped it to his mouth. He lowered the level a couple of inches, coughed, and handed the bottle back. He was a little unsteady swinging into his saddle. "I ain't used to rattler venom like that," he said.

"Better'n nothin', no?"

"Maybe."

The oasis, such as it was, was a muddy puddle maybe ten yards wide, most of which was covered with stringy pond scum. There was an apron of decent grass around the water, and after drinking, the horses began mowing the grass.

"Ya know," Austin said, "I ain't never seen so many nice, fat jackrabbits in my life."

"I know. We can't risk a shot, though. We're too close to One Dog. I figure their camp ain't but a mile or two, an' I'm goin' in tonight to look it over."

"They'll have guards out, Will."

"I'm sure they will. They'll give me a chance to test out this hog's tooth." Will slid the knife from his boot and turned it back and forth in his hand.

"We'll both go on foot an' then split . . ."

"No, you stay here with the horses. I been thinkin' 'bout this for a long time. First time, I go alone. If I don't come back, you ride off with the horses an' supplies an' my money. If I'm not back near dawn, you haul ass."

"That don't make no good sense, Will. We—"

"This ain't somethin' I'll argue about. We'll talk a bit later, but that's how it's gonna be. Hear?"

"I hear," Austin said. He shucked off his gun belt, folded it neatly, and set it on the ground. "You ever et raw rabbit?" he asked. "I'm kinda partial to it."

"I've had it. Ain't bad."

"Good. Then we'll eat right fine 'fore you go out, an' we won't burn our supplies. See, I fed my ma for some time by heavin' rocks at rabbits. I got good at it. I could tear a jack's ass off from a long ways away. I still can." He sat down and grunted his boots off and set them next to his gun belt. Any boots were bound to make more noise than a barefoot man, and even though rabbits weren't overly bright, they were intelligent enough to run from noise. "I should be maybe a hour. Don't shoot me when I come back in."

"Lookit," Will protested, "that was a bit of time ago when you was bringin' in jacks by tossing rocks at them. We got plenty of jerky an' some hardtack. All we gotta—"

"You set still an' listen to the horse tear grass. Like I said, I'll be back in a hour, give or take."

Austin walked out into the prairie, snapping a foot up when he stepped on a rock or a baby saguaro. He meandered back and forth, selecting stones that would carry well and that he could pop an unsuspecting jack with.

The sun was dropping rapidly now and the temperature came down a few—a very few—degrees. Still, the difference felt good. The absence of the glaring, merciless sun made all the difference. Will rolled a smoke and leaned back against his saddle. The pastels at the western horizon made the prairie seem inviting, benign. He remembered what an old scratch miner leading a ribby mule told him years ago.

"This prairie is like one a them real pretty hoors that look so good, an' then hand a man a dose of clap or the syph. Shit, if the rattlers an' scorpions don't kill you the goddamn sun will."

"You're out here," Will said.

"Sure. But I'm crazier'n a hoot owl. What's a man like me gonna do but what I'm doin'? Be a ribbon clerk in a fancy mercantile? Maybe go to a city an' start up a big bidness an' be rich?" He spat to the side, ending the conversation.

Will had to admit the ol' boy had a point.

Austin came in not twenty minutes after he went out, swinging a fat jack by its ears in either hand. He dropped them in front of Will, smirking, proud. "I fetched 'em in," he said. "You gut 'em. An' watch you don't nick that sack in there. I hear tell whatever's in it can kill a man, or make him awful sick. It ain't no bigger'n your thumb, so you gotta be careful."

"I guess I never cleaned a rabbit before," Will growled. "Thanks for learnin' me how. I think maybe I'll start me a goddamn rabbit ranch."

Austin took his bottle from his saddlebag, took a long glug, and handed it to Will. "Yer damn near as testy as a sidewinder in a hot skillet," Austin said, but he smiled as he said it.

"I always kinda thought of myself as a kindly man of God, spreadin' cheer an' happiness all over the world."

Eating raw rabbit isn't terribly unlike eating a cow's udder—or any other uncooked flesh, for that matter. It's somewhat stringy, but there's a singular flavor to it, almost as if it were dusted with a light spice of some kind. And there was still a tad of warmth in the meat.

"Good rabbit," Will commented.

"Got the first two I thrown at," Austin said proudly. "Stove their heads in so's they didn't run.

Thing is, I wisht we could make a fire. I cook near's good as I throw."

"Can't risk it. One Dog's men would smell the meat cookin' even if they didn't see the smoke. Then it wouldn't take 'em long to find the fire—an' us."

"Sure." Austin hesitated for a bit, as if rehearsing what he had to say. "You was sayin' you're gonna check out the camp tonight, an' maybe send one a them sonsabitches off to wherever scum like them go. But we're pards, least in this affair, an' I figure we should go together. I ain't a man to let my partner get . . ."

Will put his hand on Austin's shoulder. "We're pards OK, Austin. But all I'm doin' is a little scoutin' tonight—see what the lay of the land is. There'll be plenty of fightin'—I guarantee that. There ain't nobody I'd favor to be with than you when we come down to a battle. But I wanna go tonight. See, it'll be our first strike an' I want to be the one to do it. It's important to me, Austin. I want—need—to be the one to show One Dog we're after him, an' that I'm gonna kill him."

"Well," Austin said.

"Well?"

"I see what you're sayin', Will. First blood always counts an' I know you ain't comin' back here without makin' it flow." Austin took a quick suck from his bottle and offered it to Will.

"Nah, not now," Will said. "When I come back I'll have a sip. What I'm gonna do now is wait out a few hours an' then go for a walk. And I gotta do like you did: shed my boots. Those boys would hear boots no matter how careful I was. You have yer drink. I'm gonna rest a bit."

There wasn't much moon—a selfish crescent—when Will took his boots off. It was better than no moon at all, but the darkness was thick.

Will thought Austin was passed out or asleep or both. He was wrong. Austin said quietly, "Kill at least one a them goat turds, pard."

Will tested the edge of his boot knife with his thumb and smiled. "You can count on it."

The prairie floor was no more kind to Will's feet than it'd been to Austin's. He stumbled once and went down, and would have loved to yell out a curse, but remained silent. A jagged rock cut his face under his left eye, and the impact of his shoulder with the ground shot lightning bolts all the way to his fingertips. He stood up slowly, wiped the blood from his face with a sleeve, and flexed his left arm and hand until everything seemed to work. He went on.

The moonlight cast shadows that made Will reach for his .45, which, of course, wasn't there. The mile or so seemed like the longest stretch in the world, but Will kept walking, picking his steps as well as he could and making not a sound. The cut under his eye was weeping blood and he wiped it away impatiently with his sleeve.

He topped a gradual rise and dropped to his stomach, gazing down at the camp. There was a fire going, with the rump of a beef or horse on a spit, a man wearing a Union officer's outfit turning the crank.

A half dozen or so of the men near the fire were passing a bottle; others walked about, hanging close to the cooking fire. There was but one tepee—the rest of the gang had bedrolls and army blankets spread protectively around the tepee. The scent of the cooking meat reached Will, and in spite of himself, his mouth began to water. Raw rabbit will fill a man up, but it doesn't smell or taste like a real meal.

One Dog had a rope corral set up for the horses he was taking to Mexico—any decent horse brought a real good buck across the border—with or without legal papers. The cattle were calm, either grazing or nudging one another, shagging flies, calves stuck close to their mothers. Will saw one outrider, half asleep on his pinto, riding at a walk around the cattle, swinging over to the horses ever so often.

He knew that there must be at least a couple men standing guard around the camp; One Dog was too bright to assume he and his crew were safe. Will swept his eyes fairly rapidly all around the camp and then slowed his gaze. It took a while but he was finally able to pick out a man leaning back against a boulder, his rifle across his chest. Will couldn't tell if he was an Indian or a deserter, but it made no difference. Whoever the guard was, he was involved in the killing of Will's brother and his family. That bought the figure in the dark a death sentence.

The guard had positioned himself nicely to be killed. Although the slope to his right was steep and rocky, he had chosen the easy way—an almost gentle slope to the boulder he rested against.

Will drew his knife from his belt and grasped it between his teeth. He wanted both hands free as he crawled down the slope headfirst, moving his hands across the soil and rock in front of him, making sure there was nothing he'd loosen that would roll on down, alerting the guard.

Images of his brother floated before him as he moved cautiously. This wouldn't, Will decided, be like killing a man. It'd be like crushing a scorpion under his boot.

Will's hands touched the rock and the sandy surface pressed against his palms. He eased his legs and lower body into position and got his feet under him. Then, shifting the knife from his mouth to his right hand, he began a tortoise-paced movement around the boulder and to his prey.

Peeking around the boulder, Will could see the guard wore a Union uniform, although his hair was heavily greased and tied into a pair of braids that hung over his shoulders and almost to his belt. He smelled like rancid meat, old sweat, and whiskey.

Will crouched, knife ready in his hand, feet under him to spring him forward. He'd take the guard from the right side, grab his hair . . .

Will let his body settle, gave his heart time to stop pounding. He took the knife in his left hand and wiped the sweat from his right on his denim pants. When he grasped the knife again in his right hand again it felt as if it belonged there—as if he and the blade were partners—and he was ready. All it would take would be a quick step around the jagged edge of the rock . . .

And the battle will be on. One Dog will be seeking me as intensely as I'm seeking One Dog.

The fight would go to the death—there was no doubt about that. And One Dog was known and feared for making his captives scream for death, plead for it, beg for it. As suddenly as a bolt of lightning from a clear, blue sky, Will saw himself and Hiram as deeply tanned children of the summer, barefoot, smoking corn-silk cigarettes out behind the barn.

This is for you, Hiram.

Will stepped around the rock, snatched a greasy braid with his left hand, and sawed his blade across the man's throat. Blood spouted in a quick gush a foot or so and then slowed. It was black in the night light, but the heavy, coppery scent was always the same, day or night. Will didn't look at the man's eyes. When the blood stopped flowing Will ripped open the Union campaign jacket and carved *HW* in deep, six-inch letters in the corpse's chest. He wiped his knife on the dead man's pants, slid it back into his belt, and began his escape.

"Luke? Hey, Luke, where the hell are you?" a hoarse voice called, followed by the crunching and snapping of twigs and branches and the dislodging of pebbles and clods of dirt.

Will looked around him. There was what appeared to be a fairly deep indentation—a natural furrow—a few feet from the rock. He slithered into it on his back and drew his knife.

"Goddammit, Luke—if yer drunk again on watch, I'm gonna tear yer ass off. Hear me?"

There was more anger in the voice this time. "Dumb sumbitch! You ain't . . ."

The fellow stepped over Will and the furrow, one boot on either side, beginning to swing his right foot forward to take another stride. Will jammed his knife upward to the hilt, directly between the outlaw's legs, and then twisted it sharply.

Will completely expected a horrendous screech that would bring the entire camp up to the rock, but instead the man fell to his side, hunched over, both hands gripping his groin. His mouth was wide-open, forming a large O, but the only sound from him was an almost feminine squeak. Will rolled out of the furrow and cut the fellow's throat. The gurgle of his death was louder than his reaction to the blade in his privates, but even that wasn't loud. The man was a bare-chested Indian in deerskin pants and moccasins. Will took the moccasins and a Colt .45, carved *HW* on the well-muscled chest, pulled on the moccasins, and headed back to the camp he and Austin had established.

Will noticed his knife was still dripping blood. This time he swiped both sides of the blade on his own pants.

The walk back to the camp was a whole lot more comfortable in the moccasins. He crossed a rocky area in what he thought was almost perfect silence. Apparently, he was wrong. The sound of a handful of beans being shaken frantically in an empty tin can stopped Will where he stood. The snake was somewhere off to his left, maybe a yard or so away—maybe more, maybe less—but Will peered until his eyes teared and all he could see was a small cluster of larger rocks and scattering of smaller ones. The moon gave him no help. He'd hoped that the oily glistening of the serpent's eyes or the pale whiteness of its open mouth would place the rattler for him. The erratic but constant rattling continued. Will's mind built a fat six-footer with fangs as long as a saddler's needle, coiled tightly, ready to strike, the glistening, evil eyes focused on his calf, or his arm, or even his face.

He stood motionless for what seemed like forever, frightened sweat dripping into his eyes, almost afraid to blink. He felt a wetness in his pants without realizing he'd pissed himself.

Hot urine drained down his legs and into his moccasins. Still the snake warned him, the young-pea-sized, irregularly shaped stones dancing in the buttons at the end of its tail.

Will tensed his leg muscles, but slowly, hoping he wasn't moving. His upper body was ready to move—had been since the first sounds reached him. Both his hands were clenched into fists, but he was no more aware of them than he was of wetting himself.

His legs were beginning to tremble from the tension. He was beginning to grow dizzy.

He counted to three in his mind and hurled his body to his right, slamming painfully against the stones, and scrambled to his feet within the smallest part of a second after striking the ground.

Then, he ran.

Austin was leaned back against his saddle, smoking a cigarette but cupping his hand completely around it so that no dull red of the end showed. The bottle was next to him. His rifle was resting across his chest, locked and loaded and ready to fire. The cigarette was in his left hand, his Colt in his right—pointed at Will's chest. He lowered the weapon as soon as he recognized his friend.

"You find that guard?"

"Yeah."

"You kill him?"

"That's what I was out there for. Lemme have that bottle." He stepped closer to Austin to grab the neck of the booze bottle.

"I did another one, too." He pulled the cork and took a long swallow.

"They'll be more wary now, Will. One Dog doesn't much to take his men bein' killed 'less he does it."

"True. That bother you?"

Austin chuckled. "Hell, no, I—What's that on—? Damn, boy, did you piss your pants?"

"It wasn't One Dog—it was a goddamn rattler longer'n your leg."

Austin chuckled again. "Sure," he said.

"It went like it was supposed to, snake or no snake," Will said, sounding a bit insulted.

Chapter Four

"Any trouble?" Austin asked, picking up on a slight change in his friend's standard voice.

"No."

"You sound strange, Will. Like . . . I dunno. Jus' strange. Ain't killin' them sonsabitches what we're out here for?"

"It's not the killing. I'd as soon shoot one of them as a barn rat. Thing is . . . I marked 'em, Austin."

"Marked? What'd you mean?"

"I carved a *HW* on each of their chests with my knife—cut in real good. It'll be impossible for the rest of 'em to miss."

"HW? What's that?"

"Me an' my brother were goin' to call our operation the H&W Cattle Ranch an' our brand was gonna be a *HW*."

Austin thought that over for a while. "Seems to me, you done good, Will. You know as well as I do that the whole buncha them are pure crazy, 'specially the Injuns, what with that superstitious stuff of theirs. You gave 'em somethin' to think about, somethin' to wear on 'em while we hunt them down. Hell, boy, seems like a good idea to me."

"Maybe so. I never did anything like that before. I

killed men, but it was always face-to-face an' I never left no extra mark on 'em. I don't want to be like that loon who rode with the Earps for a bit—he usta hack the ear off a man he gunned."

"Not Holliday?"

"No—no. Doc wouldn't do nothin' like that. Some saddle tramp they picked up, name of Kid something or other. He's dead. He tried to draw on Wyatt, an' Wyatt shot his ass off."

"You didn't cut nobody's ear off. What you done is declare war, my frien'. That's what you did an' that's how One Dog and his men will see it. Like I said, you done good. All the cards is on the table now."

Both men were silent for several moments.

"They'll have more lookouts now, but they won't try to track you in the dark. They'll be lookin' for sign at first light, but not before," Austin said.

Will grinned. "You thinkin' what I'm thinkin'?"

"You bet I am," Austin answered, tugging the ten-inch blade from his boot. "What say we take out a couple more of them—an' leave the HW on them, too."

"We gotta split up, though, when we get close," Will warned. "We do what we can an' then haul ass back here an' saddle up an' light out. Right?"

"Right. An' no guns—a single shot'd bring the whole crew on us like a swarm a hornets. If the kill cain't be done quiet, it won't get done at all. We'll git him the next time."

"We got maybe two an' a half, three hours of good dark. We gotta be quick," Will said.

"Let's move then," Austin said, hauling off a boot. "We're wastin' what time we got."

Will expected at least a few muffled curses from

Austin as they set out on the mission, as bootless feet landed on a particularly sharp rock, and was mildly surprised when he not only heard no profanity, but barely heard his partner at all.

The walk seemed longer to Will than it had earlier, but the vague scent of smoke let him know he and Austin were getting close. "We split here," he whispered into Austin's ear. "There's at least one man ridin' around the cattle an' horses. He probably found the bodies from earlier. Or maybe somebody changin' guard did, but we gotta assume One Dog knows he had a visitor."

Austin nodded but didn't speak.

"You swing out to the left there, an' I'll go over where I killed the first one," Will whispered. "See you back at the horses."

The lookout at the rock was standing this time and Will could hear him shifting his feet on the gritty stone surface as he paced a short pattern. Will listened for several minutes; the shuffling pattern didn't change. The man's final step as he turned to repeat his pacing was perfect. It put his back a mere couple of steps from where Will stood, knife at the ready, blade up, clutched chest high. Will let the guard make another pass. Then he crouched slightly, extended his right hand and the knife a bit from his body, and balanced himself carefully on the balls of his feet, left moccasin slightly behind his right. He flexed the fingers of his left hand, shook his wrist to loosen any tension in it, and when the time was perfect, sprang out from the edge of the rock, left hand finding and covering the guard's mouth from the back at the same time his right hand arced out and plunged the blade to the hilt into the man's chest.

The guard was an Indian. The stench of the grease on his hair was like the pit of a privy.

He grunted as the knife struck and his mouth opened slightly, even under Will's powerful grip. Will drew the knife from the guard's chest, pulling it upward and twisting it as he did so. At the same moment—perhaps as a final act of battle or perhaps in his death throes—the Indian closed his teeth on the lower palm of Will's left hand. The pain was sharp, hot, and Will could feel his flesh tearing. Then, as quickly as the gnashing pressure began, it stopped and all the strength drained from the man: from his mouth, his arms, his chest. Will pulled his knife free and let the body fall facedown. He quickly turned the corpse over, carved the HW into the warm, blood-slick chest, and then looked at his own hand. It was bleeding freely, the blood dark in the night, spattering at Will's feet. A flap of skin and muscle three inches long hung from the bottom of the hand like a piece of torn, damp cloth. Will put the rock between himself and the dead Indian and used his knife to cut the left sleeve off his shirt. The blade, razor sharp, eased through the fabric soundlessly. Will slid the knife back into his sheath and, holding one end of the sleeve in his teeth, took a tight wrap around the wound, doing his best to hold the flap of skin to where it'd come from. He listened for a long moment and then started back to his camp.

He had the horses saddled and bridled before Austin returned. "You OK?" Will asked.

"Yeah. Killed the outrider and left him with the HW. You?"

"I got the lookout that replaced the one I killed

earlier. Sumbitch bit my hand pretty bad. Other'n that, I'm good."

Austin stepped closer to inspect Will's wound. "Still bleedin' heavy, even with the wrap," he said. "I got some latigo in my saddlebag. I'll rig you a tourniquet. Take your reins in your right hand an' hold the left higher'n your heart, much as you can."

Will looked at his friend more closely. He had a tightly strung bow across his chest and a quiver with ten or so arrows in it draped over his shoulder. "I didn't know you could handle a bow," he said.

"Might could be lotsa things 'bout me you don't know, Will. Come on—let's ride."

They rode slowly, barely beyond an extended walk, until there was enough light to see prairie-dog holes, half-buried rocks, rattlers out seeking morning warmth, and the other natural traps that awaited the unwary horseman.

With the sun came the searing heat; by nine in the morning the men and the horses were sweating copiously. Every so often one of the men would turn in his saddle and gaze at their backtrail. Miles back there was some dust rising into the air, moving at what seemed to be a steady pace toward them.

About noon they came to a wagon-wheel-sized puddle of brackish water. They loosened their cinches and let their horses drink, and they themselves sucked at their canteens, ate some jerky, and rolled smokes. Austin noticed that Will was scattering tobacco around where he sat and that he couldn't seem to get a decent crease in a paper. "Lemme see your paw," Austin said.

"Nothin' to see. It's comin' good."

"Hold it out."

Reluctantly, Will did so. "Jesus God," Austin whispered. The tourniquet had stopped most of the bleeding, but Will's fingers had turned into fat, shiny white-skinned sausages, and he couldn't have formed a fist if his life depended on it. Worse yet, tiny lines of red had begun traveling from Will's palm up toward his elbow. "Hurt much?"

"Some."

"Some, my ass. What we gotta do is free up the latigo, let some blood get to the bite. Could be some fresh blood'll clean her out a bit."

"It ain't nothin' but a little bite. It'll clear up. We ain't got time to screw around with it now." He nodded toward the dust behind them. "They're gettin' closer."

"They'll kill their horses 'fore they catch us," Austin said. "What they probably done was leave their worst drunks an' cowards to watch over the cattle an' horses, an' One Dog brought his best braves an' fighters with him. They'll ride hard 'til their horses drop an' then come on foot 'til they can steal some more somewhere." He looked back at Will. "Lemme loosen that latigo."

"It's just a—"

"Lookit here," Austin answered, almost in a snarl. "Ain't nothin' more dangerous than a human bite, 'specially from scum like them. A dog's or wolf's teeth are a lot cleaner'n a man's, an' I know that to be a fact. A friend of mine got bit by a Arapahoe on his shoulder an' it got all swole up—like your hand—an' he croaked in four days." As he spoke Austin released the knot of the tourniquet. "Let it hang at your side now."

Will did so. After what seemed like an interminably long time, some pus and blood began to drip onto the sand. Its odor was rancid, enough to make a man gag. "We gotta take the wrap off an' put a fresh one on," Austin said. " 'Fore we wrap her again, I'll pour what booze we got left into the cut—might help some."

Before Will could reply, Austin began taking turns of the sleeve around the cut. When he got to the final wrap, he warned, "Now this one's gonna be a pisser, but we got no choice. See, the cloth is kinda glued in there an' it's gotta come out. You ready?"

"No."

"Well hell," Austin said and tore the final turn of sleeve free. Will fell to his knees, his teeth grinding against one another with the pain. He didn't yell out or scream, but the deep whimpering sounds that came from his throat showed the degree of his pain. Austin fetched the quarter bottle of booze they had left, drew his knife, cut off his own left sleeve, and hunkered down next to Will. "You wanna take a slug of redeye 'fore I do this? Might help."

"Just do it—get it over with."

Austin pulled the cork with his teeth. "Turn your hand so the bite's up," he said. The flap of skin hadn't taken at all; it hung free, and its edges were turning a light greenish blue color. "Shit. That's gotta come off," Austin said, "or the sumbitch will rot your whole hand."

Will nodded. Austin drew his knife, took the gangrenous edge between his left thumb and forefinger, and sliced downward quickly, without warning. The patch of flesh hit the sand and Austin kicked it away, hoping to get some of the stench away from them.

"I hardly felt that," Will said.

"You'll feel the booze." He took a good hold on Will's wrist and poured the whiskey over the exposed tissue. This time Will did scream—and then he passed out. "Jus' as well," Austin mumbled, finishing the pouring and tossing the empty bottle off to the side. He sat beside his friend, rolled a cigarette, lit it, and waited for Will to come back to consciousness.

When his eyes finally fluttered open, Austin asked, "Where's that map at?"

Will used his right hand to push himself to a sitting position. "What d'you need the map for? We got One Dog behind us. We don't need the damned map—we need a spot for an ambush."

"Yeah, we do need the map, 'cause we need a town with a doc in it. Otherwise you're gonna lose your hand—maybe your whole arm."

The nearest town was Olympus, which looked to be forty or fifty miles due east, at least according to the inaccurate scale of the penciled map. "You real sure about that?" Will asked.

"Sure's the sun comes up in the morning. An' look." He pointed back the way they'd come. "One Dog's still comin' on strong. We got a pretty fair lead, but I'd like to get to this Olympia or whatever the hell it is before he gets too close."

"Olympus. Let's make tracks, then."

The water was a blessing. It would have stretched credibility too far to call it an oasis, but it was a pond of twenty feet long and thirty feet wide, with a scattering of scruffy desert pine standing like slouching sentries. Stunted buffalo grass spread around the water. It wasn't good grazing, but the horses didn't seem to care at all.

"Whoooo-eee!" Austin yelled. "I don't care if we gotta fight One Dog right here—I'm gonna git wet!" He swung down from his horse, shucked his pistol and gun belt, tossed the bow and quiver aside, and made a running leap into the water. It was only two feet deep, but it was cold—spring fed, obviously—and wet. Will followed more judiciously, walking out a few yards and then sitting in the water, left hand in the air, like a student asking a question.

They let their horses drink in shifts to avoid founder, filled their canteens, and settled down in the grass for a few moments. "Hell of a nice place for a camp," Will said. "Too bad we can't settle in for the night."

"No cover, though. But yeah, it's right nice. I ain't been at all wet 'cept with sweat in a coon's age. Feels awful good."

Will dunked his face and head a final time. "We'd best head on to Olympus," he said. Austin sighed and floundered back to shore.

The sun was almost touching the western horizon as they came into the town of Olympus.

"That wasn't no thirty or forty miles," Austin said. "But that's fine with me. We get you to a doc an' then find us a gin mill, no?"

Will didn't answer.

Olympus was slightly larger than most of the cattle-train whistle-stops. The doctor was a real MD, not a veterinarian or self-proclaimed medic such as were found in most towns. There was only one saloon, but it was a big one, with a restaurant and whorehouse all in one building.

"See?" Austin said. "Right there—next to the

mercantile—there's a doc's shingle. We'll get you fixed . . . Hey! You OK, pard?"

Will was slumped far forward in his saddle, his face a pallid white. His eyes didn't seem to focus, and his right boot had slipped from its stirrup and was dangling uselessly next to the leather. He'd vomited and the chest of his shirt was damp with stomach bile. Austin jigged his horse up a step and took hold of Slick's reins. "You hold on, pard," Austin said. "This doctor, he'll fix you up. Damn if I didn't tell you a bite from a human is . . . Steady now, Will. Grab the horn an' stay on your horse." He led Slick to the hitching rail in front of the doctor's office, wrapped their reins, and helped Will down.

"Jus' tired is all," Will mumbled. "I don't need . . ."

Austin half led and half carried Will into the doctor's office. "Doc," he yelled, "I got a bad case here. You gotta . . ."

A stubby fellow who'd never see sixty years old again, with pure white hair flowing well over the collar of his formal shirt, came from behind the curtain to his examination room. His pants were pressed and his shoes shined. He looked like a successful drummer. "I'm Dr. McCall," he said. "Bring that boy in here and stretch him out on my table."

Austin did as he was told. The doctor washed his hands in a large basin that smelled of raw alcohol and took Will's left hand in his own. "Decent wrap," he said, his voice calm, as if he were commenting on the weather. "This a dog bite?"

"Injun," Austin said. "We was—"

"I don't give a good goddamn what you boys were doing," the doctor said as he began unwinding the sleeve from Will's hand. "A bite like this from a man is bad news." He dropped Austin's sleeve into a trash can and examined Will's hand. "You put anything on this—do anything for him?"

"Yessir. I poured a half bottle of whiskey an' run a good tourniquet. After a while I took off the tourniquet, thinkin' maybe fresh blood would clean—"

"You did it right," the doctor said. "I'm gonna put your friend out with what we call chloroform. You in the war, boy?"

"Yessir."

"Then you know what chloroform is. I gotta clean the bite and then stitch up the tear and wrap it again. He lost some epidermis—skin—here, and it won't grow back. I'll stitch to good skin, but his hand—probably his little finger and the one next to it—won't be worth a damn for a long time, until he's healed. Is he right-handed?"

"Yessir."

"Good. Now you get out of here and let me work. Place next door will serve you beer or whiskey or ass—whatever you want. You got money?"

"Yessir. We can pay you. You got no worry there."

"I've heard that before. Go on—get."

The doc went to work. Austin took the two horses down the main street to the blacksmith's shop and livery and left explicit directions on how the animals were to be treated.

The smith was the size of a bull wooly, and he rather looked like one as well. "Yer a stranger," he said. "This'll cost you some money an' I need it ahead, 'fore I do a thing."

Austin flipped a golden eagle to the blacksmith. "You jus' do like I said: tighten all the shoes, feed these boys some crimped oats an' molasses, an' give 'em good hay. Make sure they have all the fresh water they want. You might brush 'em out a bit, as well."

The blacksmith began to raise the coin to his mouth.

"It's real. Take it to the goddamn bank. But I don't want you callin' me a liar. You bite that eagle an' I'll gun your fat ass."

The smith held Austin's eyes for a moment and then dropped the coin into his pocket. "Don't need no bank. That bow an' them arrows bothered me a bit, but I know the eagle's real. OK?"

Austin turned without a response and walked to the gin mill.

The physician did a fine job—he obviously knew his business. The line of sutures was about five inches long and the stitches were precisely spaced from one another, as neat and tight as the work of a master bootmaker—or a tailor, for that matter. Will slept peacefully through the procedure, his breathing quiet and steady.

Will awakened in a semidark room and pushed himself to a sitting position on the table on which he rested. There was a quick flash of dizziness, but it dissipated quickly. His hand was wrapped in white gauze and throbbed some, but didn't hurt terribly. There was a note tucked into the gauze.

Had to go out on a call. You're lucky you got here in time. Your hand will take 6 weeks or so to heal. You owe me $4.00 for the pills on the table. Take one a day.

Will scanned the table. Four white tablets—big ones, about the size of a dime—awaited him. He put them in his pocket and slid down to the floor.

He'd half expected Austin to be sitting in the waiting room, but he wasn't. Will didn't have to think too hard to figure out where his friend was. He left the doctor's office and headed to the saloon, feeling a little foolish in his one-sleeved shirt.

It wasn't far past dinnertime, but the joint was already doing a good business. Austin sat at a table alone, with several empty schooners on the rough wood in front of him and a full one in his hand. "Will," he called, "come on an' set an' drink some beer—best medicine in the world." Will bought a pair of beers at the bar and walked over to Austin's table.

"What'd the doc say?"

"Nothin'. He was gone on a call when I woke up. He left me some medicine to take. Fact, I better take one right now." He plucked a tablet from his pocket and washed it down with a long draft of beer.

"You might jus' notice I got two sleeves on my shirt," Austin grinned. He took another from the floor next to him and tossed it to Will. "Here—I got you one, too. You look like a damned fool with but one sleeve. The mercantile has good prices."

Will stripped out of his old shirt and pulled on the new one, buttoning it carefully. "Nice shirt," he said. "Stiffer'n a damn board, though." He tossed the bloody shirt toward the corner of the room. The men drank their beer.

"Least you could do is fetch another round," Austin said.

"You know," Will answered, "you're finally right

'bout somethin'." He strode to the bar. The dizziness settled in again but again was quickly gone. He held up two fingers to the 'tender and leaned on the bar, gawking up at the graphic nude hanging over the whiskey bottles. It took him a couple of moments to notice that all conversation, shouting, cursing, and laughter in the saloon had stopped and that the bartender had crouched down behind the bar. Will turned to the batwings.

One man stood there, just inside the saloon. He was as hairy as a buffalo, shirtless, wearing tight leggings tucked into tall boots. A pair of bandoliers of ammunition crossed his chest. A Colt .45 rested in his holster. He held a cut-down shotgun, muzzle upward. His hair was a twisted, greasy mess. His eyes, like polished obsidian, swept the saloon, passed Will, and then returned to him.

"You killed and marked my brother an' now his spirit must wander until he's avenged," the outlaw said, his voice tight, hard, trembling with fury.

Will took a step away from the bar, his right hand dropping toward his pistol. It was just then that the dizziness returned, this time accompanied by floating red motes that drifted across his line of vision. The Indian laughed. "You're so scared you can barely stand up straight, you chickenshit sonofabitch."

Will felt his consciousness leaving him, felt his right hand tremble, tried to gulp air to clear his head, but it had no effect. He wobbled in his boots as if he stood on the deck of a ship in a storm. There were more red motes now, but he could see clearly enough that the double maw of the shotgun was being lowered toward him. He fumbled for his pistol but his palm slapped the gun belt above his holster.

Then, something very strange happened. The outlaw suddenly grew eight inches of arrow from the middle of his forehead. It was as if the shaft leaped from his head. He fell forward face-first, and the impact jammed the rest of the arrow on through so that the hunting point and several inches of shaft protruded from the back of his head. Will shook his head, confused, as if he were in some bizarre dream. Everything was red in front of him now, and there was a loud buzzing sound filling his head. *Bees*, he thought stupidly. *I run right into a swarm of bees.* Then, he went down.

The corn-shuck bed is what woke Will up—that and the critters that lived in it. He slapped at his neck with his left hand and immediately regretted doing so. A searing pain traveled from his hand to his shoulder, eliciting a curse and a grimace. "Shit," he said, looking around. The bed—such as it was—was against the wall. The blanket was Union Army–surplus wool, and added to the torture of the bedbugs.

An arrow hissed past Will's face, perhaps two inches above his nose, and buried its point in the lath and poorly applied sheet wood, joining a cluster of half a dozen other shafts. Austin sat across the room, bow in hand, quiver slung from the back of his chair.

"I'll tell you this right now," Austin said, "whoever made this sumbitch put his heart into it. You seen the power it has. I never seen a arrow pierce right on through a man's head. Usually, even with a good, stout bow, they don't penetrate more'n a few inches in a skull. I'd wager that piece of trash I dusted in the saloon didn't make this here bow." Will began to speak, but Austin went on.

"An' these arrows are the best. Lookit the points—sharper'n a razor an' balanced perfect. An' the shafts—there ain't nothin' but perfectly straight hardwood, rubbed an' polished to a fair-thee-well. Them is eagle feathers, too."

"Where the hell are we?" Will's voice sounded like that of a badger with a really sore throat. Austin handed over an unlabeled quart bottle. "Have you a sip of this so's you don't sound like you do—it'd get on a man's nerves in a big hurry." Will, his throat parched and sore, sucked down a long pull. He coughed immediately, rackingly, and his throat felt as if a five-foot-long length of red-hot barbed wire had been stuffed into his lungs. "What . . . is that?" he croaked.

"Taykilla, a Mex fella tol' me. Didn't charge me but twenty cents for the whole quart. He said it's real popular in Mexico." Austin notched another arrow and began to draw back.

"Dammit, you quit that! There's no good reason you gotta shoot so close to my face, ya damned fool!"

Austin grinned and nodded. "You're right," he said. He moved the bow a bit and released the arrow. It slammed into the wall tight enough to Will's groin that had he been excited with a lady, he'd have lost something valuable.

"Idjit," Will snarled.

"Want some grub?" Austin asked. "This dump has a restaurant. You prolly should eat."

Will swallowed and quickly decided that he did need to eat and that he *wanted* to eat. "Yeah, Austin, I'm needing some food. An' my hand is killin' me, but I ain't gonna drink more of that Mex crap. Maybe you could fetch a bottle of decent booze?"

"Sure."

"Austin—was there some pills in my pocket in my ol' shirt."

"Yeah, there was. I got 'em right here in my pocket. You needin' one?"

"Toss 'em out the window, pard. Sonsabitches almost killed me."

"Sure. I'll go down, fetch up some stew—it ain't half bad. I had me a couple helpings."

"Where the hell are we, by the way?"

"The hotel—the Royal Duchess, she's called. Got grub and whores, too."

"Royal Duchess? Damn," Will said incredulously. "Might jus' as well called this fleabag the Windsor Castle."

"What's a windward castle?"

"Forget it, OK? Jus' get the stew an' coffee—lots of coffee."

Austin shook his head slowly, as if he'd just heard bad news. "Jesus, Will," he said. "You're one miserable sumbitch when it comes to givin' orders." Austin set his bow aside and stomped out the door, slamming it behind him as he left.

Will tested his hand a bit. It hurt—bad. He groaned, got his boots under himself, and weaved to the tiny table that held Austin's bottle. He took a slug, gagged, and took another hit.

After a short time, the pain in his hand and wrist dulled considerably.

Austin came in with a large bowl of venison stew, which was purely delicious, and a loaf of bread under his arm, still warm from the oven. The pot of coffee was steaming from its spout, diffusing its wonderful aroma throughout the small room.

"I didn't mean to rag on you, Austin," Will said. "I didn't mean nothin' by it."

"Hell," Austin grinned. "Had a Injun chewed most of my hand off, why I'd be kinda outta sorts, too. Here—lemme add some hog piss to your coffee." He crossed the room to Will and poured a half cup of whiskey into Will's mug.

Will ate all the stew, cleaned the bowl with chunks of bread, ate the rest of the loaf, and drank all of the coffee.

"You done stuffin' your face?" Austin asked.

"For now," Will said, clumsily rolling a smoke.

"Good. Here's the thing: I been thinkin'. We can keep on pickin' off One Dog's boys one or two at a time, but that ain't gonna get us nowhere. Dog can pick up an' hire on other losers 'fore the ones we killed have bled out." He paused. "We ain't doin' this right, Will."

"How so?"

"I'd say this: we need a man so screwed up he'd make Dog's crew look like a buncha li'l girls playin' tea party. See, we're both good—real good—but we ain't near as nutsy as our enemies. That's gonna hurt us—prolly kill us."

Will considered for a couple of minutes. "Yeah. Could be you're right. But—"

"Now, listen up. I got a good frien' name of Gentle Jane. He had him eleven notches on the grips of his Colt 'fore he was thirteen years old. He's pure crazy, Will—a goddamn killin' machine. He's part Injun and part Mex an' has the worst parts of both. You never seen a man fight like Jane—with a pistol or rifle or knife or his hands."

"Gentle Jane?" Will said.

"Jane, he took that name on his own self, hopin' men would challenge it an' him. Like I said, he's pure loopy."

"How . . . how loopy?"

"Well, see . . . if a man gives him a good fight, Gentle Jane, he'll cut the fella's eggs off an' eat 'em."

"That's pretty crazy."

"For sure. Another thing: Jane wears a string of ears 'round his neck. He likes to take trophies. He . . . well . . . he's already filled two strands, is workin' hard on the third."

"This guy sounds real dangerous, Austin."

"He is—but only if he's comin' after you with a gun, knife, or his fists. Other than that, he ain't a bad fella."

"How do you know him?"

"I shot a Union corporal who was goin' to run Jane through—from the back, mind you—with a cavalry sword durin' a bar tussle. I'll tell you this, ol' Jane is worth ten men to us, maybe more. Plus, lotsa Injuns know about him an' he scares the hell outta them. They figure he's a evil spirit."

"Well. I'm sure this Gentle Jane is all you say he is, pard. We can't use him, though. Having somebody that screwy around won't cause nothin' but trouble. Suppose he ups an' turns on us?"

"Won't happen. He calls me his brother."

"He doesn't call me his brother, though. Nope— we can't risk it."

"Kinda late, Will."

"What? You didn't . . ."

"Yeah. While you was out I wired him. I suspect he's ridin' hard this very moment to come an' give us a hand. All we gotta do is wait up a couple days, let your paw heal some, an' make sure Dog doesn't come through our door. Could be that Injun I put the arrow in was on his own, without no orders from One Dog. If that's true, the sonsabitches are still searchin' for us."

"Dammit, Austin . . ."

"There's no sense in squallin' over what's already did. We can't change nothin' now. You'll see I done a good decision, Will."

"Right. So did Custer."

Gentle Jane rode into Olympus three days later. He wasn't a big man, but he was as frightening as any man a person would care to see. His skin was a copper shade and his eyes black diamonds with a manic fire burning behind them. He wore a full beard that reached the belt of his deerskin drawers. His necklaces of dried ears rested on the beard. He had a bow over his back and a large quiver full of arrows hung from a string of latigo from the horn of his stock saddle. He had a .30-30 in a scabbard on either side. His gun belt carried a pair of Colts. Stitched to each holster was a sheath holding a bowie-type knife with blades a good foot long. His horse was large—almost drafty—with hooves the size of dinner plates and a head on him like a beer barrel. Even given the animal's size and a three day ride, he trip-tropped along like a circus pony, snapping each huge hoof up almost before it touched the ground.

Will and Austin watched Gentle Jane ride down the main street. "That a pistol butt I see at the top of his boot?" Will asked.

"Yep. Got one on the other side, too. Jane, he don't

like to be underarmed. Got him a derringer an' more knifes here an' there."

Gentle Jane ground-tied his horse in front of the saloon's hitching rail and climbed down from his saddle. "Jane don't ever tie his horse—he figures he might not have time to diddle 'round with a hitchin' rail. Ain't a bad idea, ya know?"

Will sighed. "We might jus' as well go on over an' say hello—since the man is here an' all."

"Ummm—don't offer to shake with Jane. He won't do it. He's gotta have both paws free at all the time."

"Jesus." Will sighed again.

"But let's watch from here for a minnit. See what goes on in the saloon."

"Why? What's . . . ?"

"Jus' watch, OK?"

They watched. After a few minutes a typey look-ing piebald tied at the rail swung his head back to glare at Gentle Jane's black. The big horse met the 'bald's eyes and clicked his front teeth—the size of piano keys—together with a sharp, snapping sound that reached all the way to the hotel. The piebald turned back quickly to stare at the batwings.

Five or so long minutes passed. "Look," Will said, "if we're goin' to ride with this—"

A thunderous, resonating boom, the likes of which would have made a Sharps report sound like a penny firecracker, rattled windows throughout the town. A cowhand sailed through the batwings like a diver into a deep pond, hit the street face-first, scrambled to his feet, and ran, both his nostrils gush-ing blood. His hat remained in the street where the cowpuncher had hit. There was another boom and the hat turned into a handful of confetti that rose from the street ten or twelve feet and then drifted gently, smoothly, to the street.

The shortest part of a second later a stampede of cowboys, gamblers, drunks, and saddle tramps stampeded out of the saloon and either ran or untied their horses and mounted them at a run.

"That's a eight-gauge shotgun," Austin said.

"Ain't no such thing."

"There is, though. Jane, he had it made up for him. A ol' gunsmith in Tucson put it together. You oughta see the cartridges—they're as big as a hog's snout." Austin stood from his crouch by the window. "We can go on out an' meet Jane," he said. "Now you remember—no hand shakin'."

Gentle Jane stood at the bar with a short-barreled shotgun on the wood in front of him. The stock was a deep, dark, polished wood and the trigger guard and triggers were brass. Bluish wisps of smoke were drifting up from both barrels.

"Jane," Austin shouted, "you came! I knowed you would! Good to see you, brother!"

"My brother," Gentle Jane said. His voice wasn't what Will expected. Instead, it was level, calm, and it reminded Will of that of a teacher he'd once had. "My love for you remains as the moon and stars remain." He eyed Will. "Who is this gunslinger? Does he challenge me? I'll have his ears, brother Austin."

"No! No!" Austin began to reach out to touch Jane's shoulder, and then pulled it back as if he'd stuck it in a fire. "Will, here, he's my friend—my pard. See, a crazy name of One Dog killed his brother and his brother's wife and baby daughters an' burned down his house an' barn.

"Will is set on killing them all."

"Is good," Jane said. "I have heard of this One Dog. I'd not eat his heart nor take his ears, because he's a coward. How many guns does he have with?"

"Maybe thirty-five, forty, somethin' like that. When one is killed he picks up another saddle tramp or army deserter."

"One Dog kills all black men he sees, no? He wants all blacks to remain under the white man's whip, to work and sweat and be sold like cattle to other white men, to take a man from his woman and children. Is this not true?"

"It's true," Will said. "He raids farms, rapes the women, kills them, kills the men and children, and steals the stock—cattle and horses. He sells them in Mexico."

"Austin—you and Will have killed some of One Dog's men?"

"Four. We carve *HW* on the chests of their corpses."

"What is this *HW*?"

"My brother's name was Hiram. We were going to use our first initials as the name of our ranch."

"What is this 'initials'?"

"First letter of each of our names."

"I do not read. You will need to show me *HW*. Then I too will carve it into the chests of these pigs."

"Sure."

"Is good. Now we will eat and drink and make some plans, no?"

The 'tender was still crouched behind the bar, white-faced, trembling. "Barkeep," Austin said. "You cook us up three of the best an' biggest steaks you got—blood rare, they gotta be—an' set up a couple of bottles of whiskey and three glasses."

"Three bottles," Jane said. "We will go to a table where we can see the door. Bring bucket of beer, too."

Gentle Jane faced Will for a long moment. "I see hatred and flame in your eyes, Will. That is good. We will make blood flow. No?"

"We'll do that, Gentle Jane."

"Only way is sneak attacks—like the snake after the mouse. If the three of us charge together—even at night—we will be killed."

"Yeah. Austin an' me been doin' it that way. Seems to be working good."

"How many you kill so far?"

"I dunno—eight, ten."

Jane spit on the floor. "Shit. I kill that many for you my first night. Still, for a couple of white eyes, you not done too bad." Jane took a long drink. "You are fast with your gun?"

"Yeah," Will said. "I am."

"Fast is good. Accurate is more important. How accurate are you, Will Lewis?"

Austin answered for Will. "This boy can shoot the short hairs offa a hog's back without touchin' the pork."

"Is good. If Austin say so, is true." Gentle Jane thought about that for a bit. "I am faster and more accurate with my knife than you are with your .45," he said as if he were stating a known and accepted fact.

Austin was on his feet. "C'mon, Jane—ain't no reason for this horseshit. We're all three of us goin' to ride together, no? If you an' Will get into it, there'll—"

Gentle Jane laughed. "I am not talking about fighting—I am talking about a contest, is all. No blood flows in a contest, and no one dies. Is fun, is all."

Austin sat back down.

"Here is the contest I am thinking," Jane said. "The picture there, the *puta*, over the bar. Let Austin start us and we see who puts a knife or a slug into her—how do you say?—bally button first. Is simple contest."

"Where would you draw your knife from?" Will asked.

"From my holster, just like you pull your pistol. Is fair. Is good."

"You can't win," Will said. "No goddamn way."

"Jane," Austin said, "Will's right. You can't win. An' I'm scared when you lose it'll piss you off an' you start goin' . . ."

Jane laughed. "No. No. Is a fun contest. I would have no anger if Will is more faster than I am."

"Bullshit," Austin mumbled.

"We will stand," Gentle Jane said. Both men stepped in front of the table. Will touched the grips of his Colt, lifted the weapon a bit, and let it go. Jane went through essentially the same ritual with the knife sheathed on his right holster.

"We are ready," Jane grinned. "On three, my brother Austin?"

"Sure. On three."

"Will," he said, barely louder than a whisper, "don't win, fa crissakes. I mean it."

"Count," Will said.

Austin nodded, his face showing his trepidation.

"One . . .

"Two . . .

"Three!"

Jane's hand seemed to barely move before his knife was in the air, crossing the fifteen feet to the nude. Will, on the other hand, didn't seem to hurry, although his pistol suddenly appeared in his hand. He fired once.

Jane's knife, barely two feet from its target, seemed to have been struck by lightning. The blade, bent into a useless U, clattered to the floor. The grip sailed a few feet away before it dropped.

"*Madre de Jesús*," Jane said.

Austin seated, hand under the table, drew his .45.

"You are as fast and as accurate as I have ever seen," Jane said.

"I got lucky."

"There is no luck with weapons. Only skill." He held out his right hand to Will. "I shake hands with very few men. I will shake with you."

Will took Jane's hand. The two men grinned at one another. "Is good contest, no?"

Will nodded. "Now we drink like brothers."

"And Austin—holster that pistol before I rip your hand off and stick that .45 up your ass."

Chapter Five

The three men sat at the table, drinking and talking. Austin and Gentle Jane had many memories of long rides, bloody battles, whores, and horses to rehash and, perhaps, to embellish slightly. Will tapped away at his bottle of whiskey but concentrated on scribing arcs on the wet wood of the table in front of him with the bottom of his schooner, having next to nothing to add to the conversation. Austin's and Will's bottles were a third gone when Gentle Jane's was empty and he went to the bar for another. Will noticed that there wasn't the slightest stagger or weave to his stride—it was as if he'd just downed a bottle of sarsaparilla rather than West Texas rotgut.

"It is not good alcohol," Jane said, sitting down. "But even bad alcohol is better than none at all."

"I've noticed that you speak very well—clearly and without cussin', Jane," Will said. "How did that come to be?"

Gentle Jane downed a double shot before answering. "Many years ago," he said, "the army came and took me away from my parents and carried me to a missionary school. They cut my hair off and they beat me for speaking in Arapahoe, which is the tribe with whom I lived. The missionaries told us of their

God and struck us if we refused to pray to him. They said our gods—the earth, the sky, the water, the wind—were foolish and sinful and to pray to them would damn us to the missionaries' hell, a lake of fire in which we'd burn eternally. To think of holding a girl, to envision her privates and how they'd feel, look, and taste, was also a grave and mortal sin, punishable in the lake of fire. Even thinking of these things—without doing them—was another mortal sin."

"But you learned to speak as you do, no? You—"

"I decided I'd need to speak proper English but I refused to write or read their letters. I suffered many beatings from the missionaries—particularly Brother Thomas. Brother Thomas was a cruel pig. One night I took the ice pick from the kitchen and went to his room. He was sleeping. I touched the point to his eyelid and he came awake. 'Do I need to write in your letters to tell you what will happen now?' I asked him. He started to sit up. I drove the ice pick through his eye and inside his head. He fell back on his cot. I had a barlow pocket knife in my pocket—which was, of course, forbidden. I took my first ear that night. I was eleven years old. I stole a horse from the stable and went on my way, the ear strung on a piece of latigo around my neck."

He sucked at his bottle. "I returned to the Arapahoes but they did not want me. They said I was not an Indian, nor was I a Mexican. I was a mongrel. They brought me to the tribe when I was an infant. I do not know what happened to my actual parents. They were probably tortured and killed.

"I learned to love weapons and practiced hours upon hours in using them. I stole here and there to have weapons made—like my shotgun. I learned to draw as fast as a snake's tongue flicks toward an enemy, and I armed myself with knives and other instruments of death. I killed seven men in Tombstone, and I took an ear from each. There were many others in many towns."

"Why did you fight these men?"

"Killing is what I do. My medicine demands that I kill. I do not seek prey, but when men challenge me I kill them and take their ears. This is what the gods want from me, and this is what I do."

"How many have you killed?"

"It makes no matter. I do what I do."

Will leaned back in his chair, not realizing he'd been moving closer and closer to Gentle Jane. Will took a snort from his bottle and then pushed it aside, the whiskey rising back into his throat. He swallowed hard.

"Why the name Gentle Jane?"

"You white eyes speak lies constantly. The treaties—the grants of land that were already ours, the cholera blankets, the tainted beef, Wounded Knee—all of that made me want to lie to you even about my name, lie until it came time to fight. When it came time to fight I no longer lied. My hands and my weapons and my medicine speak for me."

"But Jane—why are you with us?"

"I have said this but you haven't listened. White men rarely listen, rarely understand. Austin is my brother. I will fight to the death at his side. I will tell you this: One Dog will die, as will his men."

"One Dog will die by my hand, Jane. No other. You must understand that."

"How intelligent are you?" Jane asked.

"I've had a .45 pointed at you since we sat down at this table."

Jane grinned, showing white teeth. "And my shotgun has been quite ready to blow you in half if need be. All I need do is touch a trigger."

"Me too, Jane—and I'd split your head before you fired."

"Maybe."

"For sure."

"Say, boys," Austin interjected rapidly. "What is this horseshit? Ain't we s'posed to be brothers? This is pure crazy. C'mon. Put up the iron."

Will's eyes and those of Jane were locked, not in a threatening fashion, but in a cautious one—and an exploratory one. Both wanted to delve into the other man's mind, to see what danger he may present, to see what made him who he was.

"C'mon, dammit," Austin said. "Let's settle down here. You had your contest. I don't know what even started all this."

Jane barely showed his teeth in a smile or grin and moved his cut-down from under the table to on top of it, the dual barrels pointing at the wall. Will brought his pistol up and placed it between a collection of empty beer mugs.

"I read men through their eyes, Will," Gentle Jane said. "That's where the true window is. I will fight for you."

"I know a bit about men myself," Will said. "I gotta say you're pure crazy, Jane, but I want you with me and I want you to trust me. Can we do that?"

Jane picked up his bottle and took a long snort. He handed it to Will. Will had had enough booze—what he wanted was sleep. He sucked at the bottle and handed it to Austin. He too drank.

"I will say that now we can trust one another," Jane said. "Will we be partners? I think not. Will we be brothers? Never. But I will fight with you and Austin and we will crush One Dog the way a boot crushes a cockroach. Is this not true?"

"It's true."

"You will pay me money?"

"Yes."

Will pushed his chair back rather clumsily, picked his pistol off the table, and dropped it into his holster. "I'm drunker'n a hoot owl jus' now an' I need some sleep. If you boys want to go on drinkin', that's up to you." He dragged a golden eagle out of his pocket and dropped it on the table. "This is on me. Give the 'tender some coin—the poor sumbitch has been hidin' behind the bar forever. Tomorrow morning we can make some plans."

"Plans?" Jane spit after he said the word. "You know where One Dog is, no?"

"Prolly right outside of town," Will said.

"Is good. We attack him in the morning, just before the sun greets the sky. It is my understanding that these men smoke ganja and drink heavily, that they abuse the sacramental mushrooms. Their fighting skills—if they have any—will be dulled in the morning. That is the time to strike."

"Makes good sense," Austin said.

"It does, it truly does," Will said. "We saddle in the dark and we swing around the town until we find their camp. It's a good plan, Jane."

"We'll shoot their asses off," Austin said.

"Thass . . . that's the whole idea. I gotta sleep. I'm drunk. I'm tired. I'll see you boys in a few hours." Will stumbled toward the staircase.

"White men cannot absorb liquor," Jane observed.

"Bullshit. I'm white an' I can drink long after you fall under the table, Jane."

"We shall see."

When Will came down the stairs, Gentle Jane was seated where he'd been the night before, with a schooner of beer in front of him. Austin was sprawled next to a tipped chair, a puddle of vomit his pillow on the floor.

Will nudged Austin with his boot. His eyes slowly opened. "Damn," he said.

"Can you ride?"

" 'Course I can ride. I was jus' takin' a little nap." He began to gag and heaved again onto the floor. "There," he said, "I got rid of all that shit. Let's saddle up."

"Jane—you OK?"

"Of course. I've already saddled my pony. He awaits me."

"Pony? He's as big as—"

"He's my pony."

"Right."

Will watched carefully as Austin saddled his horse. Amazingly enough, his hands were steady and his eyes clear.

There was a bit of a tussle when Jane's horse wanted to lead and Slick didn't like that at all. The two postured and snorted and snaked their heads out to get a bite of hide, but neither reared into an actual fight.

"Idjits," Will said.

"Stop here—let them discuss it," Jane said. They drew rein. The horses sniffed and backed and snorted and pawed the ground. Slick bucked a couple times, but he stayed out of Jane's horse's range.

"Smart animal," Jane said. "He knows that my pony would tear him apart. He needs to show his manhood, but he's too bright to fight. I will be a few strides in front of your good horse." He tapped his heels against his horse's sides and they set off, Slick ten feet behind the huge animal.

"You done the right thing," Will said quietly to his horse, stroking his neck. "If there's no possible way to win a fight, you gotta back off."

Austin was pasty-faced and a bit trembly now, but he was as good as his word, and he rode without a complaint. He positioned himself a couple of yards to Will's left, his horse attempting to hold back from Jane's animal.

The plan was simple; it had been set in place the night before. Find One Dog and his hostiles and crush as many of them as possible.

"It is no plan," Gentle Jane had said, "and often no plan works most effectively. We ride to their last camp and find them there, or riding toward us. It makes no difference. We kill, and then we run back to town."

They'd been in the saddle for well over an hour when Jane held up his arm to signal a halt and reined in.

"What?" Will asked. "Why . . . ?"

"Listen more; talk less," Jane answered. He stood in his stirrups, eyes closed, face wrinkled in concentration. "They come," he finally said. "Many horses, running hard. They will soon be here."

"Shit," Austin said. "We got no cover."

"We need no cover. We spread in a line and when they're close, we attack."

"Attack? Even with the losers they left with their stock, there's got to be twenty or more of them."

Jane spat to the side. "They've run their horses too hard. The animals will not maneuver as well as ours. The men will have blood in their eyes and will make stupid mistakes in their rush to wipe us out. Listen for my war whoop and disengage and run for the town. Is all understood?"

"Yeah. I hope you know what you're doing, Jane," Will said.

"I know battle. This time, Will, we have no time for *HW*—we go in and get out."

Will nodded.

The three men spread out about ten yards apart, Jane a dozen yards ahead of the other two. Austin and Will's horses were antsy, dancing a bit, as the thrumming of the galloping enemies came closer. Jane's horse stood alert, ears forward, but perfectly still.

The prairie floor was still damp with dew; the outlaws raised no cloud of dust. But the pounding of hooves became louder, more insistent.

Jane drew a bowie knife from somewhere within his clothing and grasped the blade in his teeth. He wrapped his reins around his saddle horn. His right hand held his eight-gauge, his left a Colt .45.

Will knotted his reins, counting on knee pressure and the urging of his heels to put Slick where he wanted him. His clutched his rifle in his left hand and his Colt in his right.

Austin too knotted his reins. He held a pistol in each hand and a long-bladed knife in his teeth.

The renegades came into view suddenly, as if they'd sprung from the earth. They were riding directly into the sun and the various brass buttons and medals of the mishmash of Confederate and Union jackets reflected the sun sharply, as did the barrels of their rifles and the heads of the spears a few carried.

As they came closer, there was an unearthly silence beyond the thunder of hooves. The outlaws— even the Indians among them—held the war cries that generally led them into battle.

They closed in a ragged line, the chests of their horses white with frothy sweat. Some of the Indians, Will saw, had painted their faces and chests with war paint.

They were fifty yards out—and then twenty-five. Jane sat calmly on his horse, contemplatively, as if he were watching a particularly beautiful sunset. Slick and Austin's horse were anything but calm, their eyes wide, desperately wanting to flee from the wave of men and horses rushing toward them.

The outlaws were fifteen yards away and gunfire erupted from their line. Jane banged his heels against his horse's sides and the huge animal was almost immediately into a hard gallop, moving far faster than one could expect such a massive animal to move. Austin and Will followed, returning fire, choosing targets and taking them down, not wasting a shot.

The ponderous boom of Jane's shotgun rolled across the prairie. Two outlaws had made the mistake of riding together, and both went down as bloody masses. The shotgun bellowed again and a man, headless, rode on a few feet before toppling from his horse.

One Dog sat a tall pinto, waving his rifle and hollering orders, attempting to distribute his troops to stop the onslaught of the three men. Will swung into a swarm of outlaws and dropped a pair of them, bringing Slick into a scrambling turn. For the briefest part of a second, his eyes and those of One Dog met—and that was all it took. Both men knew immediately that only one of them would live much longer.

The barrel of Austin's rifle sizzled as a drop of renegade blood splashed onto it. He triggered another round but it misfired, the metal of the mechanism overly expanded by the heat of such rapid fire. He threw the rifle aside, cursing, and went to work with his Colt.

Jane crushed an unhorsed outlaw under the hooves of his horse and swung his bowie knife like a saber, leaning far from his saddle to skewer confused, panicked outlaws.

One Dog had gathered ten or so men near him, and bullets were whispering past Will, Austin, and Jane. Jane howled a wolf-call-type war whoop as he wheeled his horse around and galloped from the melee. Austin and Will followed, shots whistling past them, horses at full run.

Will dared a quick look back. There seemed to be more dead or dying outlaws on the ground than there were live ones on horses.

A mile away from the battle scene, Jane gave the halt signal and slowed his horse to a stop. He turned in his saddle. "Anybody hit?"

"Sonsabitches ruined my perfectly good rifle, makin' me fire too fast. She's warped to hell. Now I prolly couldn't hit a damn barn with it, even if I was inside the damned barn. I had to toss her away."

Jane chuckled. "Terrible thing," he said. "I guess the reason they charged us like that was to damage your rifle."

Will took off his Stetson. "One of them scum tore a piece off the top of a fine hat," he said. "Other'n that, me an' Slick are good."

"Why ain't they tryin' to chase us down?" Austin asked. "Was me, I'd be haulin' ass after the three pissants what caused me such grief."

"Because they're cowards and because they're un-disciplined. I expected more from One Dog, consid-ering his reputation. We rode into them and stirred them around like a bowl of applesauce. I'd wager a good number of the dead were shot by their own men. Still, we sent more than a few off to the happy hunting ground." He hesitated for a few moments. "You boys did very well, by the way."

"What now?" Austin asked.

Will spoke up. "We have nowhere to run to. Seems to me we gotta make a stand in Olympus—choose the best place an' fight from there, 'cause One Dog'll be back. You can bet on that. An' next time, he'll make sure his crew fight like men."

"I walked the street last night. The mercantile will be our fort. We can bring our horses right inside the storeroom in back. In the store are all the guns and supplies we will ever need."

"I don't s'pose the fella who owns the place will be too pleased," Austin said.

Jane smiled again. "Will can pay for the damages, no?"

There was no reason to enter into immediate negotia-tions with the mercantile owner. He—and apparently the rest of town—had scattered to parts unknown, probably to the farms of relatives and friends.

"How'd they get word of our li'l tussle so quick?" Austin asked.

"A man on a bay horse followed us out and beat us back to town. It didn't take long for the good folks here to figure out what we would do."

"I didn't see no rider on a bay."

"No. But I did."

"Well. Anyway, it's a sure thing the barkeep didn't take all his beer an' whiskey with him. You boys up for a drink?"

"Of course," Gentle Jane answered. "But after we drink we must prepare the mercantile for a siege."

"Least I can get me a new rifle," Austin said.

The mercantile was the end building of the block, and there was an alley next to it at least wide enough for a delivery freighter to pull in. There was even a pump in the storeroom the owner probably used to wash apples, carrots, potatoes, and other produce he brought in. The stream of water it produced was paltry, but it was better than nothing. The side of the structure facing open prairie had no windows, but Austin used a pickax to bash shooting ports in it every few feet. He set a rifle and a few boxes of cartridges at each port.

Will worked in the storeroom, hauling out things the horses could hurt themselves with, such as sacks of oats, corn, and sweet grain. Given time a horse could damned near eat himself to death—and if he didn't die from the overfeeding, pressure inside his hooves would make him unusable and keep him in constant pain. Will remembered the old farmers' adage about what to do for a foundered horse: "First you dig a big hole good and deep, the size of the horse . . ."

He lugged out bundles of shovels and picks, kegs of nails, and miscellaneous farm tools.

Then he filled a new trough with water and put it against a wall. He scattered some grain around to give the animals something to do. Emptied, the room was good sized, at least large enough to board three horses for a few days. Of course, Slick and Austin's horse would give Jane's behemoth most of the room, but Will didn't expect any serious fighting; neither horse would challenge Jane's.

Will led his and Austin's horses into the room, leaving Jane's where he'd been ground-tied. He went back out and approached the animal slowly, talking quietly—nonsense words with a little humming added—and reached for the reins. If he were a hair of a second slower, he'd have been a dead man: a steel-shod hoof that seemed the size of a wagon wheel snaked out toward his face. Will threw himself backward, landing clumsily and hard on his back.

Jane rushed out of the store. "I should have told you! I am so sorry—are you all right?"

He helped Will to his feet. "He's trained that way—I didn't realize you were going to try to lead him."

Will brushed off his butt. "It's a sure thing nobody's gonna steal him from you," he said. "Come on, bring him along."

Jane tossed the reins over his horse's head and began walking around the building. The horse followed him like a puppy following a boy. "Again, I apologize," Jane said.

Will waved him off. "No harm done," he said casually, but the fear in his eyes showed he knew how close he'd come to having his head cleaved open like a ripe melon.

Jane's horse immediately took over the water trough, clicking his teeth at the other two, cringing against the far wall. "They will settle," Jane said.

"You might could check on them real often," Will said. "If there's trouble, you're the only one who can do anything about it."

"I will do this."

Will was about to turn away, but stopped. "Say—does that critter have a name?"

"Of course. His name is Partner." Jane's grin showed again. "Although you know as well as I do that naming a horse makes as much sense as naming a chicken, no?"

The three men sat at the table the store owner provided for checker players. Austin was alternating between gnawing an apple and taking belts from a bottle of whiskey.

"We could use a couple men on the roof," Will said.

"Could use a Gatling gun, but we ain't got one of them, neither."

"Our biggest danger," Jane said, "is if they decide to use fire arrows to burn us out. We must drop any man who shows a flame on an arrow or a torch, immediately."

"That's what I meant about men on the roof. Be a whole lot easier to see from up there."

"Well, hell. How 'bout we chop a hole in the ceilin' an' put a stepladder there. Ever once an' a while one of us can pop up for a look-see," Austin suggested.

Jane and Will looked across the table at one another, almost stunned by the simple efficiency of
Austin's idea. Will spoke for both of them. "Boy, you're
somethin', pard."

Jane nodded toward the two broad front windows.
"That's an awful big opening," he said. "We need to
barricade it with whatever we can, just high enough
so that we can shoot over it."

The next couple of hours were spent grunting,
sweating, and cursing—even Jane said "Dammit!"
when he dropped a crate of yard goods on his foot.
The barricade was a bizarre-looking affair, but the
men felt it would be effective. It was made up of a
small piano, two desks, several barrels of apples and
carrots, a number of plow blades stacked atop one
another, four saddles upon which crates of textbooks
were stacked, a couple of butter churns holding up a
crate of canned peaches, and so forth. It was a bit
better than waist high on Will and it offered good
cover the length of the two storefront windows.

Will sat on the floor and wiped his forehead with
his sleeve.

"How's that hand?" Austin asked.

"Pretty much as good as new—fingers work good.
I figure I'll cut them stitches out in a couple more
days."

"You oughta take the ones outta your face too—
they're uglier'n a goat's ass."

"I'll give those a little more time," Will said, ignoring the insult. "I can still feel 'em pullin' a bit."

"The window glass," Jane said, "will shower us
when it is hit. The shards and pieces will be sharp
and dangerous."

Austin was the first to draw and he shot hell out of

the expanses of glass, exploding them out into the street. Will joined in, firing until his Colt was empty.

"I always liked to bust glass," Austin said. "With stones when I was a kid an' later with bullets."

"Me too," Will admitted. "There's somethin' about the way it shatters that makes a man feel good."

Jane shook his head but didn't comment.

It was hot in the store and growing hotter as the sun reached and crossed its peak. The destroyed windows would have allowed fresh air to enter, but there wasn't a breath moving outside.

Will had his Colt partially disassembled on the checkers table and was working with a piece of cloth and a can of gun oil.

"How do you think they'll attack?" Austin asked.

"One Dog is an Indian, and he won't come at night. Their initial attempt will probably be at first light in the morning," Jane said. "It'll probably be a sweep, as if they were closing in on a wagon train."

"I dunno," Will said. "I saw more white men than Indians earlier today. Seems like they might could convince One Dog to try a sneak-attack type of thing, even today. We gotta be on watch all the time."

"I can't see them scum changin' Dog's Injun ways—'specially with all that medicine horseshit he believes in."

"Will is right. We must watch constantly."

Austin pushed out from the barricade where he sat, watching the street. "There sure ain't nothin' out there now but heat," he said. "If I'm gonna set here gawkin', I'm gonna have a couple buckets of beer keepin' me company." He began climbing over a crate of goods to the street. "I won't be but a minute," he said.

"This is not wise," Jane said.

"No—but try tellin' Austin that. He wants his beer an' he's gonna get it. Tell the truth, I wouldn't mind a sip myself." Will put his pistol back together and spun the empty cylinder. It gave off a smooth, whirring whisper. He filled the chambers with cartridges and holstered the .45. Jane crossed the room to the spot Austin had vacated. Will rolled a smoke, lit it, and sat back in his chair.

The HW wouldn't be the biggest spread in West Texas, but it'd be large enough to give Hiram and his family and me, and maybe even a family for me, a real good living. We'd have a few good horses as well as our working string, and as many beef as our land could graze. We'd hire decent hands—no drifters or saddle tramps—and pay them well for their work. And we'd work with them. Hiram an' me ain't the types to set around doin' nothing. A mental picture of Hiram's daughters—whom Will had never actually seen—playing on an expanse of lush, green grass near the house was so pleasant that he dwelled on it, half-asleep, almost able to hear the giggles and screams of the girls as they chased after one another.

A rattle of gunfire down the street dragged Will from his dream as quickly as a bucket of ice water in his face would have. He rushed to the window near Jane, snatching up a rifle. The shooting seemed to go on forever, round after round, constant, nonstop. Then it stopped abruptly.

"My brother and your friend is dead," Jane said quietly. His voice was a monotone but there was great sorrow behind it.

"Maybe he got some cover. Maybe some of them shots were his. Could be that—"

"No."

A whoop—almost a screech—broke the silence, as did the pounding of hooves. A man, a white man in a rebel jacket, galloped toward the mercantile, hugging the far side of the street. He carried a spear upright in his right hand. Impaled at the top of the shaft was Austin's head, his hat still in place, his face a mass of blood, an irregular, deep red mass of meat stuffed into his mouth. It was his heart.

Jane stood, leveled his shotgun, and blew the rider off the horse to fall in a crumpled and bloody heap. Even before the rider hit the ground a dozen horsemen charged from the opposite ends of the street, firing rifles, shotguns, pistols, and a few arrows. Jane went for his rifle immediately; Will depended on his Colt until it was empty before he, too, snatched up a .30-30. Bullets riddled the barricade like a swarm of insane bees and the inside of the mercantile was a chaos of ricocheting slugs, shattering glass, tortured wood, and exploding bottles and cans.

Will and Jane fired like a combat-trained militia: steadily but not rapidly, aiming each round, making it count. It was the rare slug that didn't wound or kill an outlaw.

"Sonsabitches are crazy," Will shouted. "It's like they want to die."

"Is true—One Dog must have given them mushroom buttons. Their fighting is insane!"

Still the renegades came on, jerking their horses around when they'd galloped past the store, heading back the opposite way, fumbling loads into their weapons. There were several full-gallop collisions; outlaws and horses went down in twisted heaps of flailing hooves, arms, and legs. Survivors of the crashes were quickly dropped by the men in the store.

The street looked like the third day at Gettysburg: corpses were scattered as if they'd dropped from the sky. Small potholes and ruts were filled with blood that had seeped from men and from horses. A few attackers moaned in pain, and others writhed about in the blood and the grit and dirt. Jane stood calmly levering his .30-30. His rifle stilled those who were still alive.

The maniac charge had come to an end.

"We stopped 'em that time," Will said. "Did you see One Dog anywhere in that mess?"

"I did not—and I did not expect to. He knew it would be a slaughter. He gave his warriors those mushrooms—"

"What mushrooms?" Will interrupted. "How could a mushroom make men not care about their lives?"

"Peyote, it is called. It is strong medicine. It paints insane pictures in the minds of men, strange colors and sounds, and they follow orders, no matter how deadly to them. It makes them crazy men. At times, if they eat the mushroom buds during the day, the men will stare at the sun until their eyes can no longer see—until they are forever blind."

Will went to the back of the store, filled a bucket with water from the pump, and pulled a pair of shirts off a counter. He set the bucket down near Jane and the two men washed the blowback and bits of gunpowder from their faces. He wiped his face on his sleeve, winced at the stinging, and walked back to the slug-holed counter. He found a bottle of whiskey that hadn't been smashed and brought it up to the barricade, pulling the cork with his teeth. He took a long, deep draft and handed the bottle to Jane, who did the same.

"Think they'll leave those bodies out there?" Will asked.

"They will. One Dog cares no more for his men than a dog does about the tree on which he lifts his leg."

Will carried a pair of crates of .30-30 cartridges to the barricade and set one next to Jane, and placed one at the spot he'd occupied during the battle. "We went through a passel of ammunition," he observed.

"And we killed many snakes with it."

"How many you figure we dropped?"

"Perhaps twenty—maybe more. It makes no difference. One Dog has more and will bring in any guns he needs to hire."

Will mused for a few moments, his right hand unconsciously touching the grips of his holstered pistol. "Ya know," he finally said, "they rode off to the west, so their camp is somewhere in that direction." He paused again, for a longer time. "They won't attack at night—we know that. I'm thinking I'll slide out that way and have a look-see and make up a bit for what they done to Austin."

"Is foolish idea. Your heart—your love for your friend—talks louder than your mind, Will. I, too, need revenge. The bodies in the street are not revenge— they are the results of a battle. I will take blood for my brother's blood, but not tonight."

"You yourself said they were hopped up on that mushroom stuff. How long does that last?"

"Is impossible to say—how much is eaten, how strong and fresh the plant is."

"Is there a hangover as it wears off?"

"Often. Yes. But—"

"So," Will went on, speaking over Jane, "a bunch

of 'em will be slow an' stupid. There's some moon tonight—at least enough for me to follow their tracks. I'll go in on foot an' do a payback for Austin."

"I say no."

"An' I say you ain't the honcho on this job of work—I am. If you want to ride out of here right now, that's fine. You owe me nothing."

"I owe my brother—and in my heart, we have become friends."

"We have, Jane. You're a hell of a man. But you owe me nothing. In fact, I owe you money, which you'll get. Let me draw you a map to one of my stashes so that if I get killed you can—"

"No. This is not a job. It never was—not since I heard from Austin. Would you charge money for fighting for your Hiram?"

Will was silent for a moment. Then, regardless of Austin's warning that rang in his ears, he held his hand out to Gentle Jane. A knife suddenly appeared in Jane's hand. He took Will's hand, turned it over, and put a half-inch slit in the palm. Then he did the same to his own right palm. When the blood was flowing from both cuts he grasped Will's hand in the grasp of common blood—of brotherhood. Jane stood, carrying his rifle. "I will stand by Partner to make certain he doesn't hurt your horse as you lead him out."

The grain on the floor had been cleaned. Jane's horse stood to one side, half-asleep. Both Austin's horse and Slick had been allowed to suck at the water trough. Jane stood by his horse as Will led Slick outside and saddled and bridled him. A moment later he came back into the storeroom and shagged Austin's horse out the open loading door. He slapped the animal on the rump, setting him into a lope into the darkness. To Jane he said, "Lots of herds of wild ones 'round here. This boy'll find a home."

"It is not right that another man put a saddle on Austin's horse," Jane said.

Will nodded and stepped into a stirrup. He carried a rifle across the saddle in front of him and another in his right hand. His Colt was, of course, holstered at his side. On the left side of his gun belt was a sheath carrying a ten-inch-bladed knife, courtesy of the mercantile.

Will set off to the west at a jog. Jane shoveled the dung out of the storage room, scattered fresh grain on the floor, and replenished the water trough. He picked up a bottle behind the counter and settled in behind the barricade. He rested, but he didn't sleep.

The faint glow of a fire appeared against the sky not a full four miles out of town. Slick heard the whooping and hollered chanting before Will did, and his nervousness—tainted by fear—transmitted itself to Will immediately. There was a convenient cluster of rocks nearby.

Will tied Slick there. He left the rifle in the saddle scabbard and went ahead on foot, knife in his left hand, right hovering near the grips of his pistol.

Will walked perhaps a mile before he crouched down to make himself less obvious against the horizon. There was a gentle mound between him and the camp, and Will crawled up it like a snake. At the top he was able to look down at the gathering of outlaws. There were more of them—many more than he'd expected—and the Indians in the crew were dancing around the fire. Bottles of booze were circulating rapidly from hand to hand. Will grinned.

Damned fools.

A lookout passed in front of him not twenty yards away. The man was mumbling to himself and seemed barely able to keep his seat in his saddle. There was another pair on horseback on the side of the camp beyond Will. They were circulating, but they were much too far apart to do any real damage in case of attack. Will grinned again and watched the camp.

Either One Dog has me set up somehow, or he's a bunch dumber than I thought he was. Seems like I could ride a elly-phant in here an' they wouldn't notice.

Their weapons, Will noticed in the light of the fire, were all over the place: a few rifles here in the dirt, gun belts tossed to the ground like trash, bows and quivers of arrows scattered here and there.

Will watched as the circulating lookouts came past him. Most wore Union or rebel jackets or pants, and the majority rode pancake military saddles rather than stock saddles. For whatever reason, Will Lewis was waiting for an Indian to pass.

One did. He was riding bareback, his pony obviously fatigued, dragging his hooves. The rider carried a spear and had a rifle strapped across his chest, military-style. He sat comfortably on his pony. He wasn't drunk or drugged, but he wasn't paying a ton of attention around him, either.

Will eased in behind the pony. When he was the farthest point from the camp, he tackled the rider, brought him down, and hurled his rifle off into the prairie. The spear dropped next to the pony.

Will holstered his pistol and switched his knife to his right hand. The Indian drew his knife and faced Will.

"Looks like you an' me, outlaw. You scream all you want—they ain't gonna hear you over their dancing an' singin', now are they?"

The Indian showed no fear. "You die now," he said.

"I doubt that."

They circled one another, neither making a move, both deciding on the other's skill in a knife fight. The Indian parried; Will easily stepped to the side and swept his blade across his opponent's stomach. It was a shallow cut—little more than a scratch. The Indian stepped back . . . and then lunged forward, slashing Will's right arm below the elbow. Will caught the Indian's knife hand with a deep cut that flowed blood.

"White pig," the Indian grunted. He shifted his knife to his left hand, as if his right would no longer work, and then switched it back as Will closed in. Will missed, as did the Indian. They backed away from one another, both crouched, both knives extended.

The Indian charged again and Will ducked down, the blade hissing over his head. With his left hand he scrabbled up a handful of dirt and rushed his opponent, throwing the dirt in his face, in his eyes. The Indian instinctively raised his right hand—his knife hand—to clear his eyes. As he did so, Will drove his blade into the man's chest, twisted it, pulled it out, and drove it in again.

Will watched the life flee from his opponent's eyes. At first they were chestnut, filled with hate, but the hate diminished as the life drained. The chestnut turned slightly gray and then a curtain seemed to drop, indicating the last act—the end of all that this man was.

Will found the spear easily enough and brought it back to the Indian's body. He started twice to hack the man's head off—and he vomited both times. Finally, he finished his grotesque task. He carved *HW* into the outlaw's forehead and jammed the long, razor-sharp spearhead into the ragged opening of the Indian's head and stuck it into the sandy ground. He nudged it a couple of times to make sure it wouldn't topple. The spear and head stood well.

It seemed like a terribly long walk back to where he'd tied Slick. Will had killed before, but this was savage killing, satanic killing. *Maybe we're even for what was done to Austin. Maybe not. But I done what I had to do and I damn well showed One Dog what I plan to do with him and the rest of his killers. Justice? Shit. It was revenge, an' that's what it'll be until all of them are dead.*

Slick snorted as he heard Will coming to him. This man had meant food and water and good care to him and he was frightened by the thick, coppery scent of blood that surrounded Will. It was a different man to his feeble equine mind—his instinctual fear—but when he heard Will's voice, he associated that with good things: with sweet grain and brushing and spurless boots.

Will climbed on and settled himself in the saddle. He still held the knife with which he'd done his work. He hurled it out onto the prairie and wiped his hand on his denim pants. He rode at an easy pace back to town, checking behind him, as the dark of the night began to give way to the coming day.

I never thought I could do nothin' like I did to that Indian, but they done the same thing to a good man, a tight friend. There was no damned reason for 'em to do it—none. It was a war. Ya don't hack up an' cut the head off . . .

An uneven circle of vultures barely visible against the sky, with one or two dropping to the earth as if they forgot how to fly, caused Will to put his heels to Slick.

Austin's horse had an arrow behind his ear and his body was spotted with gunshot wounds—and the widespread but equally deadly splatter of shotgun pellets. Vultures were pulling at the corpse, tugging, fighting one another away, digging their claws into the horse's gut.

Will asked Slick for all the speed he had, at the same time drawing his Colt. They were long shots—from horseback—but he dropped two of the birds. Three of the vultures were dragging intestines from the horse. Will and Slick hit them hard, pieces of the disgusting birds, feathers, and parts of Austin's horse dropping to the ground.

One of the vultures was a little slow. Will grabbed a leg as it flapped its wings and slung it in front of Slick's galloping hooves. The vulture writhed for a moment and then was still.

Chapter Six

"Now look here, you two: this rifle was made by Confederate hands, an' it was made to shoot straight an' to kill what she hits. You miss, it ain't the fault of the Maynard—she took down more bluebellies than you two can count. I'm 'a give you both two ca'tridges an' I want you each to bring back two fillin's for the pot or there'll be hell to pay—I'll guar'tee that."

Pa doled out a pair of .50-caliber rounds to each of us, as if he was dropping diamonds into a queen's hand. He was drunk already, an' the sun was hardly up. "Y'all can take my hoss," he said.

"Shit," I mumbled, "I'd as soon ride a goddamn hog."

"Wazzat, boy?"

"I said, 'Maybe we'd better walk. Quieter that way.'"

"Walk 'r ride, I don' care. But you bring back grub. Hear?"

Hiram an' I walked out past the barn an' over the hill. I had the beat-to-shit ol' Maynard over my shoulder. Hiram handed over his two cartridges. I took 'em without sayin' nothing. Hiram, he wouldn't shoot a animal to save his life. An' he couldn't hit the ground with the rifle if he threw it down. When we butchered a pig or cow he always rode off an' didn't come back 'til the next mornin'.

We hadn't walked real far into the woods when we came

upon a doe heavy with a fawn. She was suckin' water at a little eddy where a stream had dug into soft soil. I raised the Maynard.

"Nah, Jesus, Will, she's carryin' a . . . ," Hiram said, real loud.

'Course the doe's head snapped up an' swung toward us. I dropped her clean as can be, puttin' one of them fat an' stubby .50-caliber slugs into her left eye. Hiram pushed the rifle out of the way an' punched me in the mouth, hard 'nuff to loosen a couple teeth an' get my nose runnin' blood . . .

"Will? Will? My eyes are heavy. You need to take your watch, no?"

Will swam up from his dream and sat up at the table where he'd rested his head on his arms. "Yeah, sure, Jane. Anything goin' on out there?"

"Many of the men are drunk. There was a gun-fight where a very fast gun killed a farm boy. Other than that, very little. They drink, they shoot over here when they care to. I have fired back, but my skill is with the pistol and the knife—not the rifle. Missing by an inch or so is as bad as missing by a mile, no?"

Will stood. "You get some sleep, Jane. I'll take the watch 'til dawn."

"Will they attack at night?" Jane asked.

"Who the hell knows?" Will sighed. "If One Dog tells 'em to, they will. If they get hopped up on them mushrooms again, there's no tellin' what they'll do."

"Well. Is one good thing to tell. You know Berdan Sharps?"

"The double-trigger model? 'Course I do, Jane. Been the best rifle in the world since fifty-nine—

nothin' come close to it. I know a Reb sharpshooter who picked off near a hundred blues, mostly officers. That sumbitch rifle—"

"Come here."

Jane led Will back to the storeroom. "I was looking about here to see what we could use. This case was hidden under sacks of grain. Of course, I have heard of the . . ."

Will drew his knife from his boot and began prying the nails out of the long wooden box, the top of which was stenciled SHAR—BER. He was as anxious as a kid unwrapping a Christmas gift. The box was stuffed with straw, and under the straw was a bison-skin bag, flesh side out.

"Holy God," Will mumbled as he brought the buffalo skin out and unwrapped its contents.

It was, in fact, a Sharps rifle—the Berdan '59 model with the dual triggers that fired a slug as fat as a man's thumb and was accurate—deadly accurate—for damned near three-quarters of a mile. Some buffalo hunters said it'd shoot farther with the same accuracy. Buffalo Bill Cody dropped thirteen woolies from at least a mile away with a Berdan Sharps.

At both ends of the wooden packing crate were two boxes containing twenty cartridges each. Will picked up the rifle and put it to his shoulder. It smelled of good wood, gun oil, and steel. "The storekeep, he said he didn't have a Sharps—that the wooly hunters had cleaned out his stock."

"I know why the store man would not have sold. The longer he held onto this gun, the more valuable it would become."

"I got her now, though. Damn, Jane, feel the way it fits to a shoulder, lookit the quality of the fittings."

"A weapon is a weapon. Does it matter how long the viper's fangs are? I think not. The target will be dead either way."

"You're one cheerful sumbitch," Will said, sliding cartridges into the Sharps. "You gotta realize that—"

There was a loud crash from the back room where the horses were being held. At the same time, a man in a Union general's uniform left the saloon across the street with a white flag attached to a broomstick. He marched as if in formation, waving the flag. "We will talk," he shouted.

Will hustled back to the horses. Slick was on his side, eyes closed, legs twisted under him, in a puddle of blood. Gentle Jane's Partner was slumped against the far wall, gouts of blood spurting from his throat, doing his best to raise a forefoot to fight back—and not doing well at all. When he fell, it seemed the entire building shuddered.

"They've killed our horses!" Will yelled. "They killed our horses!"

Will ran to the barricade just in time to see Jane trigger both barrels at the man carrying the white flag. The two blasts hit his upper body squarely, hurling him back six feet with a gaping hole in his midsection. The flag and broomstick vaulted into the air and then dropped to the dirt of the street.

"Both are dead?"

"Yes—throats cut."

"My Partner . . . he was a fine horse."

"So was Slick."

Will looked above barricade. "Shit. Here they come with fire arrows."

Across the street, men were firing torches—fire

arrows—at the mercantile. Both Will and Jane began shooting, Jane dropping his shotgun next to him and working the rifle Austin had left for him.

Will cranked his .30-30, rarely missing a shot.

"The roof!" Jane called. "It's on fire. They'll burn us out!"

"I ain't gonna let that happen. Keep on shootin', Jane—scare 'em or kill 'em. I don't care. I'll go up on the roof an' I'll—"

It was then that the flimsy, dry-wood roof caved in, showering Will and Jane with charred wood, snippets of flame, and years of accumulated dust that sparkled like tiny Chinese firecrackers as it ignited. A couple of renegades toppled in with the collapse. Will shot them both before they hit the floor.

"If Austin had been up on the roof . . . ," Will roared stupidly, needlessly.

"And if hogs could fly, they would nest in trees. We must get out of here before the whole place caves in on us!"

The smoke was bluish gray, and acrid, difficult to breathe, making the men feel as if their lungs were filled with searing pebbles and burning shards of glass. They both hurriedly tied their bandannas over their mouths and noses. The ladies' garments section of the mercantile was fully ablaze, as was the fabric department. Fingers of flame sprang up from the goods and from the floor, spreading quickly into sheets of fire.

The barrage from the street remained intense, nonstop, slugs whistling through the smoke and flames. Will and Jane held their positions behind a pile of plows and farm implements at the window, firing, coughing rackingly, eyes tearing copiously. A round careened into the action of the Sharps, tearing it from Will's hands. He didn't bother to pick up the rifle; the damage to the mechanism would never allow it fire again. "Sonsabitches," he cursed.

Will put his face close to Jane's. "The back's our only way out," he choked. "They're either gonna fry us or shoot us—an' I'll take a bullet 'stead of burnin' to death!"

"The fire—the damned fire! All my life I've feared fire . . . ," Jane coughed.

The two men rose and ran, trippingly, almost blind from the smoke, parting walls of flame with their bodies, gagging, throats thick and constricted by the heat and smoke.

The outlaws had smashed their way through the siding, making a hole large enough to allow a crouched man through to get to the horses, their noise covered by the fusillade from the street. Jane was a few steps ahead of Will. He performed a running dive through the hole, cranking his rifle as he did so. Will followed and crashed into his now-staggering friend—blood brother—who had two blazing arrows protruding from his chest, his beard, hair, and clothing aflame, screaming in agony. Will pushed himself up from the ground, where he'd fallen after slamming into Gentle Jane, the ungodly screeches of Jane's pain louder than thunder in his ears.

The arrows were well-placed, deadly, in Jane's chest. Will immediately saw that his friend had no chance at life. He drew his .45 and put a slug between Jane's eyes and then turned his pistol on the pair of mounted Indians who'd skewered and torched his friend. He blew the nearest one off his horse with a single shot, but when he attempted to fire at the second, the hammer of his pistol clicked on an empty cartridge. Will's right hand slammed his .45 into its holster and continued downward to his boot. He was already in a run as the renegade nocked another arrow. He hurled his body at his enemy, tackling him, plunging his knife up to the hilt in the man's guts, hot blood spurting onto his hand, carrying them both off the horse's back.

Even over the roar of the fire and the shooting into the front of the mercantile, Will heard hoofbeats, whoops, and war cries alongside the building. He vaulted onto the renegade's horse, grabbed the single rein, and put his heels to the animal's side. He'd barely gotten the horse into a full gallop when there was a tremendous crash behind him and a stinging rush of hot air and red, smoking bits of wood swept over and past him. He looked over his shoulder: the entire structure of the store had collapsed to the ground, freeing hungry flames to reach twenty and thirty feet into the sky as the conflagration sucked at and fed itself with the fire-feeding air.

Will One Dog assume I'm dead, my tomb a burned mercantile? The two dead Indians and Gentle Jane's body won't tell One Dog much, nor will the missing horse—and more than likely the first renegade down's horse ran off, too, its instinctual fear of fire easily overcoming any training it may have had.

He asked the horse he was riding for yet more speed.

Now it's not only Hiram and his family's revenge I'm seeking. I'll draw blood for both Austin and Jane, or I'll die trying.

The horse Will had taken from the Indian he killed with his knife must have been a recent steal by the renegade. Will felt some fat around the animal's withers, and the horse seemed willing enough to cover ground. He was shod; Will could tell that from the ringing sound of hooves striking bits of rock. The horses One Dog and his crew rode were unshod.

Will reined down to a fast walk after a couple of miles at a lope, figuring the gang wouldn't be able to track him in the now-full dark. The battle in memory seemed a speck of time, but in reality, it had covered several hours. Images of the fight cluttered Will's mind, clashing with one another, out of sequence, an amalgam of gunfire, flames, blood, and death.

The faces of Austin and Jane floated in front of him like mirages, one on either side of Hiram's face.

The side of Will's head tortured him—it felt as if he were still in the mercantile, forcing his way through smoke and flames. He explored the painful area with his fingertips and encountered what felt like minute strands of strings. He grasped one between his thumb and forefinger and tugged it free, puzzled. Then it struck him: the stitches! The fire had singed the exposed parts of the sutures, parting them. Within a few minutes, Will had removed the entire line. He probed where his eyebrows had been. Now there was nothing but seared flesh. He found his eyelashes were gone, as well. His Stetson was burned all the way around and it smelled strongly of scorched felt. He put his palm on the grips of his Colt: it felt fine. He wondered about his gun belt: he was carrying, he thought, thirty rounds of volatile

.45 cartridges. But as he ran his hand around his waist he found many of the leather loops were empty—he'd loaded and reloaded automatically, without realizing what he was doing. Will reached back to his saddle-bag for a fresh box of Remingtons and realized that he was riding without a saddle—without his own saddle and supplies—and that the horse he was riding wasn't Slick.

The pain struck suddenly. His face felt as if it were on fire, his arms screamed for relief from the heat, and his gut, upper body, and back felt as if he'd been horsewhipped. The crazy hot blood of the battle, the Sharps . . . and his two friends, Austin and Gentle Jane, were gone—gone for good. Will was dizzy with pain. His left hand let go of the single rein and it dropped on the horse's neck, giving the animal free choice as to where he was going.

Will mumbled to himself—and moaned, now and again—but for the most part, he sat the horse, not knowing where the hell he was, and not really caring.

The fatigue, the pain, the pounding ache in his body and in his heart, fell on Will like a heavy, impenetrable blanket. His eyes closed and he slumped forward at the waist, his face only a few inches above the horse's ears.

The animal was, of course, not saddled. Only Will's many years of riding, both bareback and in a saddle, kept him aboard the horse. Will's body shifted with that of the animal rather than against it, and although he wasn't consciously aware of it, his legs exerted just enough pressure to keep him centered.

The horse, confused, danced a bit and huffed

through his nostrils. When there was no reaction, no command, from his rider, the animal did as his instincts demanded. He headed toward the place where he'd last known safety, hay, and water: the camp where One Dog and his troops had settled prior to their siege of the mercantile.

Will wasn't asleep, but he wasn't exactly awake, either. Instead, he was in a sort of twilight, unaware of his surroundings but realizing that the horse under him was walking steadily, moving well. To where he didn't know, and it didn't really matter.

The sun had risen by the time the horse stopped. When his rider failed to dismount he became nervous. This wasn't the way things were supposed to be, the way they always were in the past. Further, there were no men and more importantly, no other horses—simply signs of cook fires, piles of manure, and remnants of bales of hay. He danced again, this time circling, raising a cloud of grit, frightened by what should have been familiar, but wasn't. He arched his back and bucked, all four hooves off the ground, and came down hard. Will toppled off his back and hit the dirt and manure like a full sack of grain tossed from a wagon. The horse trotted to the murky little puddle that provided water to the camp. After he drank, he began snuffling through the scraps of hay left behind by the renegades, salvaging what he could.

The sun flexed its morning muscles, adding its own fire to the agony of Will's face and arms. He groaned and fought his way to consciousness. He was neither hungry nor thirsty, but he realized he needed to eat and drink to stay alive. He pushed himself to a sitting position and rubbed the crust from his eyes. He recognized that there'd been a camp here, but little further registered—at least until he focused on the horse he'd ridden in on. He was what horsemen call "right pretty," a tall, well-muscled pinto with large expanses of white and equally large splotches of a deep chestnut. His nut sack looked like a tanned deerskin bag with a pair of doorknobs in it: he was obviously a stallion, and a young one, at that. But Will's eyes swung past the horse to a scrawny jackrabbit picking through the dirt for bits of spilled grain.

Will's hand found the grips of his .45 easily, smoothly, regardless of his pain. He took a breath, aimed by instinct, and squeezed his trigger. The sharp metallic snap of the hammer striking an empty cartridge was loud in the heat and the vastness of the prairie. The horse swung his head toward Will, and the jack ran ten yards or so before stopping and looking back over his shoulder, still ready to run.

"Goddammit," Will muttered through cracked and bleeding lips. He swung open the cylinder of his .45, dumped the empties, and fumbled along his belt until he found three fresh cartridges. He eased the cylinder shut. That faint click startled the jack. The pinto paid no attention.

The few bits of grain were a mighty lure for the starving rabbit. The midsummer sun had burned his usual forage to stunted brown blades with no more life to them than the arid dirt around them. Her mate had died, as had all seven of her latest litter. She'd eaten two of them but there hadn't been enough to them to maintain her life.

The jack moved cautiously back toward the spilled

grain. Will fired, taking the rabbit between its long ears and flipping it into the air in an awkward sommersault.

Will struggled to his feet, unsteady, dizzy, and within a few moments he fell on his ass. He cursed again. He needed the jack and it was a sure bet he wasn't going to be able to stroll over and pick it up.

It took him a while and a lot of hurt, but eventually, on his hands and knees, the sun flogging him, he made it to the jack. He drew his knife from his boot, cut the rabbit's throat, and drank the still hot, copper-tasting blood. He then split the jack up the middle, dumped its intestines, and gnawed at the raw, bloody, stringy flesh.

There was some shade—precious little of it—begrudgingly yielded by a few desert pines on one side of the water. Will took his jack and crawled to the shade and the water. He drank, ate some more rabbit, and then he slept.

He slept through the day until dusk, plagued by dreams of lakes of fire and flaming demons chasing him, catching him, embracing him. He fought his way to consciousness and when he was fully awake he gently touched his face, for the first time feeling the tissue-thin ripped sacks of ruptured blisters. He stayed under the scraggly trees until he felt he may be able to move.

The remains of the jackrabbit were next to him, barely visible in the fading light. The carcass was warm now, not with the warmth of life but rather with the grotesque warmth of a dead creature long exposed to the sun. He gnawed off a piece of flesh—which had already begun to stink—gagged, swallowed, gagged again, and finally kept the meat down.

Two more mouthfuls were all he could bear; he tossed the jack into the prairie.

Will's mind wasn't working properly, normally. It took him several minutes to figure out that the snuffling and crunching he heard was the pinto moving about, twenty or so feet from him. The image of the horse in his mind led to the picture of the horse drinking, and at that very moment the intensity of his own thirst almost strangled him. His tongue, fat, sandy, desert dry, filled his mouth and was a lump of foul and useless desiccated meat in his mouth.

Will realized he had to get to that puddle or he'd die. And he couldn't die; he hadn't yet taken the revenge that was rightfully his, which now included the killings of Austin and Gentle Jane. He unbuckled his gun belt and let it fall to the ground. He braced himself with a hand to either side, and with all the strength he could find in himself, he pushed to his knees. Panting as if he'd just run a mile, he scuffled his way to his feet. The earth moved under him, undulating, shifting, and jagged spots of red drifted about in front of his eyes. He fell face-first, slamming against the ground with enough force to bring an involuntary yelp from him—a feminine sound, and one he couldn't recall ever making before. He tried to curse but he couldn't force words past his swollen tongue, and the attempt started his lips seeping blood once again.

One piece of luck came Will's way: the pinto had wandered to the sinkhole and was sucking water. Will had a direction; he wouldn't have to crawl about on his hands and knees seeking the water. The horse moved away as Will dragged himself to the water.

His hands found it first and he pushed himself forward, falling chest-first into the muddy, brackish liquid, straining to keep his nose in the air, his mouth sucking water frantically.

The foul water seemed to clear not only his voracious thirst but his befuddled mind. His hands had sunk into the soil beneath the water beyond his wrists—but what he felt was neither sand nor dirt. It was clay.

Will recalled the time when, as a boy, he'd stood gawking at a barn fire and a swarm of hornets found his face and arms. Someone—a neighbor?—had plastered the stings with clay. Its coolness not only eased the fiery pain, but as it dried, it drew out the stingers the hornets had planted in him. Could it help with his burns? *Hell,* he thought, *I got nothin' to lose.*

Will glopped handfuls of the clay, which had the consistency somewhere between a thick liquid and a spongy solid, and spread it over his face and arms. The clay smelled dank, but it wasn't an unpleasant scent—it was much like that of freshly turned soil in the spring. It was wonderfully cool, and it seemed to draw the pain in the same fashion the clay had drawn the hornet stingers many years ago. He drank more water and then crawled back to the desert pines, which were now merely vague shapes in the dark. He slept deeply and dreamlessly.

The pinto eased his way to Will and, after several moments, nudged him with his nose. This man was acting like no man he'd seen before in his four years of life. The horse had been saddle broke at an early age, and sprint-raced against short horses—what some folks called quarter horses—at age three. He'd never been beaten. He'd known nothing but kind-ness and feed until the outlaws stole him and burned his owner's home and barn, and that was only a week or ten days ago. His dim mind told him that this man would eventually rise up and give him fresh, sweet hay and scoops of grain. There was no reason to run off into the prairie. Regardless of his strange actions, this man would take care of him.

He nudged Will again, with no result. After a few minutes, the pinto went back to scrounging the ground for dropped hay.

Dawn was near when a strange, abrasive sound cut through Will's sleep. Dried clay cracked from his hand and arm as he drew his Colt and thumbed back the hammer.

The sound came again, halted, and then restarted, as whatever it was came closer to Will.

The pinto huffed at the sound, stared in its direc-tion for several moments, and then went back to grazing, obviously not feeling threatened.

The sun was almost clear of the horizon before Will could see what he'd been listening to, weapon ready. A dog—underfed, its mousy coat bare in places from mange—was dragging a stout wooden post attached to its neck by a six-foot strand of heavy wire. The dog, belly to the ground, pulled himself ahead with his forepaws and pushed with his rears. He managed to move the heavy post a few inches with each attempt. Every so often he'd stop, raise his nose to sniff the air—making sure he was headed to the water, Will thought—before starting out again.

Will was on his feet before he realized he was

standing. He was weak and still in pain, but the dizziness and the red spots were gone. He approached the dog, pistol at his side.

The dog looked up at Will, its chestnut eyes neither pleading nor begging, but simply acknowledging the man's presence. Will looked more closely. Frothy blood dripped from the creature's open mouth, obviously from trying to chew through the wire to free himself. The wire, wrapped twice around his neck, had cut through his coat and into the flesh.

Will forgot his own pain. "You was either a meal or a watchdog," he said aloud, "an' them killers just left you when they deserted this camp." He eyed the post. "Musta took you some time to haul that thing outta the ground, dog, an' the scent of water musta been drivin' you nuts. But you kept right on tuggin'. You got a set of balls on you, dog—either that or you're too stupid to know when to give up."

The dog's eyes and ears pointed at Will as the man spoke, as if taking in and understanding each word. Will holstered his pistol. "Let's get that goddamn wire from 'round your neck," he said, crouching stiffly next to the dog. He needed both hands to unwrap the wire, and he fully realized that the animal might go for either of his arms or his throat as soon as he was loose.

Will decided it was worth the chance to set the poor creature free.

The wire hadn't been knotted; its end was twisted around the cruel collar and was easy enough to loosen. The dog's body trembled as Will touched the wire and his neck, but he didn't offer to growl or snarl. With a pair of quick, circular sweeps, Will got the wire free. The dog was motionless for a long moment, and then he was on his feet and in a shambling run to the water. He flung his body into it, mouth wide open, and drank, his tongue moving listlessly as the muddy water ran down his throat. When his thirst was sated for the moment he stood up to his hocks in the water and grunted as loud as a sow in warm mud.

"Good, huh?" Will grinned.

The dog turned his head at the sound of Will's voice and their eyes met. Perhaps, at least in a sense, they spoke to one another, because both understood the message conveyed by the animal's eyes: *You saved me. I'll stay with you.*

The dog left the sinkhole, stood next to Will, and shook himself vigorously, shedding water, dirt, and speckles of blood in a wide area—which included Will. The animal looked more like a drowned rat than a drowned rat would. It would have been easy enough to count his ribs, they were so prominent, and his gut curved upward almost to his spine. His tail, rodentlike, flicked from side to side a few inches each way as he looked up at Will.

His head, Will saw, wasn't half bad for a range mongrel. His snout was straight, his eyes set nicely, neither too close together nor too far apart, and his pricked ears—like those of a collie—stood alert, at attention.

"Well hell," Will said, and scratched the spot between the dripping-wet dog's ears. The dog grunted and then licked Will's hand.

"Well, hell," Will said again.

He counted the number of cartridges left in his gun belt. There were four, and he had the two he'd loaded before shooting the jackrabbit. Will needed food and so did the dog. He opened the cylinder of his .45, loaded his last rounds, and snapped the cylinder shut.

The only game available was rattlesnake, prairie dogs, and rabbit. A prairie dog wasn't large enough to waste a shot on, and snake, unless it was long and fat, didn't yield enough meat. That left rabbit.

The water drew creatures to it; it made no sense to trek about in the killing sun. Instead, Will went back to where he'd slept, clay cracking and dropping from his face and arms as he walked. If nothing else, the layer of clay had eased and cooled Will's pain, and for whatever reason, it seemed to ease the weeping of the blisters.

He situated himself in the shade, leaned back against the thin trunk of a desert pine, and rested his pistol in his right hand in his lap. The dog sat next to him on his left, and almost unconsciously, Will's hand began to stroke the animal's neck.

It was easy enough to doze off: Will's fever was still rampant and the burns he had suffered sapped any energy he may have had. The deaths of his two friends—his two brothers—had the same effect on his mind as the battle had on his body. He slept uneasily, mumbling, his gun hand flinching every so often. When he awakened, the dog was gone.

What'd I expect? The damned dog is probably wild as an eagle. The outlaws must have trapped or snared him somehow. An' what am I gonna do with a dog, for God's sake? I can barely feed myself. Be nothin' but a pain in the ass. Still . . . it was kinda nice havin' him around . . .

The pinto was hanging close by, tugging at the grass around the water. Will managed a grin. *A day*

*or so, I'll be able to ride an' I'll fetch me a saddle, a rifle,
a ton of ammunition, a couple good meals, an' some
whiskey—an' then I'll be ready to take up where I left off,
'cause I'm not even close to finished yet.*

The pinto's head snapped up from his grazing, his
ears forward, his muscles ready, tightening to run if
whatever he'd heard presented danger. Will shifted
his position a bit and raised his pistol to a shooting
position. It was a few moments before he heard what
had spooked the horse: the sound of an animal's—or
a human's—feet crushing dead grass, dislodging
pebbles. Will thumbed back the hammer of his .45,
painfully aware that the last rounds he had were
loaded into the pistol. He waited silently and very
still, moving no more than the rocks or sandy soil
around him.

The dog came up from behind Will at a lope and
swung in front of him. He stood, tail fanning the air,
a very nice-sized jackrabbit clamped between his
jaws. The blood was still running from the punc-
tures in the rabbit; it had been a very recent kill. The
dog dropped his catch on Will's legs.

"Well ain't you jus' somethin'." Will laughed.
"Ain't you jus' somethin'." He hugged the dog's head
for a moment, scratching his body. The dog's tail
waved with enough power to swing his hips and
rear body back and forth, and he whined deep in his
throat and lapped Will's face. They both ate well that
evening.

During that night Will had been vaguely aware of
the dog stretched out next to him. He wasn't aware,
though, that the dog got up several times and pad-
ded silently off into the darkness.

It was still predawn when Will was jerked from

his sleep by hands at his throat, choking him. He drew and fired automatically, his pistol close enough to his chest so that the blowback peppered his already seared and tender face. The dead rabbit he shot was launched upward a yard by the bullet and came down, bloody and torn like a child's ripped doll, and landed on his face, a length of intestine next to his head like a slimy gray braid.

The dog sat at Will's side, tail raising a cloud of dust as it swung, his face looking like he'd just conquered the world, his jaws still dripping fresh blood.

The very edge of the sun cleared the horizon as Will sat up, pushing the jack off his face. The dog stood, patting the ground excitedly, proudly: the conquering hero.

"Ya damn fool." Will laughed, reaching out to the animal, rubbing his head, his sides, telling him he'd done real good.

The jackrabbit was a fine one, a female of good size with at least a little fat to her to sweeten the meat. Will scooped the guts out and spread them on the ground for the dog. He sat for a long moment, looking at the rabbit in his lap. Then he said to himself and to the dog, "I'm damned if I'm gonna eat this jack raw. I'm gonna make me a little fire an' cook her up an' to hell with the smoke. Them outlaws got no reason to come back here. They're probably still in town drunk an' raisin' hell."

Will gathered twigs and sticks for tinder from under the trees and broke up a few storm-severed branches.

His hands and wrists were aching and he'd used every cussword he knew, but eventually a slim wisp of pale smoke rose from the piece of limb he was augering into. He nursed the tiny flame, feeding but not smothering it, tending it as a mother tends a weak infant. Before long he had an actual fire.

"You'll for sure get your share, dog," Will said. "Hell, you coulda ate the whole critter if you wanted to—but you didn't. You brought it back here."

Calling the new friend "dog" sounded strange—wrong—to Will. He tried to bring a name to mind as he turned the stick skewering the rabbit over the flames. The fire sizzled and spat as the fat dripped into it, and the smoke rose rifle-barrel straight in the still air. The sun was well risen; already the temperature was climbing.

"How 'bout Spot?" Will said. "Or Bowser or Laddie or . . . ahhh, shit. None of them fit."

He looked at the dog and the dog looked at him. "Damn," Will said. "You got a grin on you jus' like a human. How 'bout Smiley? Does that fit?" He considered a bit. "Nah. But look, how about Shark? You got the ivory of one of them critters—I seen pictures of them. Yeah. Shark, that sounds real good. That works. Fact, it works real good."

The dog understood none of the words, but he picked up on Will's enthusiasm and moved closer, licking Will's face, his feet patting the ground, his tail awag almost frantically.

In scratching and rubbing Shark, Will wasn't too surprised to see legions of fleas leaping about the dog's coat. The raw skin of mange bothered him, as well. He pointed to the water. "Let's go, Shark."

Will was amazed that the dog immediately got up and trotted to the sinkhole. Will tried some other hand signals: down, stay, go away, and so forth. Shark responded perfectly to each command. Will shook his head. "You sure had some good training, fella," he said.

Of course, Shark had been in the water a couple of days ago—and that apparently did nothing but wash a few fleas overboard. But today Will was going to use both water and mud and clay. He was going to coat Shark, and at the same time, re-treat his own face and arms. Maybe it was the clay and maybe it wasn't that made his healing so rapid, but it sure was worth another application.

Will strode into the water up to his knees and called his dog to him. Shark charged out, splashing, swimming in that foolish way dogs have. Will scooped up viscous handfuls of clay and mud and plastered Shark. The dog was curious—his eyes showed that—but he was neither frightened nor angry. Finally, so that Shark wouldn't lose too much of the muck from his coat, Will hefted the dog in his arms and carried him to shore.

The sun soon dried the clay and mud on man and dog. Much cracked off, but much stayed in place. The mange spots of exposed flesh, Will was pleased to see, remained covered.

Shark began to shake himself as soon as all four feet were on solid ground. "No," Will said, not shouting the word, not even saying it louder than a normal conversation level. The dog immediately stopped his instinctive drying ritual.

"Jeez," Will said. "You know damned near everything, doncha, Shark? Good boy. *Good boy!*"

There was one command Will hadn't experimented with, but he planned to get to that later. For now, the heat was too oppressive to do anything but hide under the trees from the malevolent glare of the sun.

Will slept soundly and didn't awaken until a jack was dropped on his chest by a clay-encrusted dog who sat grinning at him, tail raising a cloud of dust behind him. Will laughed.

"Great, Shark," he said. "You're a hell of a hunter."

There was a very feeble, dull red ember from the previous fire. Will, on all fours, blew gently at it—and put it out.

"Goddammit," he said disgustedly.

Once again he gathered up twigs and branches and went to work spinning a stick between his palms, its carved point lodged in a small notch he'd cut into the larger piece of dry limb. An eternity later, smoke appeared, followed by a miniscule orangish flame. Will fed the fire bits of dried grass and small bits of dried wood until it was ready to accept more hardy fuel. Within an hour he and his dog were eating broiled rabbit. The jack was scrawnier than the female had been, and he yielded less meat. Neither Will nor Shark complained.

Will looked closely at Shark as the dog scarfed down his meal. There'd been a picture book in grade school, Will recalled, showing different breeds of dogs, and he fuzzily recalled several of the pictures. Shark, even coated in dry and flaking clay, looked a good deal like a husky—except for his tail, which hung down, rather than curling up over his back. Shark was a good-sized dog, collie-sized, perhaps, with a broad chest. His head, though, strongly reminded Will of a breed he couldn't bring to mind—something to do with a foreign country, maybe England, maybe Germany. Whatever. Shark was Shark.

The temperature didn't drop a whole lot as the sun

began to settle in the west. Will finished his meal, sucking the suet from the jack's bones, and wiped his mouth on what remained of a burned sleeve. Looking at Shark he took off his denim pants. Strangely, the denim showed few signs of the fire and Will's stumbling dash through the flames. He tied the cuffs in sloppy knots and then filled the pants with scrub, bits of branches, handfuls of dried needles, and whatever else he could find. He stripped off his raggedy-assed shirt, filled that, too, and attached it to the pants with a young and supple limb. He wedged the creation between a pair of fairly stout branches, the stuffed cuffs maybe a yard off the ground.

Will had no idea what the signal, the command, for attack might be. *Sic 'em? Get 'em? Attack? Kill?*

Shark stood next to Will, looking up at him, his tail moving gently from side to side, his eyes curious as to what Will was doing.

Will snapped his fingers and said, "Go." Shark stood as still as a statue. He tried again with "Sic," with the same result.

"Waitaminnit," Will said aloud. "All the other stuff you did was based on hand an' arm commands." He thought for a moment, Shark still focused on his face. "What the hell," Will said, and made a sweeping motion with is right arm, his hand ending up pointing at the hastily constructed dummy.

Shark immediately dropped, stomach to the ground, and began moving slowly but steadily, like a cat stalking a bird. Shark was totally silent; there was no growling, no threatening snarl.

Will watched, fascinated, as Shark covered the few yards to his target. The big dog appeared to be hardly moving, but he was covering ground. He didn't look back at Will at all. He had his order and he was going to carry it out. When he was six feet from the dummy, he threw his body at it as if he'd been propelled by a powerful steel spring. The attack brought a quick shiver to Will's spine. It was impossibly fast, as quiet as a sepulcher, and as deadly as an eight-foot rattler.

Although the dummy was headless, Shark's jaws tore into where a man's throat would be. Still airborne, he dragged his fangs down the chest and stomach of the dummy, and then, almost before his feet hit the ground, he tore the crotch out of the dummy's—Will's—denim pants. The attack had freed the dummy from the tree and Shark went for its throat once again.

"Come," Will said, his voice an awestruck rasp. Shark stepped away from the dummy, shook away a piece of fabric that had hung on an eyetooth, and trotted over to Will.

For once, Will had nothing to say. He crouched and stroked his dog.

The next day Will waded into the water with Shark at his side. He peeled and scrubbed the clay from the dog's back and sides and was gratified to see what looked like hundreds of flea corpses embedded in the slabs of clay. The raw mange flesh looked much better: the seeping, raw spots were replaced with pinkish flesh. If dog wounds were anything like horse wounds, Will thought, it'd be a short time before hair sprouted, grew, and covered the bare areas.

Will's face and arms were still hotter than they'd normally be, even under the West Texas sun, but most of the pain was gone. He looked at the burned, ripped, and torn clothing he'd been wearing, and laughed at the crotchless drawers.

"What we need to do, Shark, is go back to town an' find some supplies—an' maybe take down a few of those killers."

Chapter Seven

The pinto had stayed quite close to Will, wandering to seek grazing but never putting a great deal of distance between himself and the man. The horse looked good: he might have dropped a few pounds from the dried buffalo grass he was eating, but he hadn't been off good feed long enough to hurt him.

Will used a handful of scrub to clean the sand and grit from the animal's coat. The pinto grunted and leaned into Will's hand. "Where the hell did those scum git you?" Will said as he cleaned the horse. "They for sure didn't buy you—so they musta killed your owner, the man who trained you. Whoever he mighta been, he knew horses. He took good care of you." Will stepped back a couple of feet. "Let's see how this goes." He drew and fired his pistol. The pinto, startled, seemed to come to attention like a soldier, but he didn't shy or run. The whites of his eyes showed momentarily, but then came back to their place under his lids as he quickly calmed.

The horse went back to grunting happily as Will finished rubbing him clean. His hooves looked good—the shoeing job was excellent. The single rein that draped from the hackamore, the leather strand around the pinto's snout, rested in his mane and gave him plenty of room to drop his head to eat and drink.

Will somewhat clumsily grabbed a handful of mane and the rein and swung up onto the pinto's back. The horse snorted, sunfished a couple of times—which Will rode easily—and was ready for work. "Gettin' a tad bored standin' around, no? Well, let's go out an' play. Shark," he said, using the "down" motion. "You stay here, pard."

He would have preferred a saddle under him, but Will rode as well bareback as did any Indian. He gathered up some rein and put leg pressure on both sides of the horse. The pinto took off fast—real fast. All four of his hooves threw clumps of dirt behind him, and he stretched to run like a greyhound. Slick had been fast. This pinto was faster, Will realized.

He leaned back a bit and tapped the horse's snout with the hackamore. The pinto broke his run in a single pace and dropped his rear legs behind him, skidding to a long, sliding stop.

"Holy God," Will whispered. For a horse to drop to a sliding stop from a full gallop like that wasn't only the result of fine training. It was an irrefutable indication of a hell of a mount.

He swung the pinto into a large figure eight, again at a gallop. The horse picked up his lead—the leg and hoof he followed as he turned—at every change. Will tightened the eight and then tightened it again, to the point where the horse was leaning far to his side making the turns, Will leaning with him rather against him, a part of the animal rather than baggage he carried.

Shark's expression showed his curiosity as to what Will and the horse were doing. When they first lit out, Shark matched the horse's speed, running a few feet to Will's right side. But when the maneuvers began—the sliding stop, the tighter and tighter figure eights—the dog moved away from the dust cloud and watched the action with all the interest and intensity of a child watching a traveling puppet show.

Will was dripping perspiration, and the salt was irritating to the healing flesh of his face and arms. The pinto's chest was frothy with sweat, and his flanks dripped water like a leaky roof during a rainstorm. Even sitting still and merely watching, Shark's tongued lolled out from between his jaws, dripping saliva—the canine equivalent of sweat.

All three of them drank from the sinkhole. Will rubbed the horse down with handfuls of scrub, but walking him to cool him down was futile: sweat broke as soon as they stepped out from the shade to the stunning power of the sun.

Will was hungry and so was his horse. Shark was doing just fine with rabbit, but Will couldn't drive the images of a beefsteak with all the fixings and a bucket—maybe two or three buckets—of cold beer from his mind.

There was another hunger, too, that was goading Will: the deaths of Hiram, his wife and his daughters, and those of Austin and Gentle Jane, which burned within him hotter than the fire in the mercantile, hotter than the hottest flames of hell.

He leaned back against the twisted trunk of a desert pine. *We killed lots of One Dog's crew. The man is crazy, but he ain't stupid. He needed to reward the men who'd lived through the battle, and what better way than to keep the town in his grasp and let the animals go to it— booze, women, whatever? Would One Dog post guards?*

Again, he's not stupid. 'Course he would, but would they be sober an' alert? Could be—but it doesn't seem to make sense. He thinks I'm dead and he knows my partners are. But we aren't his only enemies. He'll have riders out. Will grinned. *And a rider probably means a saddle, a rifle, and some ammunition for my pistol. All me an' Shark gotta do is slither in like a pair of snakes.*

While Will and his dog slept away the hottest part of the day, fat gray clouds began to gather in the east, seeming to battle one another, churning and boiling high above the prairie. The temperature dropped slowly as the front approached. The clouds brought about an early dusk. The first drops of rain were tiny, almost mistlike, with no power behind them. The following wind, however, changed all that. The temperature continued to fall like an anvil. Will was shivering—a strange and unfamiliar sensation after week after week of stultifying, unremitting heat.

Still, the weather had done Will a grand favor. The already lackadaisical and possibly/probably drunk outriders would be huddled into themselves in the rain and chilling wind, making their rounds only because they feared One Dog's punishment if they failed to do so.

Fine, jagged lines of lightning, like cracks in good glass, did little to illuminate the prairie. The thunder, distant, was more of a sensation than an actual sound: a deep, barely audible series of reports like the cannons of a far-off battle.

When it was full dark, Will grabbed a handful of rein and swung onto the pinto's back. He didn't need to call Shark. The dog was at the horse's right side, coat tight to his body and slick with rain. Will held the pinto to a fast walk as he headed toward Olympus.

He secured the horse with the rein draped over a boulder and another rock pressing on the leather. The pinto snorted a couple of times as Will and Shark went off on foot, but quickly settled down.

The lightning and thunder had moved closer, and the flashes in the sky were like the sharp white light of a photographer's magnesium. The thunder was much louder, gigantic crackling booms that seemed to sweep the prairie with the raw power of their sound.

Shark walked close to Will, and when a blast of thunder roared over them, he moved closer, his side touching Will's right leg. Will rubbed the dog's shoulder as they walked.

Shark saw the rider and stiffened. Will dropped to his stomach and motioned Shark down. The next stroke of lightning showed a man on horseback, poncho wrapped around everything but his face. His right hand held a rifle out in the driving rain.

Damn fool. There's no way in the world that thing will fire. Will drew his knife from his boot, and he and Shark moved closer, hugging the ground as lightning struck. They became part of the prairie, motionless, simply rocks and scrub in the outrider's eyes—if the man was bothering to look at all. He was a white man; Will saw that. He was riding a saddle on a tall, ribby horse.

Will didn't want to use his .45. Even in the storm the crack of the discharge would carry, and he wasn't quite sure how close to the town he was. Will clutched his knife. He could probably tackle the man off his horse, but the rider could well make enough noise to draw more men. Shark pressed against him as a blast of thunder followed a hissing, menacing streak of lightning. Will slid his knife back into his boot sheath.

"Shark," he said quietly, "get him," at the same time using the forward arm signal. The dog moved close to the ground, stopping when lightning struck. He looked like a rock or perhaps a clump of brush.

The rider paid no more attention to Shark's approach than he did to anything else around him. In fact, all he saw was the poll of his horse's head, because his own head was tilted downward to let the rain run off his hat.

The rider was apparently circling the town. He was also obviously drunk, slumped forward on his horse's back, mumbling to himself. Or perhaps he was singing. It was impossible to tell from the racket of the storm. He was moving toward Will, and Will didn't bother to do anything evasive other than quieting his dog's menacing growl.

The wind seemed to chase itself in all directions at once, first one way and then another in a bit of a second, whipping in translucent, ever-shifting curtains.

As Will watched, three events took place simultaneously: A terrific slash of lightning speared the ground not thirty feet from the rider, decimating a small boulder. At the same moment Shark threw himself at the rider, sinking his razor-sharp fangs into the back of the man's neck, just below his head, hurling him from his horse to the ground. The rider screamed but his scream was cut short as Shark, his grip secure, snapped his entire body to one side, severing the man's spine.

At the same time, the brilliant, searing white flash illuminated another rider to Will, moving in the opposite direction, hunched in his saddle, as his cohort had been. He wasn't quite thirty feet away when the lightning struck and Shark wrenched the other from his horse, and the lightning gave the second rider a view of an impossibly rapid attack—and he heard the crunching snap that ended the outlaw's life. Further, the attacking creature was flying, already in the air when the lightning struck.

"Wampus!" the rider screamed in a high-pitched, panicked voice and buried his heels into his horse's sides. Slipping, sliding, almost going down, scrambling in the mud, the horse whirled, and, running almost blindly, raced off into the storm, his rider lashing him with the reins.

Will's pistol had been in his hand the slightest part of a second after the opposite-riding man and horse came into view. He shook the rain from his .45 and holstered it. Sending Shark after the second renegade made no sense, given the storm and the darkness. Further, the rider would be constantly looking behind him and a lucky shot could drop the dog.

"What the hell?" he asked himself. "Wampus?" The word ticked something far back in Will's mind, but didn't bring an image or idea to him.

It didn't take too long to catch the dead outrider's cow pony; the animal was underfed, parasite ridden, and scarred with spur and lash welts and cuts. Will approached him slowly, murmuring to him, and was able to take hold of a rein. He saw why his pressure on the rein stopped the diseased horse so easily: the bit in the animal's mouth was a long-shanked, cruel Mexican bit that cut into the horse's mouth, stopping and turning him not through training but through pain.

Will was surprised to see that the saddle and saddlebags weren't Mex junk. The saddle was Texas made. Will could tell that as he ran a finger along the stitching, which was straight and waxed and tight, and the fenders and stirrups hung as they should. He released the cinches—the saddle was a double rig—and unbuckled the chest strap. When he hefted the weight off the animal's back the horse shook himself like a dog coming out of water. Will cut the latigo that jammed the bit into the horse's mouth and eased the bridle down the pony's snout. Both his hands were bloody as he removed the bit. He twisted the seven-inch shanks into shapes that would never allow the bit to be used again, bent the mouthpiece in the middle, and tossed the whole bloody affair out into the prairie.

It took a few moments for the horse to realize that he was free—and then he was gone, as far away from any man as he could get, hooves pounding the sloppy, treacherous mud. The only way a man would stop that horse was with a bullet.

Will went through the saddlebags. He found handfuls of .45 ammunition in each, a bit of beef jerky, a knife that was dull enough to be useless, which he tossed aside, a few double eagles, and a deck of playing cards with pictures of naked women with mules. Those, too, he tossed onto the prairie. He loaded his pistol, inserted rounds in his gun belt, and left the balance of the bullets in the saddlebags.

The dead outlaw had nothing worth taking. His .45 was a piece of junk: grips taped, rusted, trigger as stiff as an oak tree.

The rifle, a single-shot, rusted, sightless chunk of scrap metal, was no better. Will figured firing the goddamned thing would be suicide; the round would probably explode within the corroded mechanism and barrel, blowing his head off. He hurled it into the dark. The gun belt was much the same: worn, uncared for, the cartridge loops uneven and sure to scatter ammunition at a gallop. The man carried neither a hide-out gun—a derringer—or a decent knife. Will and Shark left the corpse for the vultures, Will carrying the saddle over his shoulder.

It would have made sense to fetch the pinto and ride him back to the saddle, but Will wanted some time. The word *wampus* continued to play in his mind. It was too familiar to recall, and yet it was barely familiar at all. "Damn," Will cursed as he slogged through the mud.

The storm had calmed considerably, moving on, the rain little more than sprinkles. The dark clouds that had generated the storm had, of course, scudded on their way, and the half-moon shed some light.

The pinto was as Will had left him, although stirred-up mud around him showed he'd done a good deal of nervous shifting about due to the lightning and thunder. Will eased the tattered saddle blanket over the pinto's back and smoothed it, particularly at the withers—the place where galls are most likely to occur under a new saddle. Will flipped the stirrups over the seat and settled the saddle in position on the horse's back. The fit was closer to good than to fair, and later, minor adjustments could be made to the seat, cantle, and tree. He wasn't sure that the horse had ever carried a saddle. He was an Indian pony, and most Indians considered saddles to be merely excess weight, a silly device for a poor rider who can't control his animal. The pinto stood well under the saddle, though, offering no resistance. "I shoulda known it," Will said aloud. "You was stolen well after you was saddle broke."

He pulled the front cinch and set the back cinch, leaving an inch between the leather strap and the pinto's belly. That strap was intended not to secure the saddle but to brace it and allow it to rise a bit off the horse's back when the rider was roping or descending a steep grade.

The hackamore and the single rein were fine—the animal was used to both. Will moved both stirrups down a notch. At the same time he looked carefully over the workmanship of the seat, stirrups, and fenders. The leather needed oil and the buckles were showing some rust, but all in all, the saddle wasn't a bad piece of work.

Will stepped into a stirrup and climbed aboard, setting off at a walk.

Lightning struck not far away, sluicing mud and stone into the air, dropping Shark to his crouching attack position, lips curved back over his eyeteeth, the whites of his eyes showing, his body like a tightly coiled spring. The lightning, the dog, and the blast of thunder brought *wampus* back to Will's recollection.

"I ain't scared of no horse or nothin' else," an old Indian bronc buster told him when Will was still a boy, maybe a dozen years old. " 'Cept, a course, a wampus. That's a critter the Great Spirit chased down to earth—meanest goddamn thing a man could come across. They can fly, Will, an' they can kill in a heartbeat. Once one has his eye on you, why, you're gone, boy. Ain't nobody escapes a wampus."

"You ever seen one?"

"If I had I wouldn't be settin' here. I seen drawings an' heard stories, though."

Will forced a nervous laugh. "That's jus' a superstition. Don't mean nothing."

"No? I seen the remainders of a fella, a white fella, a wampus took after. Purely tore that man apart—worse'n a painter or bear could ever do. You jus' pray to that god a yours you never cross one. Ain't a Indian in the whole of the West don't know 'bout the wampus—an' plenty of whites do, too."

Like many dog owners, Will had begun talking to his dog, sometimes in full sentences, most times in a few words. Of course the animal couldn't understand any of it, but that fact didn't stop Will.

"I'll tell you what," Will said to the dog walking along at his right side, "that wampus thing give me a good idea. All the Indians are scared, superstitious, an' them loonies they're ridin' with—deserters, gunhands, murderers, rapists, all like that—they're as crazy an' scared an' superstitious as the Indians. Here's the thing, pard: your name isn't Shark no more—it's Wampus. OK?"

The dog watched Will's face until he determined that no actual command was involved. Then he simply walked alongside the man, more attuned to his surroundings and the scents that he picked up than the words the man continued to utter.

"I figure it this way," Will said. "We make a move on the camp an' you gnaw on another outlaw. That'll build the 'wampus' thing even stronger in their booze-an'-drug-soaked minds. Then we'll haul ass away from the camp but follow the crew—hell, how hard can it be to track all those horses?—an' pick them off as we go. Sound good?"

Wampus didn't look up at Will this time. Instead, he stopped, nose high, drawing in the scent of smoke and of men. "Gettin' close?" Will said in a lowered voice. He reined in, dismounted, and led the pinto behind him. "Find 'em," he whispered to Wampus. The dog took point position, matching his speed to Will's stride.

The sound from the gathering was loud, disjointed. A couple of Indians were chanting. Will tied the pinto to some scrub and moved on.

Watching flat in the mud from a small rise, Will saw the group had built a good-sized fire from a wrecked freighter, deciding they were better off in the fire's light than continuing on to their sanctuary at Olympus in the dark with a wampus about. It was clear that the escaping outrider had brought back the news of the other rider's attack. More Indians took up the chant, while the whites, in their ludicrous army outfits, passed bottles and huddled together, pistols or rifles clutched and ready.

One Dog pushed his way into the center of the group of whites and held out his arms for silence. It did no good. He punched the man closest to him, knocking him unconscious to the ground, but the violence had no effect on the panicked jabbering and chanting. One Dog drew his pistol and found that none of his men were even watching him, concentrating instead on the grounds around the fire, each completely expecting a mythical beast to fly into the group, slashing and killing.

Will shivered in the cold mud, Wampus pressed tightly against his side. He grinned and whispered to the dog, "You pressin' against me 'cause I'm such a fine, upstanding fella, or you lookin' for a bit of body heat?"

A fistfight broke out down below, but the combatants were quickly separated by the others. It wasn't that they gave a damn if the two drunks killed one another; they didn't want to lose four eyes watching for the wampus.

Not but one way to do this. I either play on their craziness an' fear, or I don't. He sighed. *An' I'm damn well gonna do it.* Will drew his .45, which was still dripping wet. He spun the cylinder and held the pistol next to his ear, and the sweet mechanical *whirr* was as even as the ticking of a ten-dollar watch. He flipped the cylinder open and used his thumb to wipe any moisture off the rear end of the cartridges— the end that held the primer and gunpowder. He closed the cylinder into the frame of the .45 with a satisfying click, pushed back from the edge of the slope, and walked to his horse, dog next to him, gazing up at his face, feeling the tension that suddenly seemed to shroud Will.

"Might not be the smartest thing I ever did, and there's a good chance we'll both end up buzzard bait, but we're gonna take a run at it, right Wampus?" Will said grimly. The dog growled deep in his chest, knowing from the tone of Will's voice that action was coming.

Will took up his rein from the brush, mounted, and pulled his pistol. He sat for a moment, said, "Might just as well get to it," drove his heels into his horse's side, and shouted to his dog, "Git 'em, boy! Git the sonsabitches!"

The pinto leaped forward, fighting for traction, slinging globs of mud with all four hooves. Wampus, low to the ground but running hard, reached the periphery of the fire faster than the man and the horse. An outlaw standing slightly away from the rest, relieving himself, saw the dog in time to begin a scream before glinting white eyeteeth severed his jugular. Will followed a second later, riding at a slipping, sliding gallop directly at the fire, shooting randomly, dropping a pair of men too startled by the attack to even raise their weapons. Wampus was everywhere at once, tearing flesh, ghostly in the light of the fire, looking like an apparition from hell. He sank his teeth into an Indian's groin and tugged out a couple of grotesque lumps of flesh, looking like a pair of cherry apples in a blood-soaked cloth sack. The outlaw's howl of pain was louder than the fire, Will's shooting, and the panic that gripped the gang.

Will crouched low over the pinto's neck and urged more speed from him—pointing him directly at the fire. The flames were too high to clear, but the horse plowed through them, slipped and almost went down as he landed, but gathered his hooves under himself and within a couple of strides was in a gallop again. Will, turned in the saddle, wasted a couple of shots that were misses, but took down another pair with his last two rounds. "Come on, dog!" he yelled.

Wampus appeared through the flames as if he were flying and quickly caught up with the pinto.

It was only then that a barrage of gunfire erupted from the befuddled outlaws—much too late to accomplish anything.

Will reloaded his Colt as he rode, reins held in his mouth. Although he looked back several times, he saw no indication of riders coming after him—and he was sure Wampus would give him a warning if he missed anyone on his trail.

He rode a mile or so and reined to a halt. He

stepped down from the saddle and checked the pinto. There were some minor burns and the horse had lost some tail, but he was sound and uninjured. Will crouched to examine Wampus, who was delighted with the attention. The dog, too, had lost a bit of coat to the fire, but was fit otherwise. As Will rubbed his muzzle and neck his hands came away wet and sticky with the unmistakable, thickly metallic scent of blood—and the blood wasn't that of the dog.

It was logical enough that all the outlaws rode after Will—what was there to protect their saloon from? Any townspeople who hadn't fled wouldn't dare to invade the place. Will kept on riding to Olympus. The moon gave him barely enough light to see.

Will sent the dog into the renegades' bar first. The dog came out in a very few minutes, tail awag. There were no men in there. Will rode around to the rear of the gin mill and looped his rein loosely over a short hitching rail. There was some hay under a tarp behind the saloon. It was dry second cutting, but it was better than the pinto was used to. Will gave the horse half a bale. He walked around the building in the opposite direction. There wasn't a sound from inside, but the saloon's pervasive stench hung around it like a foul cloud.

Will pushed through the batwings.

The inside of the gin mill was a disaster. Bullet holes speckled all the walls, the floor was gummy with spoiled beer, and there was the stink of long-unwashed men and the cloying odor of the urine of those who hadn't bothered to step outside, much less walk to the privy. But there was treasure, too; the outlaws must have done some scrounging in the mercantile. Will found a .30-30 leaning against the bar, a pair of denim pants in one of the rooms up-stairs, and a shirt that didn't look like it had been worn yet.

There was a canned ham, several tin cans of some-thing or other—the labels were burned off—and a jar of penny-candy sourballs. In the same room there was a new slicker and a rifle kit, both of which he took. Best of all, there was a bottle of whiskey and three packs of Bull Durham. The majority of the bottles behind the bar had been used for target prac-tice, but several had been set aside. Will took a good suck at his bottle and then drew and blasted hell out of the remainder of the renegades' liquor supply. He drew himself a bucket of beer and, as an afterthought, shot holes low in the barrel and watched the beer flow onto the floor. He opened the canned ham, gave most of it to Wampus, and ate the rest himself.

Will took the time to roll a half-dozen smokes, tak-ing a belt from the bottle every so often. He lit a ciga-rette and coughed out a smog of bluish smoke, his throat feeling as if it had caught fire. He put out that fire with a mouthful of booze and took another drag. This time the smoke went where it was supposed to, and the vague satisfaction that tobacco brings—impossible to explain to a nonsmoker—flowed through him.

Nevertheless, there was an ambience to the place that made Will nervous. It was not unlike sitting in an empty viper's den, the crushed-cucumber stink still strong, and not knowing when the serpents would return. Wampus, too, was uncomfortable, pacing, panting lightly. The scent of the enemy was too strong for him to relax.

After crushing the nub of his cigarette on the floor, Will pulled on the denim drawers and board-stiff shirt. He strapped on his gun belt and tied his holster low on his right leg. He stuffed the sacks of Bull Durham into various pockets but left the bottle on the table.

Both he and Wampus drew in deep breaths of fresh air when they'd put some distance between themselves and the saloon.

Will had no doubt that the renegades could track when full light came, but with the fear of the wampus in their minds, he doubted that they would—not immediately, anyway. He loped for a few miles and then put the pinto into a fast walk. The prairie ahead of him looked as flat as a billiard table in the dawn light. It offered no cover and certainly no ambush point where he could await the outlaws. He put his horse back into the animal's easy, ground-eating lope, Wampus jogging at his side.

The elements of surprise and fear were all he had going for him, Will thought. Another attack too soon could blunt both his advantages: the renegades would soon figure out that their tormentors were merely a man and a dog—easy enough to kill. Will decided to hold off on his forays for two or three days. By then, he believed, the outlaws would be on his trail, and he'd have had time to plan out his next attack on them.

Will rode through the day, stopping only at the meager water holes he encountered. The water was generally bad—petroleum tasting—but when a man, a horse, and a dog are parched, *any* water is good water.

It was coming dark when Will saw a spurt of dust

far ahead of him, coming toward him. It was a single rider, from the rooster tail it put in the air. Any more than one horse would raise a more substantial cloud of grit behind them.

When they were a couple hundred yards apart, both men dropped their horses to a slow walk but continued to approach one another.

Will's right hand lifted his Colt a few inches above his holster and released it, letting it settle itself into its ready-to-draw position. Wampus began to growl; Will hushed him.

The rider wasn't a big man, but as they closed, from what Will could see, he was damned near a one-man armory. Twin bandoliers of rifle cartridges crossed his chest. He carried a pair of Winchesters sheathed one on each side of the saddle, in front of his knees. He wore two Colt .45s at his waist. The grips of a pair of bowie-type knives rested in sheaths sewn to the outside of each of his boots. An unstrung bow rested atop his bedroll, with a group of arrows tied securely to the bow. There was .50-caliber buffalo rifle strapped over his back. The men came within talking distance.

"Name's Gordon," he said. "Ray Gordon." His voice was deep, rich.

"Will Lewis."

"Fine dog ya got there," Gordon said. "Got more'n a little timber wolf in him, no?"

"You know dogs?"

"Some. I know a wolf cross when I see one."

"Where you headed?" Will asked.

"Olympus, I guess. From there, I dunno."

"There's nothin' there," Will said. "I just left that hellhole."

Ray Gordon shrugged. "Don't matter. It ain't the town I'm after, it's a murderin' savage named One Dog. I'm gonna kill the sumbitch an' take his scalp as well—him an' as many of his scum as I can take down."

"Why?"

Gordon swallowed and spat off to the side before answering. " 'Cause he butchered my wife an' my son. That answer your question?"

"Yeah. It does. See, I think we're both about the same task. One Dog and his gang murdered my brother, his wife—an' his two little daughters."

"Jesus."

"Yeah."

"You wasn't there?"

"I was in Folsom Prison—just about to get out. Me an' my brother was gonna . . . Ahh, shit." Will hesitated, shook his head slightly. "What about you, when your people were attacked?" he asked.

Ray looked down at his horse's mane for a full minute. "I was drunk an' passed out," he said, " 'bout eight miles from my place. I fell off my horse. When I came to an' caught him up . . . well . . ."

"You still boozin'?"

"I ain't touched a drop since then—not even a beer. My whole life now is to kill One Dog."

"You're gonna have to stand in line," Will said. "One Dog is mine."

Gordon's face flushed red and his dark eyes narrowed, locking with Will's. "Your ass, he's yours. Like I said, One Dog is mine."

The glaring contest lasted a full two minutes. Finally, Will said, "We got time to debate on it. An' 'course, either one—or both of us—could be dead 'fore One Dog goes down for good."

"Could be," Ray admitted.

Will rolled a smoke and offered his papers and sack of Bull Durham to Ray.

"Don't use 'em. Thanks anyhow."

"You drop any of them yet?" Will asked.

"Four for certain. Maybe a fifth one. You?"

"I figure about six or eight. I was in an' out too fast to keep a good count. Seems like there's always new crazies an' killers joinin' on with One Dog. I don't know how many men ride with him."

Ray grinned. "That's easy enough. Ain't hard at all. What you do is count all their arms an' legs an' divide by four—assumin' you know your numbers. If you don't, you're screwed."

Will laughed out loud and it felt good. It was the first time he'd laughed since he'd heard about Hiram and his family from the blacksmith. "Well look," he said through his laughter, "suppose you got a renegade with but one arm or one leg?"

"Easy," Ray said. "You shoot the sumbitch—even things out right nice."

"Makes good sense," Will said. "Say, how 'bout we set up camp together? My dog'll fetch us in a couple of rabbits to cook up."

Ray nodded. "I was about to suggest settin' up together, 'cept I was afraid that goddamn wolf'd tear my eggs off if I stepped down from my horse. His eyes ain't left me since we been talkin' here, an' not 'cause he loves me."

"Wampus is OK. He won't bother you unless I tell him to. He's kinda protective, is all." Will hesitated a bit. "You really think he's half wolf?" he asked.

"I know he is, Will. He's the pup of a timber, bred to what's called a German shepherd. An' I'll tell you this 'fore you need to ask: I know wolves an' I know dogs. I bountied on wolves for a dozen years—raised a couple pups myself an' bred 'em to shepherds. It's a fine mix, but they can get a bit flighty at times." Ray swung down from his saddle. "You call him Wampus?"

"Yeah. See, a wampus is—"

"I *know* what a wampus is." He gazed at the dog for a moment. "I 'magine this boy looks real scary at night. Have them renegades wettin' their drawers, does he?"

"Sure does, 'specially when they're drunk or driftin' with them mushrooms they like."

The men unsaddled their mounts and staked them out to graze on the sparse grass. They drank from a hat-sized sinkhole of water. Will sent Wampus out and the dog returned with a bleeding, still-twitching jackrabbit between his jaws. Will sent him out again. This time Wampus was gone maybe a half hour and came back with another jack and a four-foot-long bull snake.

"I ain't eatin' no snake," Ray said. "But he sure is hell on rabbits, though."

"He is. The jacks are for us an' the bull snake is his own dinner."

Ray, crouched, arranging pieces of mesquite for the fire, said, "Funny thing. I never seen a dog—I mean a full dog, not a wolf cross—eat a snake. But the crosses seem to like 'em.

"I'd 'preciate you sendin' him out a bit. Watchin' an listenin' to a critter like Wampus chow down a snake kinda stirs my innards."

"Sure," Will said. "I'll admit his table manners are none too good."

The men waited until it was dark to start their fire, in order to hide the smoke. Meanwhile, Will gutted and skinned the jackrabbits. Ray sat cleaning his weapons, with the entire arsenal spread out in front of him on his saddle blanket. Will looked on for a few minutes and then asked, "You fire all of them today?"

"Nope. Nary a one. Thing is, a weapon is like a good horse. Ya gotta look after it so's you can trust it—an' if you can't trust it, it's no damn good, horse nor gun."

They lazed about until it was full dark, and then Will started the fire and skewered the rabbits on his knife. The fat dripping on the coals sizzled like bacon in a frying pan and every once in a while flared up, and the scent of the cooking jacks had both men salivating. They ate hungrily, thoroughly enjoying the crisply seared yet tender flesh.

Will belched and tossed a leg bone out into the darkness. "Damn. I'd give my right leg for some coffee right now. It don't seem right to finish up a meal like we jus' had without coffee, ya know?"

Ray smiled broadly, looking for a quick moment like a Halloween pumpkin in the flickering light. "You keep your drawers on for a few minutes an' I'll give you coffee so strong it'd melt a anvil. I make the best coffee in the West, an' you can take that to the bank." He scuffled about in his saddlebag, taking out a scorched and obviously well-used quart tin can. Then he carefully opened a fat cloth sack and dropped three handfuls of rough-ground coffee into the can. He added water from his canteen and set the makeshift coffee pot on the coals of the cooking fire.

"You got a mess kit or cups or anything?" Ray asked.

Will snorted derisively. "Sure. I got a silver tea service and a goddamn tablecloth as well."

Ray looked at him for a long moment. "You're a right feisty sumbitch, ain't you, Will Lewis?"

Will thought it over for some time and then nodded. "Yessir," he said, "I suppose I am."

When the can was barely cool enough not to raise blisters, Ray and Will passed it back and forth.

Will smacked his lips. "Best coffee I ever had," he said.

"You bet it is."

Afterward they sat watching the coals of the little fire dim and eventually die. Will smoked; Ray worked one of his knives with a whetstone.

Will sighed.

Ray sheathed his knife. "This sure is excitin', settin' here doin' nothing," he said.

"I'm glad you said it before I had to. Wanna take a peek at Olympus? See what One Dog an' his li'l friends are doin'?"

"Damn right I do."

Riding was easy: the moon showed half its face, giving adequate illumination for the horses, at least at a walk. On the way, Will explained his rationale for holding off on attacks for a couple of days.

Ray reluctantly agreed. "But," he said, "I purely hate to let them vermin live any longer than I have to."

They began hearing gunshots when they were a mile or more outside the town. The throaty roar of a shotgun sounded every so often, making pistol and rifle fire seem puny.

"Sonsabitches are all worked up 'bout somethin',"

Ray said. "I suspect it's 'cause they brought in a new bunch of gunsels an' crazies to replace the ones we killed. Dog has a shitload of rebel gold he stole after Sherman busted up Atlanta. That's how he pays them.

"Another thing One Dog likes is to impress his recruits with somethin' so goddamn outlandish it'll stick with them."

"Like what?"

"Couple years ago he torched a little church with thirty, forty folks in it on a Sunday morning. He chained the doors shut and posted a man at each window with instructions to shoot to kill. Like that."

Will shook his head in disgust. "What the hell makes him that kinda man?"

"Beats me. But it don't matter. That's the way he is. Look—let's leave our horses here an' go closer on foot. Wampus'll let us know if there're riders about."

The men walked together while the wolf dog swept the territory in front of and around them. He returned to Will frequently, grinning, and after a few scratches behind his ears set off on patrol again.

"Damned fools don't have riders or night guards out," Will said.

"Prolly figure they're safe in town—an' they're no doubt soused, too."

As Ray and Will drew closer, raucous, braying laughter, whoops, and rebel yells reached them. "Somethin' unusual goin' on," Will said.

When Wampus next returned Will kept him at his side.

Olympus had been established in a slight dish in the prairie, which was fortunate: the terrain allowed rain and snow melt to drain downward to replenish small ponds, streams, and water tables. As the men approached the lip they crouched down to keep their silhouettes out of sight of the town.

They gut-crawled the last few yards and looked down at Olympus. Both men were silent for a moment, almost unable to believe what they saw in front of the outlaw saloon.

There were two tall fence posts planted midstreet, maybe ten feet apart. Renegades wandered about, tearing boards, slats, and doors from buildings and piling them at the bases of the fence posts. Lengths of logging chain rested in front of the posts in the dirt of the street.

A large fire—a farmer's wagon that must have been loaded with lumber from the mercantile—burned powerfully, tongues of flame reaching toward the sky and casting their eerie light up and down Main Street.

"Nah," Ray whispered, unbelieving. "Nah, they can't be planning . . ."

" 'Course they can. And they *are.*"

Two outlaws carrying cans of kerosene stumbled and weaved their ways to the posts and saturated the wood around them. One Dog, standing between the posts, arms folded, his face hard, gestured toward the saloon. The cheers and laughter of the crowd grew yet louder.

Four renegades dragged and carried two Negro men, punching and kicking them to keep them moving. Both blacks were shirtless and their backs and shoulders showed fresh welts and deep cuts from a horsewhip.

"Where'd they get the niggers?" Ray asked.

"Look: don't call them niggers. Niggers are slaves.

Ain't no black people who are slaves since Appomattox. I celled with a black at Folsom an' he was one of the finest men I ever come across. Know what he was serving eight to ten for? Gawkin' at a white whore."

"I didn't mean no harm, Will."

"I know that. But don't you say it again." He paused for a moment. "That could well be the black men's wagon burning. Lotsa freed slaves came to be settin' up little farms, building houses, out on the prairie."

"We can't let them do this," Ray said grimly. "Hell, no man deserves to die that way."

"You're right, Ray. But look on down there. There must be twenty-five new riders.

"They'd chew us up an' spit us out if we attacked— Wampus or no Wampus."

"So what do we do?"

"You know that as well as I do," Will said quietly. "It stinks, but we got no choice."

Will began to push himself back from the lip, Wampus quivering beside him.

"Where ya goin'?"

"To fetch my rifle from—"

"Screw your rifle," Ray snapped. "Jus' stay put." Ray slid his buffalo gun off his back and checked its load.

The outlaws had chained the two black men to the posts, taking several wraps around each man, binding them tightly. The fire in front of the saloon reflected its sharp yellow-orange light from the sweat-covered chests and arms of the captives. Each had obviously worked the fields in their former lives; thick muscles pushed at the skin of their arms and forearms and their guts were flat. There probably wasn't an ounce of fat between the two of them.

A ragged, drunken cheer arose as a pair of Indians stumbled out of the saloon with flaming torches in their hands.

"You want them two?" Ray asked.

Will nodded.

Ray handed over the .50-caliber weapon. "Drop the rear sight a notch an' leave the front one alone." After a moment, he asked, "You ever fired one of these?"

Will didn't answer.

"OK," Ray said, "here's the thing: the recoil's a pisser. Keep your face a hair away from the stock. Otherwise you'll end up with a busted jaw or lose a slew of teeth."

"OK," Will said.

The cannonlike bellow of the buffalo rifle was louder than thunder, louder than dynamite—louder than anything.

So powerful was the rifle that the massive slug passed directly through the renegade closest to the post's chest, leaving a gaping hole the size of a large man's fist, without knocking the man down. Gushets of blood pumped from the aperture for half a minute and then slowed and, finally, stopped. It was then that the Indian went down, but he went down slowly, as if he were dozing off. He fell a bit forward and his bare chest pressed the flaming torch into the grit of the street, but by then, he was well beyond pain—or anything else.

Will took the second renegade with a hurried, sloppy shot that hit the Indian between his neck and right shoulder. He spun a few times from the impact of the three-quarter ounce of lead, tangled his feet with one another, and went down.

"Sumbitch was dead while he was twirlin'," Ray said, "but it wasn't that bad of a shot, all in all."

A barrage of useless pistol and rifle fire dug divots of dirt out of the lip, but accomplished nothing else. The outlaws were shooting simply to shoot. They knew they couldn't put a round into the men beyond the lip.

What started out as a fistfight between an Indian and one of the new men captured the outlaws' attention. The Indian was getting his ass kicked: his nose was broken, both his lips were split, his front teeth were gone, and his eyes were so swollen that his vision was reduced to what he could see from between a pair of narrow slits. The white man danced around the Indian; he'd been in the ring before and he knew what he was doing. He moved smoothly about on the balls of his feet, bobbing, weaving, never still. He landed a few more punches to his opponent's face.

A fat renegade moved between the fighters, holding up his hands in front of the white man. Will and Ray couldn't hear what was being said, but it was obviously conciliatory, declaring the white man the winner. The white man, grinning broadly, held his arms up in victory.

The fat Indian slid a dagger between the white fighter's ribs, puncturing his heart.

"Maybe that'll—"

"Bullshit. That fight was business as usual. Gimme the rifle."

As Ray spoke, two renegades pushed through the batwings of the saloon, each with a flaming arrow nocked and bows drawn.

Their aim was good. The kerosene-saturated wood exploded into flame.

Ray stood, buffalo gun to his shoulder, regardless of the silhouette he presented, and fired twice, quickly—so quickly, the reports sounded like a single round.

The heads of both black men tipped forward loosely on their necks. Blood seeped rather than poured from the neat, oblong holes between each of their eyes. The backs of their heads, of course, were a different story.

"I ain't gonna ever forget what I had to do here," Ray said, his voice a tone of huskiness Will hadn't heard before.

"No," Will said. "You won't. But you done what you had to." He put his arm over Ray's shoulder. "Come on—let's get back to our horses." Ray slipped the sling of his buffalo gun back over his shoulder as they began walking.

Chapter Eight

They said next to nothing as they walked back to their horses. Even Wampus was subdued, walking closely enough to Will so that the dog's side touched the man's leg.

Wasn't anything else we could do for those two men once the fires started—not a single thing. Was I in the same fix, I'd welcome the bullet, the quick, clean end rather than the awful suffering, the screaming, the begging.

Still—we killed them. It for certain wasn't murder, but that doesn't make them any less dead, their bodies charred and twisted, with no more resemblance to the living men than a dead mouse has to a mountain cat.

Jesus.

A couple of guys, no doubt with women, maybe children, waitin' for their men to rattle up in their wagon loaded up with the framing for the houses the families would live in— free, *with no more shackles, no more whips, no more* "Yassuh, massa boss, sir" *horseshit.*

And then—Olympus. It must have been some time since they'd been to town. They knew nothing of One Dog.

'Course they couldn't buy a drink in the saloon, but they'd bought a whole lot of lumber from the mercantile for

cash on the barrelhead, so the clerk would sell them a bottle, carefully avoiding touching their hands. They'd probably drunk and laughed all night, headed to their homes—or what would be their homes.

Wampus whimpered quietly, plaintively, as if he were reading Will's thoughts.

Ray's skill with that .50 caliber saved those men a world of pain. It was a good thing—the right thing—to do.

Will Lewis felt like a murderer of innocent men.

They mounted and rode at a jog back to their camp. After a long time of heavy silence, Ray said, "Where do you think all them extry men came from?"

Will considered. "Well, like I said, there's always a slew of crazies lookin' to ride with somebody like Quantrill or One Dog. I'm thinkin' this might be somethin' else, though."

"What's that?"

"I had a smith—a good friend—tell me that once every year or so bands of loons meet, get drunk, eat mushrooms, smoke ganja, an' carry on—shoot one another if they get to arguin'.

"See, it's like when the mountain men meet, 'cept them trappers an' hunters aren't loons. They jus' don't like anybody but other mountain men. No harm there that I can see. A man's 'titled to pick his friends."

"Where's the army at?" Ray asked. "The raiders."

"Chasin' Indians."

"Oh."

"Yeah—forcin' 'em onto reservations or killin' 'em."

"So," Ray said, "there might could be a bunch of these raiders comin' toward Olympus? No?"

"My friend, he says there's a whole herd of the sonsabitches get together."

"No big deal. All we gotta do is kill 'em, an' we been doin' that good."

"Good point," said Will.

Neither man slept the balance of the night. Ray honed his knives on his whetstone almost mechanically, as if he were a nonthinking machine designed to do only that. The whish, whish of the blade over the stone eventually began to grate on Will's nerves, but he kept his mouth shut. If sharpening his knives is what Ray needed to do, then he should do it.

Still, it was driving Will around the bend.

Will rolled and smoked cigarettes one after another, flicking the nubs out into the prairie.

"You might could start a fire in the brush with them cigarettes," Ray said.

Will glared at him. "Don't matter. It's nothin' but scrub, scorpions, an' rattlesnakes. Let it burn."

Dawn was painting the sky with its usual glory of pastels and sharper colors, too. The men didn't notice.

Finally, as Will was lighting another cigarette with a lucifer he'd snapped with his thumbnail, Ray sheathed the knife he'd been working. "Them goddamn things'll kill you," he said.

"Bullshit. Tobacco smoke builds up lungs—makes 'em stronger. Plus, it tastes good an' calms a man down, makes him feel better. Hell, they oughta teach smokin' in grade school."

Ray grunted disgustedly.

Will stood and worked the kinks out of his back. He was silent for some time, but Ray knew from his face that some sort of pronouncement was coming. It was.

"Only one way we can get this done," Will said. "We're both good—real hardasses an' damned deadly fighters—but One Dog has about fifty men around him now. The odds are impossible."

"Could be. But what can we do? The army . . ."

"The army is a bunch of clowns chasing Indians off their own land, killin' kids and squaws an' old folks, while the warriors put arrows an' slugs into the bluecoats. If Bobby Lee hadn't screwed up so badly at Gettysburg—an' that moron Pickett didn't do what he done—things'd be a whole lot different."

"Sure. But . . ."

"We need an army of our own—of men like us," Will growled. "I know some fellas from Folsom who owe me a favor, an' some others from my robbin' days—good men who ain't afraid to pull the trigger an' don't mind the stink of blood."

"I know a few myself," Ray said. "Thing is, they ain't a real trustin' bunch. Most have posters out on 'em. They kill bounty hunters like a housewife steps on a cockroach."

"These boys friends of yours?"

"Tight friends."

"Same with the bunch I know. We gotta get 'em here, Ray."

"Ain't many who'd work for free."

"I know that, an' it's no problem. I got stashes all over the goddamn place. Plus, maybe we'd find out where One Dog's rebel gold is at," Will said.

"There's a—hell, it ain't really a town, it's a depot—but it's got a saloon, a whorehouse, an' a telegraph monkey in the depot."

"How far?"

"Hard to say. Maybe eighty miles."

"Can you find it?"

Ray grinned. "Hell, boy, I could find a nice, cool spot in hell, I needed to."

"Thing is, these men don't have addresses," Will said. "It'll be awful hard to find most of them."

"That's OK. We don't need most of them. Eight or ten'll do jus' fine. Ten of them boys is worth thirty renegades. Tell you what: you make up a list with names an' towns or ranches or whatever where your men last were, far as you know, an' I'll do the same. I'll send the wires out an' ask that they be forwarded, need be. Then we set back for a couple days an' see what happens."

"Could be no one will show up."

"Could be that pigs'll fly outta my ass an' we'll have free bacon forever, but neither one ain't likely, Will."

Will laughed. "Let's saddle up."

"No. It don't make no sense for both of us to go. You an' your wolf stay here an' watch what the outlaws are doin'. I should be back in two days."

"How long you figure it'll take these boys to get here?"

"Beats me. 'Pends on where they're at an' if they care to do some fightin'. Seems to me the ones that ain't dead will get here, one way or t'other. If I'm wrong an' they don't come, why we'll take the renegades on our own selves, just like we been doin. An' we wouldn't have lost nothin' but a couple days."

Ray saddled his horse.

"You watch your back," Will said.

"You do the same."

Ray set off at a lope. Before long he was out of sight. There was still enough dew on the ground that Ray's horse didn't raise a finger of dust that pointed at him.

Will piddled around camp after Ray was gone, accomplishing nothing more than gathering up more scrub and mesquite for the fire. He considered sending Wampus out for a rabbit, but he wasn't really hungry, and he was weary unto death of eating jacks. Wampus followed Will at his heels as he paced—so closely, in fact, that when the man stopped rather suddenly the dog walked right into him.

"Damn," Will said, "we're as nervous as a pair of ol' whores in church. This isn't what we signed on for—to sit around a camp doin' nothin'."

He shook out his saddle blanket. Once, many years ago, he'd tossed a blanket onto the back of a good horse—a blanket that had a good-sized scorpion attached to it. It'd taken him months before he could get a blanket on that horse without it going berserk. Will eased the blanket onto the pinto's back and dropped his saddle into place. Even the horse craved some action: he danced and snorted and tossed his head. When Will mounted, the pinto put on a minor bucking exhibition, sunfishing, kicking out with his rear hooves, doing some twisting and turning.

Will enjoyed the workout as much as the horse did. They rode back toward Olympus at an easy pace, and on his way he came upon a fine piece of good luck. There weren't many shaggies left—the skin hunters had shot hell out of the once-gigantic herds—but there were still wandering groups of a dozen or so.

Will came upon a gimp, a yearling with a severely twisted and damned-near-useless right front leg. He had some fat to him, although not much. Still, he'd been able to graze when the rest of the herd stopped. Something had spooked the other buffalo—probably the outlaws—and they'd stampeded, leaving the gimp behind. It was only a matter of time before the wolves or coyotes made a meal out of him.

Will untied the latigo that held his throwing rope at his right knee and shook out the kinks. He hadn't carried a lasso for some time, but Ray had convinced him to do so. "You never know when you might need to string up a Injun," he'd said.

He cut the pinto hard in front of the buffalo and dropped a loop over his head, at the same time swinging his horse in the opposite direction, pulling the gimp off his feet. Will piled off his horse and followed the rope down to the bawling yearling. He placed his knife perfectly into the critter's heart. It died almost immediately. He slit it from gut to touchhole, scooped out the innards, sawed off its head, and retrieved and coiled his rope. He tossed the heart and liver to Wampus. He'd pick up the partially butchered buffalo on his way back. "No more damned jackrabbits," he said. "Not for a few days, anyway."

They rode on. As he had the night before, he tied his horse a good three quarters of a mile from the lip, and Will continued on foot, crouching. He noticed that Wampus was trembling. "Jesus," he said, "you for sure got a taste for that renegade blood, don't you?"

The sun was fully risen now and the day promised to be yet another fifteen hours of unremitting heat. Will's shirt was soaked within a few minutes of walking. They spooked a rattler. They never saw it but they for sure heard its castanets of warning. Wampus began to trot over to the sound. Will's snapped fingers brought the dog back to his side.

Will crawled to the edge of the lip and looked down at Olympus. The two blackened, shriveled husks that had once been living men remained chained to the fence posts, almost obscured from sight by masses of flies.

Boozing for the day had already begun and there was racket from the inside of the saloon. Outside, several Indians wandered aimlessly, faces blank, hands hanging at their sides. A few mumbled incoherently.

Mushrooms, Will thought.

One of the Indians seemed intent on climbing the slight rise from which Will watched the town. He was as clumsy as a drunk on a rolling log—he fell several times. When he struggled to his feet the last time, his lips and mouth were encrusted with sand but his face retained the same expressionless, zombielike semblance.

Wampus growled, but stopped when Will elbowed him.

For some reason, this babbling, weaving, mindless creature flared Will's temper to full blaze. *This piece of dung burned two innocent men. He might have killed Hiram or his wife or daughters. If the Indian had fought those two men . . . But he hadn't. He'd burned them like kindling.*

The renegade topped the rise twenty feet from Will and Wampus and saw neither man nor dog. A sharp ammonia smell reached Will almost immediately. The front of the Indian's Union Army pants were soaked to the point of dripping. There was another wretched stink, too—that of long-dead carrion or an overloaded outhouse with a too-shallow pit.

Will snarled as he raised his arm and pointed at the renegade. Wampus was off in half a heartbeat, silent, belly close to the ground, ivory eyeteeth glinting in the sun.

Wampus hit this one from the front, his bowie-knife-sharp teeth in a death clamp on the man's jugular. Blood spurted as if from a well spigot, but amazingly, the renegade fell almost gently and completely soundlessly. After a moment the blood stopped gushing. Wampus released his grip and stepped back. He sat, staring at the corpse, almost if he were bemused by it. Will watched silently, wondering what the dog would do next.

Wampus stood, moved ahead a step, and sniffed the blood at the renegade's throat. Then he stepped back, sat, pointed his muzzle at the sky, and howled long and loud, the eerie sound echoing about the valley, washing over the town, resounding again and again, quieter each time, until it died.

There was nothing, Will realized, that was at all canine about that howl. It was all wolf, the kind of ululation that sent shivers up and down a person's spine. Ray certainly knew his critters.

"Perfect," Will smiled. "The wampus strikes again—this time in *daylight*."

He clicked his tongue at Wampus and the two of them hustled back to where the pinto was tied. Will loosened his rope once again, wrapped the loop around the front legs of the carcass of the shaggy, tied off on his saddle horn, and rode back to the camp. He was sure there was no reason to hurry. This last manifestation of the wampus would keep the outlaws huddled in their gin mill, shooting at shadows and hearing sounds that weren't there.

Will tied up to the buffalo carcass and dragged it along behind him almost to the camp. Then, he began his makeshift butchering. Wampus watched avidly, hungrily, drooling, tongue hanging out several inches. Will hacked off a section of ribs a yard long and handed them over to his dog. "Here ya go, pardner," he said. Wampus took the ribs from Will gently, but as he trotted off, he flicked his prize onto his shoulders and back—the same way Will had once seen a timber wolf making off with a lamb. Will refused to let the thought linger. Still, that instinctive movment of the jaws and head . . .

The steaks were things of beauty. Will was able to carve away six of them of about two inches or more thick. They were nicely marbled with fat. He hated to waste the chops and the other cuts of meat, but he had no choice. He and Ray had no way to carry that much meat, and it would go rotten in a day or so under the sun.

True to his word, Ray rode into camp the evening of his second day out. He looked terrible: red-eyed, dust covered, slumped in his saddle, his weariness like a weight he could barely carry.

Ray's horse had fared no better. The animal's chest, neck, and flanks were gray-white with the froth of dried sweat, and his muzzle was damned near dragging on the ground. Will watched them approach. The horse wasn't quite staggering, but he was weaving pronouncedly.

Ray rode past Will without speaking, directly to the sinkhole of tepid, foul water. He got down from his saddle like a ninety-year-old man and fell face-first into the sinkhole, his horse's face next to his, both drinking like they'd hadn't had water in years.

When Ray pulled his face out of the muck, his first words were, "You got any booze? I don't want to hear any bullshit about my pledge to myself: a man's gotta do what he's gotta do. Now, you answer my question."

Will scrounged through his saddlebag and came up with an almost-full pint of rotgut. He tossed the bottle to Ray. "Ain't up to me to judge nobody," he said, " 'specially you, Ray."

Ray nodded, pulled the cork with his teeth, and emptied the bottle in a matter of two minutes, drinking the cheap whiskey the way he'd drunk water a few minutes ago.

He pulled the saddle from his horse, hobbled him, and rubbed him down with handfuls of dried prairie grass. He let the horse drink again and then stumbled over to the fire pit.

"We got any grub?"

"How 'bout the biggest, thickest buffalo steak you ever seen? Think that'll do ya?"

"Oh, I'd jus' say so. Yep—I'd jus' say so. Get sumabitches cookin'."

"It'll put up some smoke."

"Screw the smoke. Git that shaggy over the fire." It was an order, not a request.

Ray dropped his saddle and lay down, his head resting against the seat.

"You get through?" Will asked as he snapped a lucifer into flame and lit the kindling he'd arranged earlier.

" 'Course I did. Wasn't no pleasure ride, though." He sat up, reached down to his boots, and unstrapped the pair of flat-roweled spurs he was wearing on his heels. He threw them, one at a time, as far out into the prairie as he could. "I hated to hook my good horse the way I done, but I'll tell you this: there's still a bunch of hostiles out there. Anyways, we made it. That's what counts. All the wires went out. I stood right over the monkey as he sent 'em."

Will was quiet, feeding the fire. He'd washed the meat and wrapped it in his slicker and wet it every time he thought about it—which was often.

Before long he had a pair of bison steaks skewered on the cleaning rod from his rifle kit.

The scent reached Ray, who'd been dozing. "How long?" he asked.

"Not long. Ten minutes, maybe."

Ray moved closer to Will, the fire, and the meat. "How'd you come by this feast?" he asked.

Will rolled a cigarette and explained the whole package: his exploratory trip, the dead Indian, Wampus's howl, the gimp shaggy—all of it.

"You give ol' Wampus the heart?"

"Yeah. Liver, too."

"Good. Real good. Ya know, that howlin' don't surprise me none. See, a wolf'll howl like that after he defeats a enemy in front of his pack—or when he's really proud of what he done. He won't howl when they pull down a deer or even a elk. A bear, they will, if the bear was sizable 'nuff an' a fighter."

"Why this renegade, then?"

"I dunno. Why does the sun come up? Why does a fat baby fart? Thing is, don't never try to predict what a wolf or a tight cross like Wampus'll do."

"But Wampus—"

"But Wampus, my ass! Wampus ain't no different! Look, I had a friend named Bridger—another trapper an' bounty hunter. He raised him up the sweetest li'l wolf bitch you ever seen. She purely loved that man, followed him, learned everything he wanted to teach her, slept next to him at night. She'd tear hell outta any man or animal threatened Bridger." Ray was quiet then.

"And . . . ?" Will asked.

"I swung by Bridger's cabin one spring a couple years later, 'spectin grub an' a bottle. What I found was my frien' ripped into bits an' pieces, liver an' heart gone, a arm here an' another there, tool an' eggs gone, eyes tore out . . . an' so forth. So you listen to me good, Will Lewis: Wampus ain't a puppy dog. One day he'll turn. I flat-out *promise* you that. I can't say when. I wish I could, but I can't. It'll happen, though, an' it'll be a sad thing, 'cause you ain't gonna be ready." Ray was quiet for a long time. "I can't say, though, that I ever seen a cross love a man like Wampus does you. There's always a 'ception to a rule, no?"

Will stared into the fire for several uncomfortable moments. "Looks like the meat's ready," he said.

*   *   *

The crippled buffalo was even better than the men expected—and the aroma of it cooking made them expect a lot. Because he was barely older than a yearling, he hadn't yet developed much muscle that would make his meat tough. And being a gimp slowed him way down, always trailing the herd, spending more time grazing, building up that sweet marbling meat lovers savored.

Buffalo meat isn't radically different from beef, although it has a distinctive, slightly gamey flavor that makes it yet more appealing to those who are fond of it.

After they'd eaten much more than they needed—including Wampus, who worked off his feed burying knuckle bones and other choice bits and morsels—Will leaned back against his saddle and built a smoke. Ray made up some coffee and set the tin can aside to cool to a handling temperature. He picked the can up with a pair of small branches; both began to smoke as he moved the "coffee pot."

"Oughta get you a tin can an' we wouldn't have to pass this one back an' forth," Ray said. "Ain't that I'm complainin'—there's nobody else I'd rather share my fine coffee with, mind you—but it'd make things easier."

"Yeah. I'll do that. Funny thing—any moron saddle tramp can cook up a shaggy steak, but it takes a special touch to brew real good coffee. An' I'll say this: you make the strongest, best-tastin' java I ever had the damn good luck to drink."

"Well thanks, Will. You ain't generally one to hand out compliments."

"No, I ain't. Sometimes they're deserved, though."

The men watched the embers of their cook fire fade from white to red to almost black. Wampus, asleep next to Will, whimpered, and his front paws scampered a bit, as if reaching out for something.

"Chasin' a rabbit, I 'spect," Will said.

"More likely sniffin' after a wolf bitch, doin' his best to climb on her. Them stud wolves like their ladies a awful lot."

"Ya know," Will said, "I don't know that I'm sure 'bout how much wolf blood flows in Wampus. I don't doubt there's some—maybe a good bit—but I never seen nothin' wolflike 'bout him."

"Well, lemme count for you: One—that howl. No dog howls like that. 'Course a blue tick has a howl that'll carry farther an' clearer than a wolf's, but that's a complete different thing. Two—the way he hunts—hell, Wampus could find and fetch in a jackrabbit in the middle of a ocean. And three—the way he pulls a man down an' kills him dead quiet in a heartbeat. No dog ever borned can do it like that."

Will rolled another cigarette. "You might could have some points, I'll admit," he said after lighting his smoke with a lucifer. "But look at that critter, Ray. He's got the heart of a pussycat an' . . . an' he loves me. He purely does. He coulda took off the second I got that wire from 'round his neck, but he stayed on with me. Why? Gratitude! Gratitude an' love. Ain't a wolf ever lived or will ever live that showed them two things to a man.

"I know you know wolves, Ray. I ain't disputin' that fact. Thing is, though, in any breed of animals there's one or two that's way different from the others, that goes sideways from his breed. I'd say

Wampus is that one—the strange one. Wouldn't you agree with that?"

Will waited for a response. His only answer was a grinding, nasal snore. Ray was sound asleep. Will rolled another cigarette, smoked it, tossed the nub into the moribund fire, and slept.

The next morning Ray came up on Will, who'd walked a couple hundred yards out into the prairie. "What're you doin'?" Ray asked.

Will seemed to scramble for words. "I . . . uhh . . . jus' thought I'd take a little walk 'fore the sun gets to work. Yeah—a little walk."

Ray sighed. "If any of those boys got the wires yet, it'd be a miracle. We ain't goin' to see no one for two, three days at the earliest. You standin' out here like a totem pole ain't gonna draw 'em in any sooner."

"I s'pose."

"Anyways, Wampus'll let us know if anyone's comin' toward us. Look, c'mon back. I got some coffee brewin'."

They sat close together, passing the can back and forth until it was empty.

"Wanna play some cards?" Ray asked. "I got a deck in my saddlebag."

"Ain't but two of us. Two fellas can't play poker."

"Sure they can. We jus' deal a hand and set it down an' play 'gainst each other."

"I'm not much on gamblin', Ray. I never saw no sense to it."

"I didn't say nothin' 'bout money. We jus' play for pertend. Thing is, you can't bet a hundred on a pair of threes or like that."

"OK. I'll play."

After two hours, Will would have owed Ray $125,000 if they'd been playing for real money. Will tossed his cards to Ray. "This is a pain in the ass. You bluff too good. Hell, you didn't have nothin' but horseshit an' slivers, most of them hands you won."

" 'Nother hand?"

"Hell no." Will was staring over his friend's shoulder. "We might better get ready for rain, anyway. Looks like there's a storm comin' up outta the east."

Ray turned to look. It was still a good ways off, but the sky had become slightly darker to the east. "Yeah. Nothin' we can do 'bout it but get wet, I guess." He gazed east for several minutes. "Funny. I ain't seein' no flashes of lightning at all—none. Even that far away, you'd think we'd see a couple."

"Dust storm?"

"Nah. That ain't what a duster looks like. It's too high in the sky an' there's no wind behind it. It'd be moving a lot faster if it was a duster." As they watched, the ends of the storm spread wider and the center grew darker and heavier. There was an odd, electric tension in the air, not like the calm before a summer storm, but more like that created when there's a constant, just barely audible sound that makes the hair rise on the back of a man's neck.

Both men felt it; neither mentioned it.

About an hour and a half later the horses got screwy, pulling at their stakes, arguing, snapping at one another.

"We'd best hobble them two before they get to fightin' 'an tear one 'nother up," Ray said, "or take it in their heads to run off."

For the first time since Will had known the pinto, the horse moved away from him. When he pursued it, the horse swung his back around, dropped his head, and kicked out with both rear hooves. Had a hoof struck Will, it would have crushed his head like an anvil dropped onto a cherry pie from a considerable height, or crushed his rib cage and punctured his lungs and heart.

Will moved very carefully around the horse and managed to snag the rope that led from the stake. He walked down the rope slowly, humming quietly, shushing the horse when he became fractious again. Finally, he was able to slide the hobbles on the pinto's forelegs.

Although he was turned away from Ray, it was obvious his friend was having much the same problems. "Ya lop-eared sonofabitch," Ray snarled. "Ya keep this shit up an' I'll truss your scrawny ass like a Christmas goose, goddammit!"

Ray had had quite enough. He stormed back to his saddle, his face red and distorted, and fetched his throwing rope. He dropped a clean loop in front of his horse and tugged it as soon as the animal stepped into it, suddenly pulling the two forelegs together. The horse teetered and squealed until Ray shoved his shoulder, knocking him down. He slipped on his hobbles, released his rope, mumbled, "Ya dumb bastid," and walked over to Will. They both turned their attention to the storm.

"Ain't movin' very fast," Will said.

"No—but she's gettin' bigger: wider an' taller an' darker . . ."

"Damndest thing I ever seen," Will said. "An' lookit Wampus. He's scared shitless."

The wolf dog certainly did look frightened. He stayed a few inches behind Will's heels, cringing so his gut touched the ground, his tail tucked tightly between his legs. His eyes, like those of the horses, seemed as large as wagon wheels.

"Somethin's real wrong out there," Will said. "I don't—"

Ray hushed his friend with a raised hand. "Listen careful. You hear what I do?"

Will listened intently, eyes tightly shut. The tension he'd felt earlier had translated itself into a quietly sawing buzz that was all the more ominous because of its lack of real volume. Hell, a half hundred head of beef on a run would make three times the noise. "What's . . . ?"

"Jesus Howard Christ," Ray said. "That ain't no rain storm or dust storm. Them is grasshoppers, Will!"

"Grasshoppers?" Will asked incredulously.

"Abs'lutely! I never seen nothing like this, but a fella from Missouri—another wolf-bounty boy—he tol' after he give up wolfin' an' started farmin', he lost a whole fifty acres of wheat." Ray was talking rapidly now, almost too fast to follow. "The sonsabitches et the stalks right down level with the ground. They et all the clothes his woman had hanged out to dry, much of his tack an' leather riggin's for his two-bottom plow, his saddle, a buncha kittens his kid was raisin' up, his manure pile, his—"

"How can a grasshopper eat leather an' cloth an' such?"

"One hopper can't but ninety thousand billion of them can eat any goddamn thing they come across. I hear tell they ate up a baby in Kansas. I dunno how true that is, but it's what I heard. Kinda tough on the poor baby if it *is* true."

Ray stopped talking and took several deep breaths. "OK. Here's what we gotta do.

"First, we cover our mouths an' noses with our bandannas. Then we stuff li'l plugs of cloth in our ears. If hoppers git in there . . . well . . . and then we gotta plug up the horses' ears an' their nose holes, if we can do it. Wampus need plugs in his ears, too. Here's another thing, too: every snake an' rabbit and scorpion and prairie dog in all them acres is gonna be haulin' ass away from the hoppers. We gotta keep the horses close together as we can, an' use stout sticks to whack the piss outta the rattlers an' sidewinders. See, they go nuts an' bite ever'thin' they see."

Will already had his bandanna in place and was tearing up his second shirt to make plugs for his ears and for his horse and dog. "You need some'a this?" he asked Ray. "No sense in us both ruining a shirt if we don't have to. I got plenty for me an' my critters."

"Good idear. While I'm pluggin' up my horse, how 'bout you tearin' off a couple branches to pound snakes an' scorpions with? Won't be long 'fore they're here, an' they ain't lookin' to be friends with us. Oh—and tuck your drawers into your boots an' tie one a them sleeves around your neck good an' tight. If what my friend tol' me is true—an' I got no reason to think it ain't—the hoppers'll be all over us real soon."

Neither Will's horse nor his dog put up a fight as he jammed balls of cloth into their ears. Both animals were trembling and the pinto had broken a heavy sweat. Wampus stayed in place a couple of inches behind Will, belly to the ground, following his every move.

The buzz had turned into a flapping, pounding sound—like that of the wings of a frantic bird except many, many times louder. Will hacked off a couple of desert-pine branches and trimmed them clean of shoots and suckers. He tossed one to Ray. Will stood between the horses. Ray was in front of him a few strides.

The rabbits came first, covering the ground like a dirty brown blanket, running their hearts out. It was hard to believe that there could be so many jacks in one place, but there they were, wild-eyed, many with their tiny pink tongues protruding from their gaping mouths as they sucked air.

The prairie dogs were next, scrambling, banging into one another, falling, running over each other. Then came the snakes.

Will had never seen so many goddamn rattlers in his life, and neither had Ray. They didn't glide smoothly as they generally did, but seemed to move in almost jerky, spasmodic leaps ahead, stopping every so often to raise their heads eight or ten inches above the ground as if they were periscopes on those rebel underwater ships. Ray began slamming reptiles with his stick, yelling and cursing at them. Only a few got past him and Will handled those easily enough. The horses stood stock-still, paralyzed with fear, the scent of the snakes reaching their brains even through the cloth jammed into their nostrils. And then, suddenly, there was nothing in the world but grasshoppers, impossibly massive numbers of them, with virtually no space between them. They came on with a roar composed of millions—billions—of the miniscule abrasive sounds each made, amplified by a figure too large to imagine.

In a matter of seconds both horses, both men, and the wolf dog were blanketed with foraging hoppers. The horses, now beyond panic and into a state of raw instinct, wanted nothing but to run, to get this horror behind them. They reared and bucked in spite of the hobbles, their piercing squeals barely audible over the infernal racket of the insects. Will was pulled from his feet, blinded by the hoppers sheeting his face, afraid to open his eyes, and had to release the ropes he had on each horse. Without the use of their forelegs, the horses stumbled and fell and were unable to get up, their hooves sliding on the crushed grasshoppers that now covered the prairie floor like a grotesque green snowfall from hell.

Wampus was rolling wildly, digging his shoulders into what should have been ground but was, instead, two inches of grasshoppers, the thick brown exudate—tobacco juice, as the cowboys called it—staining his coat. He snapped futilely at the hordes, accomplishing nothing but filling his mouth with hopper parts and guts. Will and Ray slapped at themselves ineffectually. Even with pants tucked into boots and bandannas tight to their necks, the cursed hoppers got into their clothing and the sensation of the beating wings, the sharp-edged legs, and the seeping flow of tobacco juice was enough to drive a sane man 'round the bend. Will tried rolling on the ground—forgetting there was no ground, beyond millions of grasshoppers. He stumbled to his feet with more hoppers touching his flesh than he'd had before he attempted rolling.

It was impossible to see; the cloud of insects was so thick that there was no space between them. They were a writhing sheet of foul, tremendously destructive creatures that brought forth a driving, atavistic fear in man and animal alike.

The onslaught ended abruptly. One moment the very air was crawling with hoppers and the next only a few stragglers leapfrogged past. Even the mass of hoppers on the ground moved after those in the air—except for those that'd been crushed, rolled on, or stomped into paste. Dead and dying snakes littered the ground; dead prairie dogs and jackrabbits were scattered about. There hadn't been many scorpions—at least that the men could see. They'd stamped on those.

The men stripped down and shook their shirts and pants vigorously, emptying their clothing of hopper corpses. They picked the crushed ones off their skin as if they were scabs, often gagging as they did so.

Will tossed his bandanna on the ground in disgust, first holding it out in front of him. "Lookit this goddamn thing," he said, "dripping with 'bacco juice. Damn! It'd make a shit fly puke."

They looked around them, awestruck. There was nothing green—or even brown and dessicated by the sun—left on the prairie. It was as if a giant scythe wielded by a demon spirit had attacked the area as far as the eye could see.

The horses, still hobbled, hadn't gotten far and now stood together, heads hanging, breathing heavily, insects glued to their panicked sweat. Will and Ray cleaned their mounts using the edges of hands as scrapers. Wampus, finally standing erect, cleaned himself, except for those his paws and teeth couldn't reach. Will took care of those for him.

"Ya know," Ray said, "as bad as this was, some good's goin' to come out of it."

"How so?"

"Think about it, Will. The whole wampus thing. See, the redskins believe a wampus can control nature, control the weather. They gotta see the hopper attack as a plague ordered by the wampus."

Will considered that. "Then we oughta plan an attack real soon—hit 'em while they're still seeing visions of hoppers an' wampus comin' after them."

"Right. The grasshoppers headed right for Olympus. The outlaws could stay in their saloon, but most of the windows—maybe all of 'em—were shot out, so that cesspool was just a-crawlin' with hoppers. We know how they react to your wolf dog, an' if you up an' add that to a plague of bugs they figure the wampus set on 'em, well, we got us a buncha scared enemies—real scared."

"I dunno, Ray. One Dog jus' hired on a herd of new guns. We don't know where they come from or who they are—or what they can do with a pistol or rifle."

Ray grinned derisively. "Sure. I 'magine they hired on the Earp brothers, Billy Bonney, John Ringo, Bill Hickok, ol' Doc Holliday, all them Clanton boys, an' the goddamn Pope, right?"

Will laughed heartily. "Thing is, the Pope could never fan a .38 or .44 worth a damn. But yeah, you're right. Still, they got a army and we got us. We're better an' faster an' a whole bundle smarter than they are, but they can put a awful lot of lead in the air.

"Seems to me you got a plan, Ray."

"Oh, yeah. An' a damn fine one."

"Tell me."

"First I gotta show you somethin'." He led Will

over to their saddles, their boots crunching on dead hoppers. The grasshoppers hadn't had time to do any real damage to the saddles, although both were splotched with amber saliva from them. "I got some neat's-foot erl," Ray said. "We'll clean our tack later." He crouched down and opened his saddlebag, from which he removed a wooden box about sixteen inches long and six inches wide.

"What's that?"

"Now, jus' hold on an' I'll show you."

Ray worked the three latches on the box and swung its top open. There, on a layer of straw, were six flat, blunt-ended darkish brown strips, each about a half inch wide. "This here is black powder," Ray said, "mixed with some chemical or another, so it ain't loose—ain't really a powder. A feller named Du Mont or Du Pont or some such come up with it for the Union Army. Then the war went an' ended an' he kinda give up on the idear."

"But what's it for?"

"I'll show you in a minute. But first, when I went to send them wires, I seen posters nailed to the wall of the depot on three of the boys I was lookin' for. Then, the ol' buzzard runnin' the 'graph key tol' me two of the boys was dead an' he knew it for a fact. Anyhow, we got to jawin' an' I mentioned One Dog. I tol' him me an' my group was Pinkertons disguised as reg'lar saddle tramps an' cowhands, an' our job was to kill One Dog. Well, that lit up the ol' fella. Dog had killed some relative a his, a farmer. He—"

"Jesus, Ray, will you cut the horseshit an' tell me what you're thinkin' an' what them sticks are for?"

"Porky sumbitch," Ray mumbled. He took one of

the sticks and hurled it overhand out into the prairie. "Now you pop that fella with a rock," he said.

Will drew his pistol.

"No, dammit! Toss stones 'til you hit it."

"Look here . . ."

"Jus' do it an' keep your yap from flappin, OK?"

Will waited for a long moment and then gathered up a good handful of pitching stones and began throwing. Will didn't have much of an arm for throwing stones—he had the strength, but his accuracy was abysmal.

"Gonna be dark in a few hours," Ray remarked.

Will grumbled some obscenities but kept on pitching. Finally, one of his stones ticked the very end of the stick. The explosion blew him off his feet and onto his ass on dead grasshoppers.

"Holy God," he said reverently.

"See, a decent-sized man's weight—a single step—will set one of these sonsabitches off. All we gotta do is slide in there and plant some sticks an' we got them outlaws by the eggs, no?"

"Sure! We plant some 'round the saloon, some where their horses are—lots of places. Damn, Ray, you're a genius!"

"Ahh, hell," Ray said modestly, "ain't nothin' the great Bobby Lee couldn't have did, had he these sticks."

It was a long wait until full dark. Will leaned against his saddle, smoking a cigarette after clearing the insects out of his space, thinking.

Ray has become an awful good friend. He's a good fighter, he's got the balls of a bull buffalo, and a sense of humor that's really somethin'. Sure, he yaps a tad too much—but lookit his plan with those sticks of black pow-der. Hell, if we launched an attack, both of us an' Wam-pus's blood would be drawin' flies on Main Street.

I've seen Ray handle a rope, too. He don't look at it as he builds his loop, and he throws better'n average—not a top-notch roper, but not half-bad, neither. Better'n the usual cowhand, anyways. Ain't afraid of some work. Lookit that ride he made.

Ray's a good man. I wonder if he's ever thought 'bout ranchin'?

Chapter Nine

The saloon was cryptlike in its silence. One Dog stood atop the far end of the bar, arms folded, war paint on his face and his naked, sweating chest.

"One Dog has more power than the wampus," he said. "I will meet him and kill him and take his hair and his head and hold his bleeding head in front of you, whether he calls upon his powers to appear as a man or a wolf or a lowly grasshopper. Remember my medicine."

There were at least two heavily armed men at each window frame, the glass having been long ago shot out. A dozen or more men spread around the bat-wings and the front windows. The floor of the saloon was a carpet of dead and dying hoppers, puke, urine, and shell casings.

"We have new and powerful warriors to help us in our battles," Dog went on. "Let me ask this: who is the fastest and most accurate of the new men—the one who has the balls of a cougar and has killed many men?"

There was some mumbled conversation among the men, but it only lasted a moment until a raspy voice called out from the back of the group, "That'd be me.

No goddamn doubt." The speaker was a rifle-barrel-thin tall man wearing a black shirt and black hat and a pair of .38s tied low on his thighs, the butts of the pistols facing outward. The bone grips of the pistols were scored with neat little notches—many of them. He grinned, although it was a false smile, and he had the eyes of a man who didn't care if he lived or died.

"I ain't here to listen to your horseshit, One Dog. I'm after the gold an' that's all. I'll kill you an' any 'r all of these clowns who need killin'."

"Good," One Dog said. "Come here and stand before me. I will hand you my pistol and then I'll kill you and take your hair."

This time the gunman's laugh was real. "An' when I drop you—ya bigmouth Injun—I'll take over this band of sows an' use them to make money. No?"

"Perhaps," One Dog said quietly. "And perhaps not."

The gunslinger pushed his way forward and stood below Dog at the end of the bar.

"You said you don't need a iron to kill me. Hand over that Colt, ya damn circus Injun, flappin' your yap about how tough you are, how your medicine is gonna kill me. Don't use nothin' but your left hand—I see your holster's on your right side. Tug her out nice an' easy an' hold 'er upside down. Fair 'nuff, Chief?"

"It is fair."

One Dog reached across his waist and slid his .38 from its holster. He held the weapon upside down, and the very tip of his index finger eased into the trigger guard.

"OK so far," the gunman said. "Now, drop it."

"I do not drop fine weapons as a goat drops shit."

"Yeah, ya do—when I tell you to. Now!"

One Dog fired the .38 upside down with his off-side hand, putting all six slugs into the gunsel before the man hit the floor.

"You see?" he said to his men. "My medicine is a shield before me. It is stronger than the gunfighter, and it is stronger than the beast, wampus. I will kill it in its man shape. I saw that happen in a vision with the help of the sacred mushroom. You will all join me. Those who fail to help I will kill and take their hair and ears."

Dog let that settle for a long moment. "Keep good watch. We know not when the wampus will come, nor what shape he will be in when he does come. The one thing we know is that he will be in a man shape when I take his life."

"Way I see it, if we can plant them strips of black powder around the saloon an' start raisin' hell outside, the 'splosives will do lots of our work for us," Will said. "Plus, Wampus'll be tearin' throats—tonight I mean." He paused for a moment, his face suddenly worried. "Is Wampus heavy enough to set off one of them strips?"

"How much you figger he weighs?"

"Maybe eighty, ninety pounds. A tad less than a hundred-pound sack of grain."

Ray shook his head sadly. "He'd set one off sure as God made li'l green apples. We gotta leave him here—an' he ain't gonna like that, and I ain't either. I'm kinda used to havin' him with us. He's a fighter worth a half dozen of them renegades."

"He is. But maybe we don't need to leave him behind. Gimme one a them strips."

Ray took one of the innocent-looking devices from the box and gave it to Will. "Better back off," Will said. "I dunno how this is gonna go."

He placed the strip on the ground. Naturally enough, Wampus trotted over immediately to investigate the thing, sniff it, see what it might be.

Will let him get a stride from the explosive, muzzle down, getting its scent. He began to take another step.

"NO!" Will bellowed in a voice and tone the wolf dog had never heard from him before.

The word—the rawness and command of it—hit him like a lash across his back. Wampus didn't cringe. Instead, he stood as still as a marble statue, his eyes showing his confusion, his grief at displeasing Will.

"Ray," Will said, "put a good handful of jerky chunks on top of the stick an' then back off again." Ray did as he was asked.

Will walked off a few yards and then called the still-frozen Wampus over to him. He made a big deal over the dog, rubbing his head, tussling with him, scratching behind his ears, talking to him, until the flatness, the pain, left the wolf dog's eyes. Then Will began to walk, Wampus, as ever, at his side. Will stopped ten feet from the little pile of jerky and waved Wampus on.

Jerky—particularly beef jerky, which this was—had become Wampus's favorite treat. He trotted a few feet toward the dried meat and then stopped so suddenly he fell forward, his muzzle digging a furrow in the dirt. The scent of the strip, even over that of the meat, had reached his sensitive nose.

Will bit the inside of his cheeks to keep from

laughing. Ray turned his back on the scene silently, his shoulders shaking. Both men knew full well a creature like Wampus had all the pride of a good, strong man. Wampus trotted back to Will. "Good boy," Will said. "*Real* good boy."

"Well," Ray said, grinning, "I guess there's no problem there. Tell you the truth, I'm gettin' right fond of that ol' fleabag. Don't tell him that, though— he's liable to git a swelled head."

The men, as they drank their after-dinner coffee, decided not to use the strips that night.

"I say we take down a couple guards an' mark 'em, maybe scatter their horses if we can, an' then call it a good piece of work," Will said, rolling a smoke. "We got somethin' to discuss, though."

"Yeah," Ray said. "We been kinda sweepin' it under the carpet for a while. Who gets One Dog?"

"Seems to me this's been my show all the way along. I told you right up front that Dog was mine," Will said.

"I never noticed there was a boss an' a hired hand involved here. An' you got her wrong. I told you *I* was gonna take One Dog down."

"Ain't gonna happen, Ray. I'd hate to have to jerk guns against you, but if I had to, I would."

"You think you're faster, better'n me?"

"I know I am."

Ray spat off to the side. "Faster? Sure. Better? Hell no. Fast don't count for a fart in a hurricane if the slugs don't go where you need 'em to."

"Are you sayin—?" Will began hotly.

"Waitaminnit! Goddammit, waitaminnit! There's a real good chance one or both of us will die in this mess with them outlaws—in which case, we both lose. Or maybe only one of us catches lead. That leaves One Dog to the other, no? So let's quit this horseshit 'bout slappin' leather 'gainst men who've become friends. It don't make no sense."

Will attempted to build a smoke but trembled tobacco all over his lap. After a bit of time he said, "I was way the hell outta line, Ray, an' I 'pologize. You're right. An' for what it's worth, I'd no sooner pull iron on you than I would on my grandma."

"Why? 'Cause I'm old, beat up, slow, an' half-blind?"

" 'Zactly. She's deaf, too."

The two men laughed together and then reached over and shook each other's hand. The handshake meant something important to both of them far beyond the burying of an argument. Both knew that now they were partners in the true sense of the word. At times they'd argue and curse and call each other idjits and pissants—but each knew his partner would always have his back. How men become pards is a mystery, but that's what happened here.

The sky had cleared as the men drank their coffee after their rather unsatisfactory evening meal.

"Too bad we couldn't make that gimp last," Will said. "Jerky an' warm water ain't a great meal."

"Right. I'll tell you what. Nex' time we set off after a horde of bloodthirsty outlaws who outman an' outgun us, we'll haul along three, four fifty-gallon barrels of salt to preserve any shaggy calf you might come across."

Will chuckled. "You're one porky sumbitch, now aren't ya?"

When it was full dark, it wasn't *really* full dark. The stars glinted like millions upon millions of perfectly cut diamonds clustered on pure black velvet, and the moon was close to full and hung in the sky and was not unlike a gigantic eye seeking out what was happening on earth.

"Too much light," Ray observed, "but what the hell. Wampus will only look more scary with more light on him. Let's use some scorch from the fire to cut down the glare of our faces."

"Good idea," Will said. "Night like this one, the outriders might top the rim on their rounds. We'd best tie our horses back farther than we have been, an' keep a real sharp eye out. 'Course, we got Wampus . . ."

"Wampus came over to me this afternoon for a scratch. First time he done that," Ray said.

"Still think he'll turn?"

"Yeah, Will, I do. It's in their blood. It ain't Wampus's fault—it's jus' in his blood."

"Bullshit."

Ray sighed. "You ready to ride?"

The strange quality of the light cast the entire prairie in a silvery hue that transformed things into what they weren't: boulders became lurking bears, the soil itself became shimmering water, large clumps of scrub became hunched riflemen, drawing a bead.

"Lookit that," Will said, pointing off to one side. Wampus had given a half-hearted chase to a jackrabbit that had saved himself by diving down one of the countless rabbit-warren tunnels of the area. Wampus stood looking back at the men and his entire body seemed iridescent—a softly silver color that made the wolf dog an unearthly creature. But it was his eyes that'd caught Will's attention. They were viridescent ovals that glowed from within, making them a pale emerald shade.

"Damn," Ray said. "If any of those guards get away after seeing Wampus, they're goin' to be carryin' a load in their drawers as they skedaddle."

They left their horses and continued on foot.

It was a good night for outrider hunting. One Dog had been smart enough to post four riders above the rim surrounding Olympus. There would have been five, but Dog shot the fifth in the back as he rode out of town lifting a bottle to his mouth. One Dog had ordered no booze, and he meant what he said.

Will and Ray heard the steady clopping of a horse at a fast walk before they saw the rider. They dropped behind a cluster of scrub. Wampus, next to Will, was trembling in anticipation, his lips curled back over shining white eyeteeth but not growling, not making a sound. The guard rode past the men and dog, and Will gave him several yards before he whispered to Wampus, "Go."

Wampus snaked his way across the prairie floor like a moving light, seeking cover a few times to watch his prey, and then continuing on after him. He went into a jog eight or so yards behind the rider's horse; the jog rapidly evolved into a flat-out gallop. He launched himself onto the horse's rump and tore into the back of the rider's neck, carrying the both of them to the ground. Wampus quickly shifted his grip to the jugular. In moments the man was dead, his horse galloping frantically away, stirrups flapping, reins dragging. Will approached the rider, told Wampus he'd done good, and ripped the man's shirt open. He was getting good at leaving his *HW*—it took him only a couple of seconds. The corpse's .38 seemed to be in good shape; Will stuck it in his belt.

The rifle was a piece of a junk; that Will left. The rider had nothing else worth taking.

Will was walking back to Ray when Ray motioned "down." Will dropped and lay perfectly still. Another outrider was approaching from the opposite direction. One Dog's idea had obviously been to have the riders intersect with one another, so that if there was trouble it would be immediately known.

When the rider passed, Will sent Wampus to Ray with the order to stay.

He tugged his knife from the sheath in his boot and jogged after the guard, hanging twenty feet back, careful of his footing. He didn't realize Ray was a few strides behind him until he stopped. Ray tapped him on the shoulder. Will pivoted, knife at chest level—and then grinned. "Sneaky sumbitch," he whispered.

"If you'd been payin' attention, you'd a heard me," Ray whispered back. "Was I a renegade, we'd be eatin' your liver tonight." He held out his hand. "Gimme the knife."

Ray balanced the knife in his palm, looking for the midpoint of its weight. He found it easily; it was a good knife. He tested the keenness of the blade with his thumb and smiled.

His mouth formed the word *good*. He leaned close to Will and whispered into his ear. "You stay here. I'm 'a show you how this kinda killin' should be did."

The rider, of course, had kept on moving. Ray had to trot for several minutes to catch up to him. When he was twenty-five feet behind the guard, Ray took the tip of the knife flat between his right thumb and forefinger. He raised his arm and stretched it well behind him. When he threw his motion was smooth, fluid, and very rapid. The knife, looking like a silver bird as it flipped over several times, buried itself to the hilt in the back of the ourider's skull, making a sound much like that produced when a pumpkin is struck with a stout stick. The man toppled from his horse soundlessly, slowly, almost gracefully. His body twitched twice and then he was still.

Ray scurried up, hauled the knife from the man's head, turned him over, and tore open his shirt. He scribed the *HW* and then, after looking at his work for a long moment, carved a smaller but still readily discernable *R* under the larger marking. He jogged back to Will and Wampus, wiping blood, bits of bone, and gray matter from the blade onto his pants.

"Where'd you learn to throw like that?" Will asked.

"My pa." Ray said he was about half Cree. "They like their knives. They hunt with 'em an' so forth—an' not jus' rabbits, neither. Three or four good men could bring down a deer faster'n a arrow would. See, a arrow is liable to miss a vital spot. These Cree knife men don't miss."

"You think you could maybe teach me?"

"If we live long enough, sure I can."

"Fair 'nuff. Look, we done some good work. Wanna call it a night?"

"Hell, no! Let's go over to the other side of the rim an' see if we can't make sure one a them guards sees Wampus. In this kinda light, he even scares *me*."

They walked, saying little, setting a good pace, Wampus slightly ahead, tasting the air for scents. The wolf dog stopped suddenly and at the same moment bits of stone and dirt spit into the air around the men. It was mostly pistol fire, but there were rifle reports as well. A couple of slugs snarled over their heads.

"We got no goddamn cover!" Ray cursed. "Sonsabitches . . ."

There was a slight dune of a rise a hundred yards away. It wasn't much, but it was better than no cover at all. "We'd best haul ass," Will shouted. "C'mon, Wampus!"

Wampus was ready to do battle, already advancing toward the gunfire, but he responded to Will's call.

"Maybe you shoulda let him go—scare them snakes off," Ray gasped, running hard.

"Not if One Dog is there, an' I suspect he is. His crew wouldn't have the balls to fire on us and the wampus if Dog wasn't pushing them real hard. Come on, Ray—run!"

They threw themselves over the dune, panting, their legs feeling like rubber and their lungs screaming for air. Their cover was barely enough to stop slugs and keep the men—at least to some degree—hidden.

"We gotta git to the horses or we'll git circled—and then we're screwed," Ray said when he had enough breath to speak.

"Maybe not—r'member, we got the wampus and there's a ton of fear that goes back lots of years on the parts of them loonies—particularly the Indians," Will said. He reached next to him and rubbed Wampus's back. "This boy could be our bes' weapon."

Ray began to respond when a voice sounded from the outlaws. Will peeked over the dune.

One Dog sat—bareback, of course, on a gray stud horse that was decorated with war symbols:

handprints, arrows, fire, dead enemies—slightly ahead of his crew.

"Hear me," he bellowed. "Your wampus is a wolf dog—not an evil spirit. He obeys you like a cringing camp cur. The wampus obeys no man. My medicine is far stronger than that of an egg-sucking dog. A bullet will take down your cur—your phony spirit you used to frighten the trash I ride with—who will die with you both."

"You're a feeble woman, One Dog," Will yelled back. "You ride with cowards—and you, too, are a coward. You crawl under the blankets of your cowards at night and play the woman for them. I will kill you, Dog, just like my partner an' me have killed your drunken guards and outriders. And my wolf dog has more courage than the whole godforsaken bunch of you swine!"

One Dog hawked his throat and spat. "This is for your dog. I will tear his heart out and piss in his chest. Such is what a sneaking chicken killer deserves."

"Think we can get a shot at him?" Ray asked.

"Not with a pistol. He's outta range."

"OK. Let's git to our horses. If they decide to charge, we're well and truly screwed."

They backed away from the dune, jumped to their feet, and began to run, hoping the renegades' line of vision was broken. Will tripped, fell, and got a face full of dirt—and knocked the breath out of his lungs.

"I'm . . . gettin' . . . mighty . . . tired of this . . . running shit," he gasped.

"Ain't far now. An' tomorrow night we won't be doin' no runnin'."

The day that followed was interminable, and as

hot as a smith's-forge fire in hell, to boot. Wampus, tongue lolling, moved frequently, following the stingy patches of shade afforded by the desert pine.

Will rolled and smoked cigarette after cigarette, one after another, lighting the next one from the nub of the last.

Ray, his Colt resting on his chest, more or less slept.

Finally, Will spoke, his voice unusual in its tone—neither accusatory nor conciliatory.

"I . . . uh . . . seen your initial on that Indian," he said.

"Yeah. I figured you would."

"You had no goddamn right to do that, Ray."

"I killed him. He was mine, jus' like when a man takes down a deer or elk."

"That's not the point."

Ray's voice was tight, heated. "Then what is the point?"

"This: That little pissant *R* was too small and was in the wrong place. It shoulda been the size of the big letters and tagged right on the *HW*—shoulda been *HWR*."

Ray's smile could have lit up a very dark night. "You mean . . . ?"

"Yep. I give it lots of thought. I surely do mean it."

"I . . . I got nothing to bring to a spread, Will."

"You lazy, Ray? Stupid? You gonna steal the operation blind?"

"Why hell no. I ain't none of them things. You know that, Will."

"There ya go, then."

"HWR," Ray repeated, almost reverently. "Damn, if that don't sound good."

"Sounds good to me, too." Will held out his hand and Ray took it in his own. They shook solemnly, as if they were sealing a pact or maybe a major business deal—which, in fact, they were.

"One more thing we gotta settle," Will said. "One of us is goin' to kill One Dog. We don't know how the battle will go—there's no way to tell where Dog'll be. There's only one rule we need to agree to. Whoever kills him can't use a rifle and drop him from a hundred yards away. One of us has got to look into that pig's eyes as he dies—whether we kill him with a knife, a pistol, or a damn club don't matter. But One Dog's gotta know it was one of us, and why he's dying."

"I want him awful bad, Will," Ray said.

"An' I don't? Like I said, it all depends on how the final battle works out. I'll take him if I can; so will you. But face-to-face."

"Well hell," Ray said, "it ain't impossible that the pair of us get our asses shot off an' One Dog rides off with our hair after chowin' down on our hearts."

Will grinned. "I'd say that *is* impossible—but I guess we'll see."

The day dragged on. Will dozed, smoked, and dozed again. Ray piddled around with his equipment, not because it needed attention but because he needed something, anything, to do. There was a tension in the air—a storm coming, although not of the natural sort—that both men pretended to ignore. It was an anticipatory kind of desire/dread; neither of them was frightened, and neither was terribly confident.

Once, as Will dozed, Wampus sat up and flapped his rear paw under his ear, chasing a flea. Will's Colt was in his hand before he was actually awake, with the hammer thumbed back. Ray looked away as Will reholstered his pistol.

In the late afternoon Ray tossed his saddle on his horse. Will watched through sleepy eyes. "Where ya goin'?"

"I'll be back in a bit—an' I'll bring a meal." He stood next to his horse and took a roll of latigo from his gear. It was half an inch wide and maybe twenty feet long, and it was very nicely tanned and oiled. A knife appeared in Ray's hand and he centered the latigo on the blade and began easing it through. The leather split into two equal-width pieces its entire length, as neat and clean as if it'd been cut by a coat-maker's machine. He gathered up the latigo, mounted, and rode off at a jog.

Will dozed again, his mind playing with the leather strips. *Trip wires? Neck busters?*

When Ray rode in less than an hour later, his bow was strung and swung across his back.

He held a decent-sized jack by its ears.

Will got a cook fire going. "Screw the smoke. After tonight smoke ain't gonna matter, anyways."

"Well, yeah. But we got a problem," Ray said.

"Oh?"

"Your wolf dog, Will. The crazies know now that he ain't a spirit from hell—One Dog said so. Them renegades will fill Wampus with enough lead to bust a damn bridge."

"Damn."

"We can sink a post, Will. I got some metal-core rope—not much, but enough—an' I got some laudanum, too."

"I hate to do it," Will said quietly.

"So do I. But we'll dope him first an' then take care of the post an' rope."

Will shook his head. "Suppose the two of us get killed?"

"Then all three of us played our cards wrong, Will."

The deeply buried post was a fine idea—except there was nothing that would serve as a post. The men decided they would secure the wire-cored rope around the base of one of the desert pines, the only option they had. Getting the laudanum into Wampus presented no problem. Ray poured all of his remaining jerky into a pile and then dumped the laudanum over it. The label on the brown bottle read:

Dr. Lucian Golden's Positive Cure For All Human Ailments

(Being a highly efficacious medication absolutely guaranteed to treat and cure cancer, blindness, disruption of the bowels, vapors, rickets, pneumonia, tuberculosis, flatulence, male performance problems, malaise, and all other problems that afflict men and women.)

Directions:

Ingest up to three tablespoons of Dr. Golden's Elixir several times per day, as required. Upon even the first dosage, the patient will immediately notice a recession of symptoms and a sensation of good health and physical and emotional well-being.

—Dr. Golden's Elixir is available in convenient one-quart glass containers—

"Hey!" Will said, looking at the bottle. "Wampus ain't sick! He don't need no medicine. Why do you want to go an' give him . . ."

"Will," Ray said, "this stuff ain't no more medicine than rotgut whiskey is. Fact, it's almost pure laudanum. It'll give Wampus a nice ride whilst we're gone."

"You sure?" Will asked dubiously.

"Positive."

Will waved the drooling wolf dog to the jerky. The medicinal/alcohol scent didn't deter him for a second. He gobbled down all the jerky as if he hadn't eaten for a month and looked at Will for more. When none was forthcoming he began to walk to a blotch of shade—and began weaving, as if he couldn't keep his balance, his tongue hanging out of the side of his mouth, with a singularly goofy look in his eyes. He collapsed halfway to his piece of shade. Will picked him up, grunting at the wolf dog's weight, and carried him to the desert pines. There he took a double wrap around Wampus's neck and did the same with the best of the poor selection of trees. Wampus slept without moving, snoring sibilantly, his breathing even and strong.

"How long is Wampus goin' to be out?" Will asked.

"Hard to say—a few hours, at least. We'll be back or dead by the time he wakes up. If we're dead he'll get through that rope after a good bit of work an' maybe a couple busted teeth."

Will nodded. He didn't like the idea, but it was all they had.

Dusk was beginning to turn to night when the men saddled up. "I guess we might jist as well have at it," Ray said.

"Let's ride, pard."

"I s'pose," Ray said, "you was wonderin' what I was doin' except fetchin' a jack when I rode out."

"I figured you'd tell me sooner or later."

"I'll show you in a bit, is what I'll do."

Although not as bright as the previous night, there was good light. The shadows were a bit deeper and visibility wasn't quite as long, but it was a good night to hunt outlaws—or be hunted by them.

When they were a hundred yards from the rim, they saw the first outrider. Ray held up his hand to indicate a halt. The man on horseback could barely be seen, but his movement made spotting him easier.

"Watch," Ray said quietly.

He slid his bow off his back and pulled an arrow from the quiver attached to his saddlehorn and handed it to Will. Will looked at it carefully. An eight-inch piece of black-powder composition was lashed neatly to the shaft of the arrow with latigo.

Ray wet a finger in his mouth and held it up over his head. "No breeze 'tall. That's good." He nocked the arrow to the bowstring and pulled the string back to full draw, bending the stout bow so far Will was certain it was going to snap. Then he released the missile, aiming high.

For a couple of seconds nothing happened. Then a slash of light as bright as a photographer's magnesium lit up the sky and all that remained of both the horse and the outrider was an explosion of dirt and rock and a reddish pink mist that faded with the residual light of the flash.

"Holy God," Will said. "You got enough arrows?"

"Plenty."

"Then let's git them sonsabitches!"

They rode on a short distance and left their horses secured to rocks. The stink of scorched hair and burned flesh and leather hung heavily in the still air as they walked to the rim.

Twenty or so renegades stood in front of their saloon, many looking dazed, others firing pistols and rifles uselessly toward where the explosion had taken place.

Ray began firing arrows as smoothly and with as much accuracy as a good rifleman operates his weapon. The saloon was immediately ablaze and several men ran out through the batwings on fire, screaming.

A cluster of a half dozen men partially hidden by the charred hulk of the freighter went up like Fourth of July skyrockets, arcing ten feet into the air, clothes and hair flaming, ammunition in their gun belts firing from the intense heat.

Will was prone, firing his .30-30 quickly but carefully, aiming each shot and rarely missing. Dead and dying outlaws littered the street—and burning things that may or may not have once been men were scattered about.

Ray set his bow aside and reached for his rifle. "Clear outta—" he began.

That's when the battle ended for Will and Ray. The impact of rifle butts on the backs of their heads removed them from the fracas and everything else.

A bucket of water from a trough brought Will and Ray back to consciousness. They were on their backs, hands tied behind them, with heads that hurt more than either man thought a head could possibly generate pain.

One Dog stood at their feet, muscular arms folded,

face painted with war paint, the red hand of death imprinted in dried blood on his forehead.

"Sit up."

When the two bound men didn't comply immediately a group of about twenty men moved in, prodding and kicking Ray and Will with their boots. They struggled to sitting positions, legs extended in front of them, hands already becoming numb from the tightness of the rope around their wrists.

A thought flashed through Will's mind as he looked about him. *This is all that's left of One Dog's army. We killed the rest of them—and they all deserved to die. Now, if I can get my hands on One Dog . . .*

Will had heard that Dog constantly smoked ganja and that he used the sacred mushrooms almost daily. He looked closely at the Indian's eyes but saw none of the dilation and wet glistening the drugs brought.

One Dog spoke again. His voice was calm, but there was an obvious tone of hatred beneath his words. "I will fight and kill each of you with my friend, the serpent's fang." He held out a knife in one hand. It had a fairly narrow, double-edged twelve-inch blade. "The second to fight will watch his friend die—and I will not kill quickly."

"We gonna stay tied while you kill us, you chickenshit savage?" Will snarled.

"Just like you tied women an' kids when you killed them?" Ray said.

"You don't have the balls of a prairie dog, you woman who wishes to be a man but cannot, because she's a coward." Will spat toward One Dog. "I'll fight you to the death right now, with or without a knife. A coward dies easily. I won't break a sweat."

"The coward will piss himself," Ray added. "That'll be fun to see."

Dog took a step closer to Ray and swung his right fist hard, connecting with the man's mouth. Ray spit out blood and bits of smashed teeth. Still, he managed a bloody-lipped, derisive grin. "Your type of fightin', no? When your enemy is tied an' helpless. Your sow mother gave birth to a worm, a cowardly worm that—"

One Dog swung again, smashing Ray unconscious, head lolling to the side, draining blood and enamel.

"Cut me loose an' we'll fight," Will shouted. "Any goddamn way you wanna fight—jus' cut me loose!"

"We will fight," One Dog growled. "Here's how, white-eyed snake. A short piece of rope will be tied to our left wrists. In the other we will hold knives. The winner lives. The loser's guts are fed to the coyotes and vultures." He fingered the deerskin belt around his waist with many globs of hair attached to it. "Thirty-one times I have fought in this manner. My belt holds thirty-one scalps. Yours will make thirty-two."

"Don't bet on it, coward."

One Dog took a quick step behind Will. Will wasn't at all sure whether the Indian was going to slash his throat or free his hands. He breathed in relief as his hands fell to the grit of the road.

The Indian motioned to a renegade wearing a Union officer's hat, a rebel shirt with several bullet holes in it, and a pair of men's dress trousers several sizes too large for him held up with a length of baling twine. He carried a piece of rope about six feet long.

Will struggled to his feet, the pain from his head almost knocking him back to the ground. His hands were numb. He shook them—hard—to restore sensation to them.

The renegade moved to One Dog, who held out his left arm. "Pew! You stink, you swine," Dog said as the man took two wraps around One Dog's left wrist and secured the rope with a knot. The outlaw did the same with Will, leaving five feet or so between the two combatants. One Dog had been quite right about the stench of his man; he smelled like a rotting corpse under a long day's hot sun. Will shook his head to clear it and immediately regretted the move. What was left of Dog's army formed a rough circle around the bound-together fighters.

One Dog nodded and an outlaw handed Will a knife. It was a decent piece of work: twelve-inch single-sided blade with a smooth blood channel and finely worked bone grips. Will tested its weight and balance and was satisfied.

"We will fight," Dog said grimly.

"You bet your red ass we will."

They circled each other once and then again, the rope taut between them. Then, surprising Will, One Dog tried a sucker's move: an attempt to kick Will's knife from his hand. Will hacked downward with his blade, opening a gash on One Dog's forestep that showed bone through the blood.

One Dog's kick had been a ruse. His blade slashed a six-inch groove across Will's throat, barely opening the skin. But another couple of inches and the fight would have been over.

They circled again, this time a tad more cautiously, bent slightly forward at the waist, on the balls of their feet, ready to move in any direction, their knives in front of them chest high, extended a couple feet from their bodies.

One Dog's eyes swung for the briefest part of a second to his audience and Will took that fraction of a moment to attack with a direct thrust at the Indian's gut. One Dog was both agile and fast—but not fast enough to completely evade Will's blade. They stepped apart, Dog with a five-inch laceration slightly above his waist, blood flowing copiously onto the scalps on his belt under the wound.

One Dog countered immediately, again aiming at Will's throat or chest. Their wrists met, and each man exerted all the power he had against his opponent.

Will felt a jarring bolt of raw fear. His wrist was being pushed back toward his body minutely, almost imperceptibly, but it was moving toward him.

One Dog is stronger than I am.

Will slipped the wrist contact, dropped into a crouch, avoiding the Indian's thrust, and delivered a bone-revealing slash to Dog's calf—the same leg he'd stuck early on in the fight.

But I'm smarter than he is.

They circled again. One Dog feinted low and then impossibly fast brought his knife upward to open a gash across Will's chest, crushing two ribs with its force. Blood erupted the length of the cut and pain screamed from the fractured ribs.

The impact slammed Will to the ground and he scrambled to get his feet under him, but he was a heartbeat too late. One Dog fell on Will's chest, one knee pinning his right arm—his knife arm—to the ground.

Now the Indian had all the time he needed to play with Will, to kill him slowly. "First," he said, "I'll take your ears." He brought his knife down so that the edge didn't quite touch the flesh of Will's upper ear. "Now, white eyes with your false wampus and your partner and his bombs, you'll pay for those you've killed. I can gather fifty men in a week to replace those you've murdered. You've accomplished nothing, white eyes. *Nothing.* And you'll scream for mercy as I kill you." He lowered the knife and began slicing into the top of Will's ear. "Ehh—where is your wampus now? Cringing somewhe—"

It was then that a silver-gray juggernaut with a bloody mouth and a piece of rope hanging from around its neck slammed onto One Dog, knocking him off Will. The wolf dog struck first at the jugular, which was revealed for a half second when One Dog was still falling. Gushes of blood spurted but quickly slowed to strong flowing rivulets. But this time, Wampus wasn't finished. As One Dog fell forward, the wolf dog sank his teeth into the back of the Indian's neck and snapped his spine. Then he began to saw with his teeth into One Dog's neck, shaking the body, bearing harder and harder until his trophy was free. He took One Dog's head from his body, carried it to Will, and dropped it in front of him.

Most of Dog's troops had run for their horses when the wolf dog appeared. The balance of them now ran after their peers.

"Holy mother of God," Ray croaked, barely back to consciousness. "Holy mother of God." He took some deep breaths. "You ever tie that boy again an' I'll draw on you, Will Lewis," he said.

Will stumbled to Ray and cut his hands free.

"Gimme a hand with these cuts an' fetch our horses. I can't walk worth a damn. We got ranch work to do, pard."

Wampus lived to be fourteen years old and died quietly, sleeping next to Will's bed in the ranch house Will and Ray had built. The wolf dog was never much good with cattle—too aggressive—but he followed the men each morning as they saddled up to check on their stock.

Wampus never "turned."

INTERACT WITH DORCHESTER ONLINE!

Want to learn more about your favorite books and authors?
Want to talk with other readers that like to read the same books as you?
Want to see up-to-the-minute Dorchester news?

VISIT DORCHESTER AT:
DorchesterPub.com
Twitter.com/DorchesterPub
Facebook.com (Search Pages)

DISCUSS DORCHESTER'S NOVELS AT:
Dorchester Forums at DorchesterPub.com
GoodReads.com
LibraryThing.com
Myspace.com/books
Shelfari.com
WeRead.com

T.T.T

CPSIA information can be obtained at www.ICGtesting.com
Printed in the USA
269852BV00002BA/1/P